T0152989

Virgin Territory

Kenna White

BELLA
BOOKS

2016

Bella Books, Inc.
P.O. Box 10543
Tallahassee, FL 32302

Printed in the United States of America on acid-free paper.

First Bella Books Edition 2016

Editor: Katherine V. Forrest
Cover Designer: Judith Fellows

ISBN: 978-1-59493-515-2

Other Bella Books by Kenna White

Beautiful Journey
Beneath the Willow
Body Language
Braggin' Rights
Comfortable Distance
Romancing the Zone
Shared Winds
Skin Deep
Simple Pleasures
Taken by Surprise
These Two Hearts
Yours for the Asking

About the Author

A Lambda Literary Award winner and best-selling author, Kenna White resides in Southwest Missouri and enjoys traveling, creating dollhouse miniatures, her family and writing with a good cup of coffee by her side. After living from the Rocky Mountains to New England, she is once again back where bare feet, faded jeans and lazy streams fill her life.

Acknowledgments

I'd like to thank the physical therapists, limousine services, construction companies and medical community for providing information and support, without which Elise and Jan's story couldn't be told.

Dedication

This book is dedicated to those amazingly courageous and self-reliant individuals who accept life's disabilities and deformities with grace and good humor.

A heartfelt thank you to those who shared their stories and struggles with me.

CHAPTER ONE

Elise Grayson spun her leather desk chair around to face the view of downtown Boston from her sixth floor office. She held the phone to her ear and waited for the call to be answered.

Low-hanging clouds had settled over the city. Rain was in the forecast, welcome rain to cool the late summer heat wave. But neither the threat of rain nor the heat diminished the number of tourists clogging the sidewalks, snapping pictures of anything and everything they saw. Elise found it amusing that travelers came thousands of miles to a city renowned for its history and architectural culture only to take pictures of high-rise buildings, sailboats on the Charles River and a pub's staircase immortalized on a TV show.

This was her city. She knew everything about it intimately. She was born here, grew up here and attended Harvard. That seemed like eons ago. Now in her forties, she was vice-president of Grayson Construction, a multifaceted company offering turnkey commercial building services throughout the Northeast, everything from site development and architecture design to the finished product. She was the fourth generation Grayson to sit behind a desk in the business. It was the only job she'd ever had, started in the purchasing department to get a feel for the business. Her father, Forest Grayson, had joined his father, Henry Grayson, and grandfather, Charles Grayson in running one of the most respected companies in Boston. Their clientele included some of the most prestigious and influential New Englanders.

She glanced over at the antique mantel clock on the bookshelf. It had been her grandfather's. He had given it to her when she graduated prep school with a note that read, "Whatever else you manage, time is first." She didn't fully appreciate his remark back then but she did now. And she was wasting precious time.

"Come on, Cramer," she mumbled impatiently into the phone. She uncrossed her legs and crossed them in the other direction to the familiar swish of her pantyhose as she pulled one knee over the other. She picked a piece of lint from the hem of her skirt and rolled it into oblivion between her fingers.

"Elise, I need to talk with you when you have a minute," Jake said from the doorway. He was dressed in jeans, a polo shirt, work boots and a ball cap. He had a dark tan and had a pair of sunglasses perched backward on his cap. He looked like he belonged on a construction site. Which he did.

"Come in, Jake, and please tell me you have the results of the soil test," she said, hanging up the receiver and quickly jotting a note to herself about the unanswered call.

"What soil test?" He frowned suspiciously.

"You have got to be kidding me. You don't have it?" She glared up at him.

He held his frown for a long moment then slowly pulled a smile.

"Yes, I have it." He dropped a printout on her desk. "We're fine. No problems."

"You just love doing that, don't you?" She grabbed it and read it. "One of these days I'm going to have a heart attack and it will be your fault."

"Can I tell Seth to deliver the equipment?"

"No. Not yet. I have a meeting with the Tanners this morning and they still aren't sold on the parking situation so let's hold off until we get an okay on that."

"What's to discuss?"

"Burt wants it in front. But Mrs. Tanner wants the parking lot on the west end. More aesthetically pleasing, she said."

"Elise," a white-haired man called from the doorway.

"Good morning, Dad. Come in. I got your message. What's up?" She looked at Jake and added, "I'll let you know when we're ready. Hopefully this week."

"Gotcha," he said and strode out the door, nodding hello to the well-dressed man as he slipped past.

At sixty-eight years old, Forest Grayson was still a handsome man with a narrow white moustache and thick hair combed back in undulating waves. He had on dark suit pants and matching vest over a white dress shirt. A silver and red striped tie billowed slightly above the top of his vest, held in place by a black onyx tie tack. Black onyx cuff links completed the customary look. A few decades ago he probably would have been dressed in clothes more suitable for visiting a construction site. As a senior business executive he spent more time at his desk than wearing a hard hat and tromping around a job site.

"Harris and Mills changed their minds. Again. They want nine thousand square feet instead of seventy-five hundred. They want that second conference room."

"Do they have room for nine thousand? That's going to cut into the parking capacity."

"Don't worry about it. I think they can acquire the adjacent lot. It's not vacant but I think we can make it happen. But that's not why I'm here. I need you to attend that gallery opening in Cambridge this evening. The mayor and the president of the university will be there."

Elise had been jotting notes to herself and looked up with a scowl. "I'm flying to Buffalo this evening. I'm delivering the final blueprints and specs for the riverfront condos. Besides, I thought you were attending the gallery opening. We both don't need to be there."

"I can't go. I'm having dinner with John Hartwell. He wants to discuss a remodel on some of the executive suites in the Gillette Stadium."

Elise removed her reading glasses and leaned back in her chair, staring up at him curiously. "New England Patriots. Hmmm."

"Don't start, Elise. I don't want to hear it."

"What did I say?" She shrugged then offered a smug grin.

"Money's money and this reno is money. Anyway, I need you in Cambridge. They'll expect at least one of us to be there. You'll have time for an appearance and still make your flight to Buffalo. It's at ten thirty, right?"

"Seven thirty."

"Have Lorraine reschedule you. United has a ten thirty out of Logan. The gallery opening is from seven to ten. You'll have plenty of time for both." He dispatched his orders without regard to any problems his last minute changes might entail. Ignoring the exasperated look on Elise's face, he pulled the door shut behind him. It wasn't the first time he'd turned her plans upside down.

She had just reached for the phone when there was another knock on her office door and her secretary peeked in.

"I understand changes are in the works," Lorraine said with a smile. A round-faced woman with dark brown hair neatly restrained by a paisley scarf at the back of her neck, she was a few pounds overweight—at least she thought so, and complained about it frequently. She had been with Grayson Construction for twenty years and was good at her job. She had an amiable smile and pleasant telephone voice and was exceedingly professional. She didn't have to work. Her husband was a retired military officer with a handsome pension, but she had been Elise's secretary for six years and seemed to enjoy the challenge. Like a mother hen, she kept the details of Elise's business calendar running with military efficiency.

"It looks like I'm attending the gallery opening in Cambridge this evening. I'll need a car and driver."

"Six thirty-ish?" Lorraine offered as if she already knew the plans.

"Yes. And can you check on a later flight to Buffalo? Something after ten."

"Is Ginger going with you?"

"No, she's still in Trenton until Sunday night."

"Wow, that's some conference. Maybe I should be a real estate agent."

"Can you make my reservations first please?" Elise looked up and smiled.

Elise went back to work. It wasn't worth being mad about the change in plans.

Returning to her office a few minutes later, Lorraine said softly, "The Tanners are here early. I showed them into the conference room. By the way, there's a ten-fifteen flight to Buffalo. Seats are still available."

"Sounds good."

"So a limo to the gallery opening around six thirty and a ride to the airport afterward?"

"Yes. Just enough time to sip a glass of pretentious wine, shake a few hands and still get to Logan by nine. When you call for a car ask for a different driver. I'm tired of that disgusting little man in his lint covered uniform peering at me in his rearview mirror. He spends the entire trip trying to see either up my skirt or down my blouse."

"I did some checking. You weren't the only client with concerns about that company. So if it's all right with you, we're using a different service. Bay State Executive Car Service comes highly recommended. They've been in business since 1982 with a five star rating. And just so you know, your driver will be a woman. She's fairly new but she has an impeccable driving record and she's fully licensed and vetted."

"A woman limousine driver. That's different. Maybe she won't have wandering eyes." Elise envisioned a matronly looking woman with deep wrinkles and chubby fingers gripping the steering wheel as she whizzed along at a breakneck twenty miles an hour. She collected a stack of papers and a rolled set of blueprints and headed out the door, her high heels clicking a determined pace down the hall.

"Would you like for me to bring coffee to the conference room?" Lorraine offered as she followed.

"Yes, please."

Elise opened the door to the conference room and stepped inside, a welcoming smile on her face. An elderly couple sat at the table with their hands in their laps and their backs to the window as if they couldn't care less what was going on in downtown Boston.

"Mrs. Tanner, Mr. Tanner, I'm so sorry to keep you waiting." She shook their hands then closed the door and took a seat at the table.

Elise would be with the Tanners for over an hour. They would take time for pleasantries and coffee before getting down to work. Without children to leave their sizable estate to, they had decided to build a retirement center on property they owned on Cape Cod. Uncluttered functional units, energy efficient, easy access bathrooms, relaxing views of the ocean. Cost didn't seem to be the limiting factor to the project. Mrs. Tanner's attention to detail and aesthetics was.

Rain finally came sometime after lunch, turning downtown Boston into a steamy sultry sauna. Elise finished with the Tanners, conducted two conference calls, read and sent emails and dictated three letters. Lunch was a ciabatta sandwich with some unidentifiable cheese melted over salami and pesto sauce. She hadn't ordered it. It just appeared at her desk somewhere between an email from the North Adams planning and zoning office and the call from the Brattleboro sewer department that their site runoff wasn't being properly contained.

"I hope this is a good stopping place," Lorraine said, peeking around the edge of the office door. "Your car is here."

Elise quickly finished typing a sentence before looking up. "What time is it?"

"Twenty five after. You said for me to remind you when it was twenty five after, so here I am." She cocked an eyebrow. "Your chariot and the pretentious wine await. The driver is downstairs."

"How do I let my father talk me into these things?"

"You're a good daughter. You know how to take care of business."

Elise quickly read over the email she had composed. She wasn't satisfied with it but saved it as a draft, shut down her laptop and slipped it into her briefcase. She collected her wheeled suitcase from the corner of the office and headed for the door. Lorraine followed, carrying the tube of blueprints.

"Lorraine, we're smart people. Surely we can find an acceptable excuse not to attend these little soirées." She strode down the hall and out into the lobby, her briefcase strap on one shoulder, her purse strap over the other and her suitcase rolling along behind. "We're developers, not social arbiters. They're always crowded. The food is unpalatable. And someone inevitably spills their drink on my shoes. No wonder my father didn't want to go."

"A legit excuse? Hmmm."

"Yes."

"I'll get right to work on a prospectus for that." Lorraine pressed the elevator button. "Concerning said excuse, do you want medical or non-medical?" she asked, playing along with the silliness.

"Something that doesn't require a note from a doctor."

"So, nothing broken or dislocated."

"Preferably." The elevator door opened and Elise stepped in, maneuvered her suitcase over the threshold and stood facing the opening. "I think we can avoid concussions, whiplash or venereal disease as well."

"I'll keep that in mind." Lorraine handed Elise the tube and smiled dryly. "Enjoy Buffalo."

The elevator door closed as Elise's cell phone rang in her purse.

"Hello Fred," she said, recognizing the caller. "Please tell me we're ready to pour the foundation."

She listened to the man's protestations as the elevator descended to the lobby. Fred was a detail freak. Consumed with OCD, he often felt the need to go to the top of the food chain for answers and that meant Elise.

"Good evening, Ms. Grayson," the security guard at the desk in the lobby said as she stepped out of the elevator.

She was still listening to Fred when the guard pointed to the woman standing just inside the revolving door, a woman Elise assumed was her driver. She looked like a limousine driver. At least, she was dressed like one. Black suit, white shirt and black tie. Her black shoes were polished to a mirrored gloss. She wasn't wearing a hat like most drivers but she looked the part. Clean, humbly confident as she stood waiting with a black umbrella in her hand. She was a tall woman and wasn't wearing makeup. Her hair was blond, gelled and combed back on the sides. She nodded and offered a discreet smile as she reached for Elise's suitcase.

"Good evening, Ms. Grayson," she said quietly as if not to interrupt Elise's phone conversation. She pushed the revolving door to start it moving then stepped back for Elise to enter. She followed and opened the umbrella, protecting Elise from the evening drizzle as they stepped to the curb and the waiting car. It wasn't a stretch limousine, the size capable of transporting an entire wedding party from the church to the reception with conspicuous excess, the kind Elise often thought was overkill when she just needed a reliable car and driver to transport her from point A to point B on time and without stress. It was a sensible sedan, a luxury sedan, but a sedan. Not a party barge. So far, so good.

The woman opened the back door and kept the umbrella over Elise's head.

"Just a minute, Fred." Elise cradled the phone to her chest. "Do you have the address in Cambridge?"

"Yes, ma'am. Your secretary gave me your itinerary for the evening. The Steinberry Gallery at the corner of Massachusetts Avenue and Holt."

"And you know how to get there?" Elise remembered Lorraine mentioning this woman was new. She didn't need a navigationally challenged driver when she was on a strict time table.

"Yes, I do." She handed Elise a business card. "This is my cell phone number. You may call when you're ready for me to pick you up at the gallery."

"Jan Chase, is it?" she asked, studying the card.

"Yes. You may call me Jan if you like."

"I don't plan to be at the gallery very long. A few minutes at the most. I have a flight to catch this evening."

"Yes, ma'am. United flight 8126, scheduled to depart at ten fifteen."

"You can put that suitcase in here with me," Elise said, her cell phone still pressed to her chest. "I need to get something out of the zipper compartment."

Jan waited for Elise to get settled before closing the door then carried the suitcase around to the other side. Elise didn't think it was that heavy but the woman seemed to stumble, nearly falling as she maneuvered it into the backseat.

"I'm sorry, Fred. Now, you were saying..." Elise went back to her call but watched as Jan climbed in the driver's seat and discreetly blotted the raindrops from her face with a tissue.

The car's air conditioning was left on, set at a comfortable temperature against the hot and sticky evening air, unlike the last driver, who seemed to intentionally leave it on high to see what popped up.

"Fred, go ahead and get a half dozen more pumps. We need that water pumped out ASAP. We'll bill the city later. I already told them that. The city crew broke the line. They can pay to get the water out of our foundation. We're on a timetable even if they aren't."

Jan pulled out into traffic and headed for the Bunker Hill Bridge across the Charles River into Cambridge. Elise went back to listening to Fred but her attention was divided between his insistence on detail and the mass of blond curls clustered at the back of the driver's head. It was a pleasant change from the nondescript hat bands and crooked hairlines of the male drivers she was used to. Pleasant enough that she lost concentration on the call all together.

"Say that again, Fred. My cell service is acting up." Elise noticed Jan tossing a look at her in the rearview mirror.

The phone call, tedious as it became, was a convenient distraction from the heavy traffic and lunatic drivers that clogged Boston streets. Elise hated driving in the inner-city. She didn't like having to anticipate who was going to cut her off or fill the space she had allowed between her and the car ahead of her. She rode mass transit in the morning, or the T as the Bostonians called it, unless she had a meeting that required a driver. She was perfectly happy to sit in the backseat of a professionally driven car and be delivered to her destination. Ginger teased her about it. She loved to drive in Boston and was responsible for their transportation on evening or weekend outings.

"Keep me posted, Fred." She ended the call and noticed two emails waiting in her cell phone's mailbox. She started to open one of them but closed the leather case around her phone instead. She needed the last few minutes of the ride to decompress.

It had been a long day. It started at five thirty with an incoming text sent to the wrong person. Once awake, Elise's brain engaged and she couldn't go back to sleep. Like always she kept her phone on the nightstand and like most nights she lay in bed checking and sending last minute emails and texts before drifting off to sleep. Ginger occasionally played games on her phone before going to sleep, mind-numbing games with exploding gumballs or monotonous card games. There were no game apps on Elise's phone. She didn't count the one Ginger's niece had put on it by mistake thinking it was Ginger's phone. Every time she tried to delete it, it performed an update instead. Ginger had been out of town for six days, leaving Elise alone in the king-size bed. They talked or texted everyday while she was away. Elise gave updates on projects and shared glitches to their progress. Ginger reported on what seminars she had attended. They were usually short communiqués but at least they kept in touch.

Elise took a deep breath as the car pulled up in front of the gallery. A crowd was already forming inside the glass-fronted lobby. She checked her looks in the mirrored reflection of her cell phone. She laced a lock of brown shoulder length hair behind each ear, checked her teeth for trapped food particles then cleaned the corners of her eyes. Her pale blue silk blouse and gray skirt would have to do for this event. There hadn't been time to go home and change. She knew these openings attracted an eclectic array of attendees with diverse ideas of what was fashionable. Her business attire would fit right in between cocktail dresses and yoga pants. She didn't plan to be there long enough to make a fashion statement anyway. She was representing the company, nothing more.

The driver opened the door and extended a helping hand, which Elise took as she climbed out, leaving everything but her purse in the backseat. It had stopped raining.

"Don't go very far," Elise said.

"I'll be nearby. Call or text when you're ready." She continued to offer the supportive hand as Elise stepped up on the curb.

Elise smoothed her skirt and blouse then blew an exasperated breath.

"You look very nice, ma'am," Jan said at Elise's hesitation.

"Thank you. Good thing my aversion to these things doesn't show." She swallowed and headed inside.

Elise accepted a glass of wine from a waiter's tray and stood near the door, sipping and deciding how far into the abyss she wanted to venture. It didn't take long for someone to recognize her.

"There you are, Elise." An elderly woman in a bright red sequined pantsuit took hold of her arm for support as much as a greeting. She had erect posture but had the thin face and deeply wrinkled complexion of an octogenarian.

"Olivia! Hello, dear." Elise kissed her cheek and hugged her warmly. "It's so good to see you. I heard you've been under the weather. I wasn't sure you'd be here."

"Lord, yes. I come to all these things. I wouldn't miss it." The woman rested her wine glass against Elise's arm to steady it from the tremors her age had gifted her.

"I love this color on you. You look wonderful." Elise discreetly plucked a clump of hair from the old woman's shoulder.

"I feel old," she said with a labored chuckle. "But a glass of wine or two and a little socializing and I feel seventy again." She sipped demurely. "Elise, dear, I think I'm going to wait a few months before we tackle that remodel I was thinking about. I'm just not up to it."

"Absolutely, Olivia. You let me know when you're ready and we'll sit down and discuss it." Elise had forgotten about Olivia's on again, off again remodeling plans. With several projects currently demanding so much of her time, Elise was relieved it was once again on the back burner.

"Oh, Lord. Here comes that insufferable little man who always wants money and can't take no for an answer." She smiled disingenuously toward the man in a blue suit weaving his way through the crowd. "I really do dislike him, and at my age I'm entitled to say so." She released Elise's arm and strode off in the opposite direction.

Elise watched as the man noticed Olivia walking away and veered in that direction, a determined look on his face.

"Appetizer, miss?" a waiter asked, holding out a tray of tidbits.

Now that he mentioned it, Elise was hungry. She selected a toothpick skewered shrimp and dipped it in the little dish of cocktail sauce.

"Thank you," she said then looked for a place to discreetly discard the toothpick. "Why do these things never put out wastebaskets?" she mumbled and added hers to several other toothpicks dropped into a large flower pot.

Elise lost track of time. Minutes ticked away unnoticed as she visited with former clients. It wasn't her favorite place to talk business but like previous events and grand openings, it was hard not to listen to multi-million dollar project proposals. What bubbled to the surface over a glass of wine and a caviar-topped cracker was often more boastful than substantive.

"An appetizer?" A waitress extended a tray of chocolate dipped fruit bites.

Elise waited for the couple she was visiting with to make a selection then reached for a strawberry. Something caught her eye. Jan stood just inside the door, the folded umbrella in her hand dripping a wet spot onto the marble floor. She stared back. Elise wondered how long she had been there, looking like a wallflower at senior prom.

Elise excused herself and moved through the crowd toward her.

"I told you I'd call when I was ready," she said in a quiet, stern voice. "You may wait with the car." Elise looked around to see if anyone was listening. Common chauffeur etiquette did not include eavesdropping on the client, regardless of whether it was raining.

"Yes, ma'am." Jan nodded submissively. "Perhaps you'd like to confirm a later flight," she suggested then stepped outside, leaving Elise with the shocking realization of why she'd come inside.

"My flight!" she gasped and checked her watch. An hour and a half had slipped away. She should already be at the airport or at the very least be on her way.

Elise quickly turned toward the door, spilling wine down the front of her blouse. She handed her glass to a passing waiter and rushed out into the rain. Jan met Elise on the sidewalk, covered her with the umbrella and walked her to the car. She opened the back door and waited while Elise climbed in.

"My flight is at ten fifteen. Do we have time to make it?"

"I'll see what I can do." Jan closed the door and circled the car, again with an awkward, almost leisurely pace.

"Can we hurry please?" Elise asked anxiously as Jan settled into the driver's seat. She didn't seem to be in any great hurry.

"Yes, ma'am." She checked the rearview mirror then pulled out into traffic.

Elise dug a tissue from her purse and began blotting the wine spot on her blouse. The more she blotted the more she realized it was drying to a large and noticeable stain, one that accentuated her left boob and trailed down her skirt, suggesting she wasn't fully potty trained. She hated the idea of wearing ridiculously stained clothing but there wasn't time to stop and change. It was decision time.

"Driver, these windows are tinted, right? No one can see in?" She glanced out the window at the SUV in the next lane. Even though it was dark outside she didn't want to attract attention.

"Yes, ma'am. They're tinted." She tossed a glance in the mirror. "Do you need something?"

"I need clothes without wine stains that make me look and smell like a sloppy drunk," she mumbled as she slipped out of her shoes and pulled the suitcase closer. She took a quick look at the driver. Jan seemed preoccupied with maneuvering through traffic. There was no divider between the driver and the passenger compartments, but her eyes were on the road, right where Elise expected them to be.

Elise unzipped her skirt and wiggled it down over her hips, taking the slip with it. She pulled a pair of black slacks from the suitcase. She didn't always wear pantyhose with slacks but she left them on since she wasn't wearing panties. She hated panty lines and frequently didn't wear them on days she wore smooth fitting skirts. She wrestled herself into the slacks, turning in the seat to get them up over her hips, illuminated only by the occasional streetlight. She hadn't worn this pair of slacks in several months. She didn't remember them being so snug. It had to be the awkward position she was forced to use that made them seem snug. Her weight hadn't changed in twenty five years; she was the same one hundred fifty-one pounds she had been in high school and in college. Her ample breasts were still perky. Her rear was still tight. And the skin on the underside of her arms hadn't yet sagged into what Ginger called bingo flaps. Elise hadn't done anything to keep them that way. They just were and she was grateful for it. She didn't have time to work out. The four thousand dollar treadmill in her home office hadn't been touched in over a year. Or was it two years?

Elise unbuttoned her blouse. She sorted through the tops folded in her suitcase, looking for something long sleeved but lightweight, something comfortable for the flight. She chose the lemon-colored scoop neck Ginger had given her, the one she had admired in the boutique window on their last trip to Provincetown. She peeled out of her blouse, rolled it and the skirt into a neat little bundle and placed both in the corner of the suitcase. She pulled the top over her head and smoothed it around her waist. She swapped her high heels for a pair of low heeled shoes. She finger-combed her hair into place, once again composed and ready for her trip. It wasn't until she zipped her suitcase and looked up that she saw Jan's eyes on her in the rearview mirror. Elise hadn't considered she'd stare, but she had just performed a striptease for this woman. How much had she seen? Her unbuttoned blouse? Her lacy bra and cleavage? Her pantyhose and the triangle patch of curly hair clearly visible in her lap? Their eyes met for an awkwardly long moment. Jan didn't seem embarrassed for being caught staring. Not like the beady-eyed male drivers who would sneak a lewd, almost sinister look when all Elise was doing was sitting there, with nothing more than her kneecaps showing.

"I beg your pardon. Shouldn't your eyes be on the road?" Elise asked indignantly.

"I'm sorry." Her glance returned to the road as a tiny crinkle formed at the corner of her eyes.

Jan followed the traffic through the airport and pulled into a reserved parking spot in front of the terminal. The rain eased to little more than a drizzle as she opened the door for Elise and offered her a hand when she swung her legs out. Jan retrieved the suitcase from the backseat, set it on the curb and opened the retractable handle.

"Well, it was an experience," Elise said, juggling the blueprint tube and briefcase as she straightened the hem of her top. "I understand you're relatively new to limousine driving. A word of advice. Staring at the passengers in the rearview mirror could be considered an invasion of privacy."

"I'll remember that." Jan caught the strap of Elise's purse as it began sliding down her shoulder and put it back in place.

"I'm willing to overlook it this time since you did get me to the airport. We'll chalk it up to inexperience."

Jan closed the back door and said nothing, but the muscles in her cheek were clearly rippling as if she were withholding—with effort—some smart aleck retort. Elise took hold of the handle of the suitcase and started for the terminal door without another word. She had made her point and she had a plane to catch.

"Excuse me, Ms. Grayson." Jan drew a deep breath then stepped up on the curb awkwardly.

"Yes?" she said impatiently.

Jan stepped closer and lifted a clean handkerchief from her jacket pocket. She folded it over her index finger then wiped it over Elise's chin.

"What are you doing?" she demanded, touching her chin.

"Removing what looks like cocktail sauce." She showed her the small red stain on the handkerchief.

"Is it gone?" Elise rubbed again.

"Yes." She cleared her throat and added, "One other little detail, if you don't mind."

"What?" Elise's eyes widened, wondering what else she had on her face.

Jan reached around and lifted the back of the yellow top. Elise could feel Jan's hand inside her waistband.

"What are you doing?" she demanded and pulled away.

"I don't think you want a bunny tail following you around the airport." Jan held up a white lacy bra. "I can put it back if that's where you intended to wear it." She cocked an eyebrow.

"Oh my God." Elise snatched the bra and stuffed it in her briefcase as she blushed bright red. "No wonder my pants felt snug."

"In my defense, that is why I was staring. I was hoping you'd notice before we got to the airport. And for future reference, there is a mirror in the drop-down on the back of the seat." She stepped back and smiled respectfully. "Have a pleasant trip, Ms. Grayson."

"Thank you," Elise said, still embarrassed.

Elise was well inside the terminal when guilt overtook her. She turned and headed back outside, but Jan and the black car were gone. Elise stood in the rain, angry at herself for not apologizing. The woman had done her job and then some and Elise hadn't been the least bit appreciative. And she knew better.

CHAPTER TWO

Jan stood in front of the bathroom mirror in her sports bra and jeans, working gel through her hair. The obstinate waves and curls refused to cooperate as she finger-combed the sides in an attempt to draw it back. She continued to rake her fingers through the thick blond stuff until she was satisfied she had done her best. Her Levi's sat low, exposing her belly button and the top of her hipbones. She had no tan, at least nowhere other than her forearms and face. As a teenager she had proudly boasted a rich bronze tan, the result of summer trips to the beach. She had been a good swimmer and still had swimmer's shoulders and well-defined arm muscles, but she hadn't been to the beach in years. She pulled on a Boston Red Sox T-shirt and headed for the door.

It was the first Saturday she'd had off in a month. She could use a day at home to catch up on chores but she was due at her parents' house for dinner to celebrate her twin nephews' eighth birthday. There was no way she could miss it. The whole family would be there. Her sister and brother and their spouses.

Jan didn't want to listen to the twins practice their demonic screams and wrestle over the video game controllers. And she didn't want to hear her mother complain she looked too thin or wonder why she wasn't dating someone. You shouldn't be alone, Jannie, dear, she would undoubtedly say. But there was no way out of it. No excuse short of death was acceptable for missing a family birthday dinner. Her brother found that out last year when he and his long-time boyfriend had opted out of a birthday dinner for Grandma Nowak.

Grandma Nowak was eighty-five. Everyone in the family called her Baci, the bastardized version of the Polish name for grandmother, Babcia. She had lived with Jan's parents since her mini-stroke that left a permanent arch to her right eyebrow.

Jan leaned back in the seat of her SUV and steered with two fingers as she headed west on the Mass Pike and the eighty miles to Indian Orchard, the blue-collar community just east of Springfield. She didn't like her mid-size SUV. It was comfortable, energy efficient, all-wheel drive and it rated well on crash tests. It even had heated seats that came in handy during the frigid New England winters. But it wasn't her candy apple red Mustang with a rear spoiler and black leather interior. Even though it had been a gas-guzzling and pricey-to-insure car, she'd liked the way it handled. It was eager and responsive the moment she released the clutch. The roar of the exhaust was like an adrenaline rush, although on ice and snow it was a challenge not to spin out. Someone had told her it was a chick magnet. Maybe it was. She'd had her fair share of make-out sessions in it. Now she drove a sensible Toyota. Maybe it would grow on her. She hoped so.

She took exit seven, paid the toll and wound her way through the residential streets before pulling to the curb in front of a two-story frame house built in the late 1920s. It had pale yellow siding with white shutters, a bay window in the living room, a driveway that ran next to the house and ended at the detached garage and chain-link fencing around a very small backyard. It was a typical New England working class family home on a quiet tree-lined street in a predominantly Polish neighborhood—at least it had been for most of her childhood.

Jan and her siblings were only half Polish. Her father was a mix of Irish, German, English and a little Swedish. It was her mother's Polish heritage that bubbled to the surface during these family gatherings. She and Baci would be in the kitchen, stirring, tasting and hovering over whatever was for dinner. And there would be the typical mother/daughter bickering over how much salt to add to the kapusta, a traditional cooked cabbage dish. The men would be in the living room, watching the Red Sox or whatever local team was in season, and staying out of the way until it was time for dinner. The house would be noisy and busy and smell like sauerkraut and garlic, but that was the way she was raised. Even now in her forties, Jan still found comfort knowing her family was there for her if she needed them.

"Hi Mr. Czerbowski," she called to the chunky man carrying a bag of trash to the barrel. "Red Sox ahead?"

"Hell no. The bums are trailing six to two." He gave a disapproving wave.

"What inning?" she asked as she retrieved sacks from the backseat and headed up the driveway.

"Seventh."

"There's still time."

She climbed the three steps to the back door and stepped into the mudroom. Like many hundred-year-old two-story homes in New England, the enclosed back porch was a shelf-lined catchall for anything too important for the garage but that didn't have a spot somewhere else in the house. Ironing board, out-of-season boots, extension cords, step stool, spare crock pot, electric roasting pan for the holiday turkey, stacks of newspapers waiting for the recycle truck. A hodge podge of mementoes and accessories of everyday life filled the shelves, hooks and corners of the room. Even the broken trophy Jan won her senior year in high school for cross-country track had been rescued from the trash in favor of the mudroom.

"Hello. Anyone home?" she called, returning a canvas cooler she had borrowed to its rightful hook.

"Is that you, Jannie?"

Harriet Chase was a gusher. A middle-sized, middle-height gusher with short salt and pepper hair and a welcoming smile. She gushed over any accomplishment. She gushed over pregnancies, weddings, job promotions and the occasional ten-dollar winning lottery ticket. Even Baci's successful gall bladder surgery was worthy of a gush. Standard gush was a hug, a kiss on the cheek and a loving moan. Variations included a double-sided cheek kiss and a sway with the hug, something bordering on a dance step. She rushed up to Jan, wiping her hands on her apron. "Hello, sweetheart. How's my baby?" She gave her a kiss and a hug, and went back to the stove. "You're late."

Like Jan, Harriet had a mass of curls at the back of her head, although hers were thinner and nearly white. She wore pink elastic-waist capri pants and a matching floral top tucked into her waistband. Her apron was bright green and imprinted with script lettering: *Grandma's cooking, Don't complain.*

"You said three o'clock. It's quarter to three. Here's the mustard you wanted." She set two jars of seeded mustard on the counter, the only kind acceptable for a meal that included kielbasa.

"Hoffmeyer's?" She grabbed up one and examined the label.

"Yes."

"Hello, sis," Lynette said, tossing an air kiss in Jan's direction. She stood at the sink washing and slicing cucumbers. She was a shorter version of Harriet, except for the hair: shoulder length, brown and pulled back into a thick ponytail. She wore tan shorts, a navy blue polo shirt and sandals.

"Hi. Where do I put these?" Jan held up two identical gift bags.

"What did you get them this year?" she asked in a critical tone.

"Jigsaw puzzles with three thousand tiny little pieces."

"Jan!" her mother groaned.

"You better not have," Lynette warned.

"I got them…" Jan looked toward the hall to see if anyone was coming then lowered her voice. "Remote control helicopters. They're not very big and the controls are super simple. They'll hover and do stunts and everything. The receipt is in the box if they don't like them. You can exchange them for video games but I thought they needed something that required a little fresh air."

"Like the skateboards you got them when they were four?"

"Hey, I gave them helmets and elbow pads too."

"Shawn tried to ride his down the stairs."

"Don't blame me. I just buy the toys. You're the warden." Jan gave her sister a playful poke and carried the gift bags into the dining room, adding them to the pile on the buffet. Baci, wearing a flowered dress and slippers, was arranging silverware at each place at the table.

"Hi Baci." Jan gave her a kiss on the cheek then took a celery stick from the dish. "They have you working too?"

"Hello, dear," she replied without looking up from her task. There was a shaky hesitation to her voice, another result of the stroke.

The dining room table was extended to its full length and a card table had been added at the end. A mix of wooden and folding chairs was crowded around the table to accommodate everyone. In spite of the mismatched china and ugly striped glasses, the table setting brought a contented smile to Jan's face. She patted Baci on the arm and returned to the kitchen to see if she could help.

"Where's Pop?" she asked.

"I sent him to Chmura's for rye bread." Harriet poked a fork in the simmering potatoes.

"Hey Jan," a thin-faced woman said, striding into the kitchen. Wearing black yoga pants, an over-sized Green Peace T-shirt and barefeet, she looked like a much shorter version of Jan but with long blond hair. Beth was often included in family dinners even though her parents, Jan's aunt and uncle, hadn't accepted her bisexuality. Harriet and John said she was family regardless and accepted her warmly into their fold. She was a staunch vegetarian but there were always plenty of dishes to her liking.

"Hey Beth. How's my favorite cousin?" They shared a fist bump, an elbow bump then turned sideways and executed an awkward hip bump, as if it was a ritual.

"I'm great. How's the limo biz? Have you driven anyone important? Movie star? Rock star? Alien from Mars?"

"I took a senator's wife for a mani-pedi last week."

"Which one?"

"I can't tell you that. Client confidentiality."

"It's not as if I'm asking for her medical history. And who am I going to tell? Was she a good tipper?"

"Not particularly."

Beth picked several cucumber slices from the bowl and returned to the living room.

"I thought I heard your voice." A smartly dressed man in khaki slacks and button-down shirt came at Jan with his arms wide for a hug. "Hi, sweetheart. How are you?"

Keith was the youngest of her siblings. He had been out since college, although he had confessed his sexuality to Jan his freshman year of high school. Theirs was a special bond. It had taken their parents a few years to fully accept and understand their homosexuality, but now it was just who they were. The Chases loved all their children and defended them equally, in spite of the Catholic church's opposition.

"I like that aftershave. What is it?" Jan sniffed his neck.

"Polo Black. Isn't it nice? Jefferson gave it to me for our anniversary. He said he was tired of me smelling like fruit salad."

"Where is Jefferson?" She looked past him toward the living room.

"He's losing at Super Quest or some video idiocy."

"Who to?" Lynette asked, overhearing their conversation.

"One of the boys."

"Which one?"

"I have no idea. They're twins. They look exactly alike."

"No, they don't," Lynette and Jan said in unison.

"Shawn is taller and Shannon's eyes are darker," Lynette explained.

Raucous laughter erupted from the living room.

"Keith, your turn," someone yelled.

Keith refilled his water glass and returned to the living room.

"Did you hear? Keith and Jefferson are talking nuptials," Lynette said softly.

"For real?"

"That's the rumor. Why don't you ask them."

"Why me? You ask them." Jan ate a cucumber slice.

"What will we call Jefferson? Keith's wife or Keith's husband? I heard it depends on who's dominant in the bedroom, if you know what I mean." Lynette raised her eyebrows.

"Well, I'm certainly not going to ask them that. I do *not* want to know who does what to whom."

"Aren't you curious?"

"God no." She chuckled. "No more than I want to know what Mom and Dad do in the bedroom."

"Jannie, sweetheart, can you call Uncle Leo?" her mother asked as she came out of the pantry with a jar of pickles. "Tell him fifteen minutes and tell him to put his teeth in. He's not going to sit at my table looking like a toothless fool."

A wooden shutter hung next to the wall phone, the same harvest gold telephone that had hung there since Jan was a toddler, the one with the long curly cord that dragged on the floor. The shutter had tiny pieces of paper with phone numbers taped to the slats, some scribbled over and rewritten several times. Jan scanned down the slats until she found Leo, Baci's only surviving brother. He had lived across the street for fifty years and was included when family events grew large enough that one more didn't matter. He was a difficult man. That was the way the family referred to him, the polite way. But he was family so he was included for birthdays, holidays and backyard cookouts. He didn't have anyone else.

"He wants to know if you made kapusta," Jan asked, although the kitchen smelled like it and she couldn't imagine a family dinner without it.

"Yes. I made kapusta." Harriet lifted the lid to a large pan as if showing the man on the other end of the line.

"With onions?" Jan added, caught between Uncle Leo complaining in her ear and her mother's angry response.

"Yes, there's onion in it. Whoever heard of making kapusta without onions?"

"He says onions give him gas."

"If he doesn't like my kapusta, don't eat it." Harriet scowled then turned away from the conversation.

Jan did her best to reassure Uncle Leo there were other choices without onions. He would probably eat kapusta anyway. He usually did. She ended the call and heaved a sigh of relief.

"Everything makes Uncle Leo fart," Lynette said. "He doesn't need onions."

Jan let her gaze drift out the window as her sister stuck out her tongue and made farting noises. The glint of sunlight off a car's bumper caught her eye. She did a double take, squinting at a white Camry.

"Son-of-a—" she muttered through clenched teeth.

"What?" Lynette tossed a quick look out the window.

"What is she doing here?" Jan turned her back to the window as if she could will away the red-haired woman by ignoring her. But a knot was already forming in the pit of her stomach. "Ma!" she yelled.

"What?" Harriet returned to the kitchen, using her apron to wipe out a small serving bowl.

"Did you invite her?"

"Who?"

"You know who." She nodded toward the window and the woman climbing out of the car.

Her mother gave a quick look. "Oh, doesn't she look nice. I like her hair. I've always liked red hair. Aunt Cecilia had red hair. It came out of a bottle but it looked nice on her."

"Ma, why did you invite her?"

"I didn't, dear. I might have mentioned you'd be here for the twins' birthday is all."

Jan cocked her head and stared at her mother.

"Okay, I might have said if she wasn't busy she was welcome to stop by."

"You invited my ex to dinner."

"Fine. So, kill me. I invited her to dinner."

"You should have asked me, Ma." She took the jar of pickles from her mother and popped the lid.

"If I had asked you'd have just said no. She's a nice girl. What's the harm in inviting her to dinner?" She shrugged then poured the pickles into the dish.

"I don't need a girlfriend right now. And I certainly don't need my mother fixing me up with my ex."

There was a knock at the back door.

"Put a smile on your face and let her in." Harriet pointed to the back door.

"You invited her. You let her in." Jan crossed her arms and leaned back against the kitchen counter.

"Lose the attitude or I'll take a switch to you, young lady." She wiped her hands on her apron and went to answer the door.

Lynette leaned over and whispered in Jan's ear, "I warned her you wouldn't like it."

"You knew?" Jan turned an angry glare toward her sister.

"Yeah. But I told her it was a bad idea. Don't be too hard on her. She's just trying to help. You know how Ma is." Lynette giggled wickedly.

"What's so funny?"

"When she's trying to help you she doesn't have time to meddle in my life." She grinned.

A freckle-faced woman appeared in the doorway. A large turquoise purse slung over her shoulder was decorated with an oversized chrome belt buckle and metal studs that looked like something a cowgirl would carry. She wore tight fitting jeans and a denim vest buttoned over ample breasts. If she had a tank top on under the vest Jan couldn't see it. All she could see was the two inches of cleavage above the top button, pale cleavage covered with freckles.

"Look who's here," Harriet announced cheerfully as she followed her into the kitchen.

"Hi Allie," Lynette said with a smile then turned to Jan.

"Hi Lynette." Allie's gaze fell softly on Jan, slowly moving down her body and back up, ending with an affectionate smile. "Hi Jan."

"Hey Allie." Jan's arms were still folded defensively, more a statement against her mother's invitation than against this woman. Their relationship was over and had been for nearly three years. She represented no threat. That didn't make this meeting any less awkward.

"Oh, come on. You big goof. Get over your cheap self and give me a hug." Allie threw her arms around Jan, crossed arms and all, and squeezed tightly. The top of her head and fluffy red hair fit under Jan's chin, stray locks of hair tickling her nose. "How have you been, sweetie?"

"Good. I'm good." She heaved a reluctant sigh. She knew what was expected of her and finally said it, hoping it sounded sincere. "How are you?"

"I'm okay. Had a cold last week but I'm okay. You look good, Jan." Her eyes did another run down and up her body. "I like these jeans." She hooked two fingers in the front pocket of Jan's jeans and gave a tug. "Very good look on you."

"Thank you."

She stood close enough for Jan to see down the gap in her cleavage to the soft rounded form of her breasts. Allie seemed to know she was looking and took a deep breath.

"Your mom told me you're driving a limo in Boston. How do you like it?"

"Can you reach that platter on the top shelf?" Harriet interrupted, as if to bump Jan out of her defensive posture.

"I like it. It's easy and I get to meet people. Great way to drive fancy cars too." She handed down the platter. It was the first time she had unclenched since Allie had walked into the kitchen.

"You two are in the way," Lynette said, nudging them aside as she reached for serving spoons from the silverware drawer.

"What can I do to help?" Allie said happily. "Give me a job." She thrust her hefty purse at Jan. "Put this somewhere, sweetie. And move out of the way." She elbowed her toward the hall.

"Find the parsley in the spice cabinet." Harriet nodded in that direction. "Jan, get the new package of napkins from the pantry. Two at each place."

"I'll do it." Allie set down the jar of parsley then winked at Jan. "Go stand over there out of the way."

Like making homemade sausage, preparing a big family dinner in the Chase household was messy and fraught with near disasters. Through all the confusion and chaos, the end product promised to be delicious. The menu varied only slightly from summer gatherings to holiday feasts, usually consisting of the family's favorite Polish dishes, the ones they grew up on. Comfort food.

"Bread's here," Lynette said as a bald-headed man passed under the kitchen window.

John Chase came through the back door with an armload of paper sacks. A tall man, taller than anyone else in the family, he had bushy eyebrows and deep c-shaped wrinkles on either side of his mouth. He wore a white snap front shirt with a glasses case, a pen and a small screwdriver with a clip on the barrel in the breast pocket. His sleeves were rolled up to the elbow, exposing long thin arms covered with white hair. A tuft of white hair curled out the top of his shirt, suggesting a hairy chest.

"What did you get?" Harriet met him at the door, peering inside the sacks.

"Two seeded rye. One plain rye. One marble rye. All sliced. And half a dozen bagels for breakfast," he answered in his deep voice. "Hey, kiddo," he said, smiling over at Jan. "How's the new job?"

"It's good, Pop. Really good." Jan helped her mother carry the sacks to the counter. "You were right. The mini-fridge in the party van does have room for an ice tray. But I'm not sure it gets cold enough. We'll find out next week. I'm taking a group of sorority girls to the Cape."

"Which sorority?" Lynette asked eagerly.

"I don't know. Kappa Snooty Pooh." They both laughed.

"I love Chmura's rye bread," Allie said and turned to Jan. "Remember when we bought a dozen rolls to take to Gina's party but ate half of them before we got there?" She smiled as if inviting Jan to share the memory. "That was right before…" Allie's eyes met Jan's then turned away. It was a private memory no one else seemed to notice.

"Uncle Leo's here," Keith called from the front door. Uncle Leo was the only one in the family who didn't use the back door, in spite of instructions to the contrary.

"Allie, could you put the bread in the baskets?" Harriet said, setting two loaves next to the breadbaskets. "Jan, put these bowls on the table and call the boys."

It took several trips but finally all the food was on the table. Kielbasa, parsley potatoes, kapusta, cabbage and spinach pierogi, pork roast as well as several vegetables and salad dishes. More choices than could fit on a dinner plate. But it was tradition. And there would be leftovers well into the week.

Jan's father sat at one end of the table, a twin on each side of him. It wasn't a ceremonial honor for them to sit there. It was to keep them from picking and sniping at each other. Grandpa John didn't allow horseplay at the table and he wasn't above saying so. Harriet sat at the other end nearest the kitchen, ready to spring into action if anything had been forgotten or needed refilling. Baci usually sat on the corner next to Jan but Allie snagged that spot, so she nabbed a spot beside one of the twins. Lynette sat next to her husband, Mike. A high school teacher and soccer coach, he was a quiet man and fit like a glove into the family, a now boisterous, laughing and loving family.

"Everything smells so good," Allie said, leaning into Jan. She helped herself to the bowl of peas and carrots, offered some to Jan, then sent it on its way around the table. "I can't get over how good you look."

"Thanks." She raked some sliced kielbasa onto her plate. "You look good too."

"Have you been seeing anyone?" If Allie tried to make it sound like an innocuous conversation starter, she failed.

"No."

"No one? It's been three years. Why not?"

"Who are you dating?"

"No one right now. Carol's sister asked if I wanted to go to the Melissa Etheridge concert. I said no." In spite of the typical dinner chitchat around the table, it was clear Lynette and Harriet were eavesdropping.

"Why didn't you go?"

"I don't know. I guess I wasn't in the mood." Allie turned a soft smile to Jan. "I was going to ask you to go with me."

"No, thanks," Jan said stiffly and passed the potatoes. She felt her cell phone vibrate against her waistband. It was the limousine service. She excused herself and stepped into the hall for privacy and so she could hear.

"Hi, Glenda. What's up?"

"You're off today, right?" the gravelly voiced woman said.

"Right. And before you ask, no, I can't come in. I'm out of town."

"How far out?"

"Far enough."

"Okay, not this one." Glenda sounded like she was reading the schedule. "How about tomorrow? Pick up at Logan. Delivered to the Fairmont Copley Plaza. The flight is due in at seven thirty but they're calling for rain tomorrow afternoon and evening so you might have to wait. I know it's last minute but are you absolutely sure you can't come in this afternoon?"

"Can't, Glenda."

"What's so important you can't cancel it?"

"Sorry, can't help you. I've got a family thing."

"You realize I'm going to have to send Ramone."

"So what's wrong with sending Ramone?"

"They specifically asked for you, or rather they asked for a female driver."

"It's not my fault you have twelve drivers and I'm the only female. Besides, I couldn't get there in time. Who is it, anyway?"

"That woman from the other night. The one you took to Cambridge then to the airport. Grayson."

Jan took a quick breath, surprised Elise would have asked for her. But maybe she wasn't particularly asking for her. Maybe she assumed the car service had other women drivers.

"Jan, are you there?" Glenda asked at Jan's hesitation.

"Yes, I'm here. I'll see you tomorrow." She ended the call. "You can pick on somebody else, Ms. Grayson. 'Cause it ain't gonna be me," she muttered to herself as she returned to the table. In spite of her efforts not to go there, the image of Elise Grayson in her bra sitting in the backseat of the limousine came into focus.

"Is everything all right?" Allie asked, passing the breadbasket.

"Sure. Just a reminder about a pickup tomorrow."

"You work on Sunday?"

"I work whenever they need me. People go places and do things on Sunday just like any other day."

"I guess that's true." Allie sounded disappointed.

The dinner conversation moved from the twins' birthday to Baci's doctor appointment to Uncle Leo's car problems. Mike and John discussed kitchen faucets. Harriet and Beth compared rising grocery store prices. Jan tried to ignore her but she could feel Allie's eyes watching her every move and every bite she took. It wasn't a loving look. It was an overbearing protective look, as if Allie were poised to wipe her chin or cut her meat if Jan wasn't capable of doing it for herself. And it made her uncomfortable.

"What?" Jan finally asked.

"Nothing." Allie smiled fondly, like a mother encouraging a toddler's first steps. "How about some more veggies? I remember you love carrots."

"No, thanks. I've got some." She pointed to the helping on her plate.

"Kielbasa?"

"No, thanks, Allie. I'm fine."

"Allie, help yourself to the pickled beets," John called.

"That's okay. I've had plenty."

"When he says help yourself that's code for please pass the beets," Jan whispered.

"Oh!" Allie obliged then rested her hand on Jan's thigh. "Why didn't you tell me?"

"I just did." She pulled her leg away but the hand came with it.

For over an hour they sat around the table eating, laughing and watching the twins open birthday gifts. When her father and Uncle Leo left the table it meant the dinner was over and it was time to clear the dishes. Jan stood, ready to help carry plates to the kitchen.

"You sit and visit with Allie," her mother said and looked over at Beth and Lynette. "Come on, girls. Grab a plate."

"I can help," Allie offered although not very vehemently.

"No, you stay at the table and talk with Jannie. I don't have room for everyone in the kitchen anyway." Harriet headed into the kitchen to package leftovers while Beth and Lynette carried dishes and loaded the dishwasher.

"Are you spending the night at your folks'?" Allie asked Jan.

"No. I have to be in Boston in the morning. I'll head back after a while."

"I was hoping you'd stay over."

The twins came running into the dining room. "Thank you for the money, Allie," they said in unison as if they had been instructed to do so.

"You're welcome, sweethearts," she said warmly. "Happy birthday."

They both disappeared, seeming satisfied they had done what they were sent to do.

"They're cute boys," Allie offered. "They look just like you."

"They look like Keith when he was eight. It was nice of you to give them a gift."

"I remember when they were four, or was it five? They followed you everywhere. You were their rock star. They loved to wrestle around on the floor with you."

"They're too old for that now. They're more into video games and soccer." Jan drank the last swallow from her water glass. "Allie, why did you come?"

"Your mother invited me. It was very sweet of her. She's a wonderful cook."

"Okay, now answer the question honestly. Why did you come? What did you think was going to happen?"

Allie took a deep breath, diverting her gaze.

"I wanted to see you. I wanted to know how you were." She drew her eyes up to meet Jan's. "I miss you."

Jan rested her arms on the table and gave Allie a sideways glance. "It's not going to happen, you know," she said softly.

"What? What's not going to happen?"

"You and I. I don't know what my mother told you or what you thought you'd find here today but you and I aren't happening again."

"Oh, I know. I know," Allie quickly acknowledged. "I know." She finally took a deep cleansing breath. "It's late and I've got another appointment. Walk me out, okay?" she asked quietly.

"Okay."

"Harriet, it was wonderful. Thank you so much for inviting me," Allie said as they walked through the kitchen.

"I'm so glad you came, dear." She gave Allie a hug then tossed a glare up at Jan. "You're welcome anytime. Isn't she, Jan?"

"Sure." Jan wasn't going to argue with her mother. Not now.

Allie went out the back door and down the steps first then waited for Jan. She locked her arm through Jan's as they strode down the driveway together.

"It really was great to see you, sweetheart. I know you don't want to hear that but it was," Allie said, leaning her head against Jan's shoulder. "Please don't be mad at me for coming."

"I'm not mad."

"You're not mad but you don't want us to be friends anymore. Is that it?"

"I didn't say that. But I know you, Allie. If I say I'll see you around or I'll see you the next time I'm in town you're going to assume something that isn't there."

"No, I won't. I tried to make you happy. I truly did. I don't understand why you shut me out. Do you even remember?"

Jan turned her face up to the afternoon sun and took a deep breath. Along with her mother, she didn't want to argue with Allie either. They'd done that three years ago and all it had accomplished was hurt feelings.

"I don't need another mother to take care of me. I have one and that's enough."

"I didn't mean to smother you. I just wanted…" Allie's voice cracked and she began to cry.

"I know." Jan wrapped her arm around her. She hadn't meant to upset her. She walked her to her car and opened the driver's side door. "Take care of yourself, Allie." She wiped a tear from Allie's cheek.

Allie smiled up at Jan, her chin still quivering. She pulled Jan's head down and kissed her on the lips then climbed in, closed the door and drove away without saying a word.

Jan shoved her hands in her pockets and stood in the street until Allie's car disappeared around the corner. She wondered if she'd handled that as diplomatically as she could have. She also wondered how long before her chest didn't tighten at the mere thought of Allie staring back at her. She shrugged and went back inside.

CHAPTER THREE

"Good morning, Lorraine," Elise said, looking up at the sound of footsteps outside her office.

"Good morning." Lorraine looked surprised and glanced at her watch. "You're here early."

"I couldn't sleep so I decided to come in and see if I can get a head start on Monday. Have we used Hudson Flooring before? Do we have a track record on them?"

"Hudson? That name doesn't sound familiar. Is that the wholesale place in Worchester advertised on TV?"

"Yes. Mrs. Bales saw some tile there she likes for the lobby of the clinic. I want to know if they're an outlet store where we can't reorder matching goods. I don't want a place that only sells end of the run or odd lots."

"I'll check it out." Lorraine smiled brightly. "What time did Ginger get home last night? I bet it was good to have her home."

"Her flight was cancelled. She'll be home today."

"That's too bad. What happened? Weather in Jersey?"

"Mechanical I think. The airline put them up in a hotel and is flying them out around noon."

"So she should be home by dinnertime."

"Probably. She's going to call when she lands."

"Do you still need to go to Springfield next week?"

"Yes. I'm meeting with the city about the hospital expansion. And while I'm there I'm supposed to look over a piece of property Dad thinks has good apartment potential."

"Are you driving or do you want a car and driver?"

"The last time I drove to Springfield I ended up in Connecticut. And I got a ticket for an illegal left turn. Definitely a car and driver. Definitely. Let's make it next Monday," Elise said, flipping the page on her desk calendar. "By the way, when you ordered the car to pick me up at Logan did you ask for the same driver I had last week?"

"I asked for a female driver. You said that's what you wanted. Was there a problem?"

"They sent a man." Elise raised an eyebrow. "A greasy-haired man with a lead foot."

"Really? I specifically asked for a female driver."

"That was my fault. I should have told you the driver's name. Next time ask for Jan. At least she didn't drive sixty miles an hour along the Boston Common."

"Do you want me to let them know you weren't happy with the service?"

Elise leaned back in her chair and thought a moment.

"No, not this time. We'll just remember not to include Ramone on the Christmas card list."

"I'll take care of it this morning," Lorraine said.

Elise added the Monday trip to the appointment calendar on her cell phone. Bright red letters on Saturday caught her attention.

"Is that this week?" she mumbled and picked up her desk phone. She touched one of the speed dial numbers but hung up before it started to ring. "She won't be up yet."

She went back to work. An hour later she leaned back in her chair and hooked one of the temples of her glasses at the corner of her mouth while she waited for an answer.

"Hello," a woman said with a gasp.

"Hello, Mother."

"Elise. I was expecting the caterer."

Caterer. That word unto itself meant her mother was going all out for her dinner party. But then, it wouldn't be the first time, nor would it be the last.

"No, Mother. It's just me. How are you?"

"In a word, frazzled. The guest list is growing as we speak. Your father insisted I invite the Henleys *and* the Martins. If I invite Lenore Martin I have to invite her sister. There's no getting around it. That woman is insufferable."

"So the dinner is still on for Saturday night?"

"Yes, Elise. It's still on for Saturday night," she said with an exasperated groan. "If you see your father *please* tell him not to invite anyone else. The caterer is beginning to think I'm insane."

Elise chuckled. Her father wasn't the problem. It was her mother's insatiable desire to maintain status in Boston society.

"How many are on the guest list so far?"

"Let's see, two, four, hmmm. Twenty six. Twenty eight counting you and Ginger."

Elise was tempted to proffer an excuse why she and Ginger couldn't attend but she knew better. It was expected she be there. She *and* her partner. It took her mother long enough to accept Ginger. She wanted to take advantage of that fact before she changed her mind.

"What can I bring, Mother?"

"Nothing, dear. My menu is set. I really need to get off the phone, Elise. We're finalizing the details this morning. I'll see you both, Saturday, sixish." Her mother ended the call.

Elise spent most of the afternoon with the company's architectural designer working on revisions for several project plans. It was half past three when she heard her cell phone chime an incoming text. It was from Ginger.

Hi, El. Just touched down. Long day. I'll see you at home. Luvya.

Elise remembered Ginger took a cab to the airport last week instead of leaving her car in the parking lot. She tapped out a reply and sent it on its way.

Glad you're back. Do you need me to send a car to pick you up? We could meet at The Grotto for dinner.

No, I'll take a cab on home. I can catch one at the curb. I'm exhausted and I need a shower. Why don't we order in later? Ginger added a frowny face to the text.

I'll see you at home later then. Welcome home, by the way.

There was no reply from Ginger. But a few minutes later another text chimed its way onto Elise's phone. It was from Ginger but it read as if it wasn't for Elise.

Mal, you were right. The extra days were amazing. I'm glad you suggested them. They were, how shall I say it, magical. Thanks for everything. There was a little heart shaped emoji at the end of the text as well as one of a tiny house.

Before Elise could question Ginger about the text she received another.

Oops, sorry, El. That text was meant for Mallory. She was so helpful at the conference, helping me decide which seminars to attend. She even invited me to participate in the one she moderated. It was great. I learned so much. See you at home, sweetie.

Elise dismissed the text and didn't bother to reply. She herself had sent a few errant texts. The one she'd accidentally sent to a job foreman ordering a pizza and a mocha latte still created a few giggles.

It was after seven when she finally unlocked the front door to the two-story condo where she and Ginger lived in Boston's Back Bay. It had been a foreclosure investment Elise's father insisted she make years ago, long before owning a home in a prestigious part of Boston would possibly come across her radar. He had guaranteed she'd double or triple her investment someday. Fresh out of college, single and working for her father, she had agreed. For the first few years she'd wondered if she had purchased the proverbial money pit. All of her spare time and money had gone into remodeling. What emerged was a comfortable two bedroom, two bath home with hardwood floors, spa tubs, high ceilings and a modern kitchen that suited her mature and successful lifestyle completely. And was worth three times her investment.

"El, is that you?" a voice called from upstairs.

"Yes. Just little ol' me." She set her purse and briefcase on the hall table and went to the bottom of the stairs. "What's for dinner? Shall I call Jimmy John's?"

Ginger appeared at the top of the stairs. She looked freshly showered and was dressed in fluorescent green running shorts and a white tank top. Elise looked at her appreciatively. At fifty-two, Ginger Lindquist was a handsome woman. She had a square jaw and dancing hazel eyes. Her brown hair with blond highlights and radiant complexion, even without makeup, gave her the youthful appearance of a thirty-five year old. Even Elise's mother, a woman consumed with appearance and the woes of aging, was surprised at how old Ginger really was. She came bouncing down the stairs with her laptop under her arm and braless under her tank top. She wasn't as well-endowed as Elise but she bounced nonetheless, the imprint of her areolae and nipples dancing with every step. Elise felt her breath quicken. "Hi," she said with a glowing smile.

"Hi." Ginger stood on the bottom step and looked down at Elise. "How's the woman in my life?"

"She's good. How are you?" She couldn't contain herself and hooked a finger through one of the straps of Ginger's tank top. "I'd be even better if you'd go back upstairs and bounce down again." She gave a saucy grin.

Ginger laughed and gave Elise a quick kiss on the cheek.

"I'd love to but I have to be online in exactly three minutes. We're having a conference call to go over the listings that came in while we were gone. I think I'm showing one in a couple days."

"What would you like for dinner?"

"I brought home a calzone. I put the rest of it in the fridge. Spinach and mushroom. Your favorite," she said, touching Elise's arm then heading into the living room. "Sorry I didn't wait for you but I was famished. That little baggie of pretzels on the plane was all I've had since breakfast."

"That's okay. Calzone sounds good."

Elise poured herself a glass of wine and took a sip while she waited for the calzone to heat in the microwave. By the time she took a seat at the counter with her plate Ginger was online yakking away with her colleagues. Not exactly the welcome home dinner she'd envisioned but at least Ginger was home.

It was after ten when Ginger shut down her laptop and came upstairs. Elise had spent the evening catching up on email, doing laundry and wondering what she was going to wear Saturday. Whatever it was, dressy or casual, her mother's critical stare would have her wondering what else she should have chosen.

"Remember Saturday is dinner at my folks'," she said as she climbed into bed. Elise didn't wear pajamas, at least not until the dead of winter when even the hardiest of souls acquiesced to the elements and donned flannels. It had been a long day and she was tired but Ginger was home after having been gone for over a week and Elise fully expected her to initiate sex. For the past few months they seemed to be ships passing in the night when it came to intimacy. Between busy work schedules, out of town trips and monthly menstrual cycles, they had been living an almost platonic relationship. Elise couldn't imagine Ginger would let a golden opportunity like this go by. Neither of them was on her period. Both were home, in bed and, at least for Elise, horny. She couldn't remember the last time she'd had a partner-induced orgasm.

Ginger came to the bathroom door with her toothbrush in hand. She gave a quizzical look. "When did that happen?"

"This is the one I told you about last month. Mother decided to have a dedication dinner for her new remodel."

"What did she have remodeled that needs a dedication dinner? The Louvre?"

"The kitchen and breakfast room. She went Tuscan this time. I know. It's not that big a deal. Mother just wanted an excuse to have a party."

"First of all, your mother and kitchen don't belong in the same sentence. She doesn't cook. She reheats. And second, Tuscan is *so* last year. How much did she spend on this little remodel? Probably more than I paid for my car. And that's assuming Grayson Construction did the work."

"I saw pictures of it. It does look really nice. She had one of those huge six-burner gas stoves put in."

"Tell her I'm happy for her." Ginger went back to the sink to rinse.

"You can tell her yourself Saturday night. She'll love to hear it." Elise did one last check for email on her phone then set it in the charging cradle. "We'll leave here around five."

"El, I can't go. I'm helping Mallory with an open house. It's the one we had to postpone a couple months ago. She specifically asked if I wanted to co-hostess this one. It's a great house on a great street. Almost two million dollars. Even with a shared commission, it would be a nice piece of change."

"The dinner is Saturday. Not Sunday."

"Right, the open house is Sunday but we're going over on Saturday to help the owners stage the house." Ginger squirted a glob of moisturizer onto her hand and began working it into her arms and elbows. "They have no idea what they're doing. We are talking major clutter. We ordered one of those mobile storage units and hopefully one will be enough."

"It seems like that's waiting until the last minute. Shouldn't that have been done already?"

"All I know is Mallory is picking me up at noon on Saturday and she said dress casual and be prepared to work late."

"Ginger, I told you about the dinner weeks ago. Mother is expecting us both to be there. You'll have to tell your boss you've got a previous engagement on Saturday. Tell her you can be there Sunday for the open house but Saturday is out of the question."

Ginger set her phone in the charger on her side of the bed and turned back the covers.

"I'm sorry, Elise, but my work comes first. If I don't go Saturday Mallory will ask someone else for Sunday and there goes my commission."

"It's an open house. Not a sale. There's no commission on an open house. And you know as well as I do, a two million dollar price tag means you'll have gawkers, not serious buyers."

"Yes but say someone does make an offer, my commission could be almost fifty grand." She checked the mute setting on her phone then snuggled down. "Besides, your parents don't like me anyway."

"Yes, they do. Where did you get that idea?"

Ginger turned her head toward Elise and frowned. "New Year's Eve. Last year. Don't tell me you forgot."

"She didn't mean it. Mother just had too much champagne. You know how she gets."

Ginger cleared her throat, as if preparing for an announcement, and began a shrill imitation: "Ginger, dear. That color does absolutely nothing for you or your complexion. When you get home, take that blouse off and throw it away. Try a neutral color, dear. Something inconspicuous."

"Hey, when we got home you said she was right. Persimmon wasn't your color." Elise had to smile. It was an ugly color.

"That wasn't the only time. She just doesn't like me."

"She does too." Elise turned out the lamp on her nightstand and moved closer, expecting to feel Ginger's hand under the covers at any moment.

"Well, she'll have to wait for another evening to pick on me. I'm going with Mallory. I just can't cancel. It's too good an opportunity. Please don't insist, El. Okay?"

Elise heaved a resolute sigh. "Okay. I'll make your apologies. If I tell her you're showing a multi-million dollar house she might forgive you." She wanted to put her mother and her confounded dinner party out of her mind.

"Thank you, sweetie." Ginger kissed Elise's forehead then turned on her side, facing the window. She yawned loudly. "I'm beat. Night night."

"Good night," Elise said, hoping to hide her disappointment. She understood. Ginger had had a busy week and she needed her rest. They'd find time for lovemaking another day. Soon, hopefully.

CHAPTER FOUR

Elise decided not to forewarn her mother that Ginger wasn't coming to dinner. Her mother was already stressed enough. With a house full of guests maybe she wouldn't really notice. Or at least not care. Elise had hoped to find a convenient opportunity to mention the dinner again in hopes of changing Ginger's mind. But Ginger seemed totally consumed with the big plans about the big house. It was all she could talk about. Elise conceded that she couldn't be dissuaded and chose not to even mention it. She had her own job details to handle, including a last minute meeting with a client at a job site Saturday morning.

She hoped to be back before Ginger had to leave but the meeting ran on and on. It was Elise's job to answer the client's questions and quell all their worries about the project, and she could not appear impatient. But the longer the meeting ran the more she worried about having enough time to dress and get to her parents' by six.

By the time she showered and was ready to leave she wished she had ordered a car and driver, perhaps Jan Chase, that is if she could keep her eyes on the road. At least she'd be delivered on time and without the obnoxious smell from the backseat of a taxi permeating her clothes. But there wasn't time. She'd have to settle for a taxi.

Elise could hear voices inside as she climbed the two steps to the front door. She rang the doorbell then let herself in.

"You're just in time to hear your mother's story about how she selected the granite for the countertops," her father said, rolling his eyes.

"Hi Dad." She kissed his cheek. "Do I have to?"

"Come with me." He took her by the hand and led her into his office, a mahogany-paneled room off the foyer with a pair of leather chairs facing an oversized desk. He stopped at a tall cabinet with an open drop-down door. Inside was a small but well-stocked minibar. "What'll you have, Elise? Bourbon? Scotch?" He dropped ice cubes in two glasses. "I'm going to have Four Roses and stay out of your mother's way." He poured an inch of bourbon in one glass, looked at the level and poured a little more. "Four Roses for you too?"

"Sure. Why not?" Elise wasn't a liquor connoisseur but she knew what bourbon, gin, vodka and the rest of her father's collection tasted like. It wasn't unusual for him to invite their better clients over for a drink. He said it was good business to make them feel like part of the family. Build their confidence and trust. Forest Grayson wasn't above opening a thousand dollar bottle of premium reserve and toasting a client's multi-million dollar project. Elise had sipped many a toast for the sake of the business.

He poured her glass and handed it to her. "Here's to your mother and her travertine tile." He tapped his glass against Elise's then took a drink. "God love her," he added with a chuckle. "By the way, have you looked at that piece of property in Springfield yet?"

"No, not yet but I'm going out there Monday. I'm meeting with the city planning board about the hospital addition. I'll swing by and take a look at it while I'm there."

"Good. That location has good access to shopping and restaurants. Let me know what you think. Maybe a pair of matching three-story buildings? Brick and stucco maybe. There's a couple of units a mile or so away built in the eighties. They slapped them up with vinyl siding and exterior wooden stairs. They look trashy. I think we can tap into people's need for better housing choices."

Forest Grayson was a good judge of property potential. As a construction company, most revenue came from building projects for specific clients. But once in a while an opportunity to purchase property presented itself. They had kept their losses to a minimum through shrewd negotiations and careful choices.

"I'll look it over. It's currently a strip mall, right?"

"Not really a strip mall. More of a row of older commercial storefronts, most of them empty or about to be."

He refilled his glass and gave it a swirl. "Should I ask why Ginger didn't come with you? Your mother is going to want an explanation."

"She wanted to but she's showing a house. Big one. Two mil." Elise took another sip, hoping to camouflage her fib, or at least make it palatable.

"Uh huh." He sipped, his eyes on Elise.

"Okay, so Ginger and Mother don't always see eye to eye."

"Hey, keep me out of it. I'm an innocent bystander." Forest held up a hand. "Your mother just wants you to be happy. We both do. She has a little trouble conveying that sometimes. If Ginger makes you happy, then we're happy." He hesitated then asked, "Does she make you happy, Elise?"

"Sure. Yes." Elise felt an awkward ambivalence to his question.

"Good. Shall we join the others?" He led the way into the spacious living room, where guests were visiting and sipping from wine glasses.

Suzanne Grayson had several guests crowded around her, listening to her every word. She wore a gold and black bolero jacket and flowing black gaucho pants. Her platform sandals were covered with sparkles. She reminded Elise of a flamenco dancer or maybe a bullfighter, except for her hair, which was platinum blond and stylishly asymmetrical.

"There's my gorgeous daughter," Suzanne announced and waved her over.

Elise crossed the room and gave her a hug. "Hello Mother. You look wonderful."

"Thank you, sweetheart. Oh, I see you wore this again. It's lovely. Always in fashion. You can never go wrong in a simple gray pantsuit. And I love the scarf. Just a splash of color." Elise's outfit seemed to pass muster; she gave her daughter a kiss on the cheek as approval. "Where's Ginger?" Suzanne asked.

Elise tossed a look at her father. He gave a soft chuckle then sipped his drink.

"She couldn't come, Mother. She wanted to but she's working."

"Working?"

"She's showing a house and she just couldn't get out of it. It's quite a house I understand."

"Oh?"

"List price is two million." She could have described the house's size and square footage but the price was sufficient to distract her mother's disappointment. "She really wanted to be here but there was no way around it. She had to be there."

"Of course. I understand. The client comes first. Your father has missed many a dinner because a client had a problem. We'll miss her, dear." Suzanne patted her daughter's arm and smiled warmly.

Elise noticed her father's nod, as if to say *That went better than we expected.*

Dinner was served as a buffet. Linen covered tables were set up on the patio. With the Tuscan décor as the backdrop, not to anyone's surprise, Suzanne chose an Italian cuisine for the meal. A selection of seafood, pasta dishes, imported delicacies—some Elise didn't recognize. She ate her meal, visited with guests and was thankful she didn't have to further defend Ginger's choice not to attend. She texted Ginger twice to give her updates and offer encouragement. When she didn't hear back from her she assumed they were busy moving knickknacks, fluffing pillows and arranging furniture.

It wasn't until Elise's third yawn that she realized she was exhausted. She had eaten, drunk and talked all she could for one evening. Her father had disappeared into his office and closed the door, presumably talking business with a potential client. Elise discreetly pulled her cell phone from her purse and called a cab, instructing them to wait outside for her.

"Mother, everything was wonderful. Your remodel is spectacular." She hugged her mother's side. "I love the travertine tile and the backsplash." She turned for the foyer.

"Elise, you can *not* be the first to leave. You're family," her mother said, taking her arm and leading her away from the hall.

"I'm not the first. Doctor Fish left an hour ago. So did the Bowmans. I'm tired and I have nothing to say to these people. I don't even know most of them."

"Elise, I made excuses for Ginger not attending or even acknowledging my invitation. It was rude and inexcusable. But you are my daughter. I don't want to have to make excuses for you too." Suzanne took a deep breath, as if suppressing her anger. "Let's not fight, dear. Yes, you may leave and go home. I'll handle it. I always do."

"Mother, please don't nail yourself to the cross over this. If you want me to stay, I'll call and cancel the cab."

"No, no," Suzanne said in resigned martyrdom. "You run along. It's late."

A car horn couldn't have come at a better time.

"Good night, Mother." She kissed her cheek and went out into the night. She didn't want to be mad at her mother or at Ginger. But she was. Deeply.

CHAPTER FIVE

A text was waiting on her phone when Elise woke Sunday morning. She rolled over to say good morning to Ginger but her side of the bed was empty. Elise could hear the shower running from behind the closed bathroom door. She retrieved her phone from the charger. The text was from Lorraine.

Quick update. I forgot to tell you on Friday but the car service confirmed for Monday, 7 a.m.. And yes it's the same driver you had last week. Jan Chase. Are you sure that's who you want? You said she was clumsy.

Elise sat up in bed and tapped out a reply.

She's wasn't exactly clumsy. It was more awkward. She had a limp. Anyway, she's a good driver. That's all I care about. She doesn't give me a panic attack driving like a maniac through downtown Boston.

Lorraine replied immediately.

Maybe she has arthritis or lumbago. I get that in my hip. Some days I can barely walk on it until I've had my ibuprofen. Or maybe she strained a muscle. She could be one of those exercise geeks. Why don't you ask her?

That's none of my business!!!! Elise texted back.

Maybe she has one of those neurological diseases, like MS. Or maybe she has vertigo. But if she did she shouldn't be driving a limousine, right?

I'm sure she doesn't have MS. I repeat…her personal life is none of my business. She seems to be a safe driver so I'm satisfied.

Okay. Have a good day, Lorraine replied with a smiley face.

Ginger opened the bathroom door. She was naked and riffling her fingers through her wet hair. Even at fifty-two her body was still a thing of beauty.

"Oh, good morning, El. I thought you were still sleeping." She went to the dresser for a pair of panties and a bra.

"Morning. You were out late. How did it go?" Her eyes followed Ginger, reacquainting herself with the parts of her body she hadn't touched in weeks.

"We worked our asses off. By the time we finished you'd have thought the Queen was coming to visit. It was awesome."

"So you're ready for the open house?"

"We better be. The yard signs are going up at noon. Mallory decided to go with a four hour showing instead of just two. She thinks we'll have a good steady crowd. She ordered a couple trays of cookies and little pastries and is having Panera bring out an urn of coffee as well."

Elise was about to invite her back into bed when Ginger's cell phone rang. Still naked, she scrambled to answer it.

Ginger sat on her side of the bed, her body within easy reach. But Elise waited. "Yes, I had them printed at Staples and Donna was supposed to pick them up. Why are they in her car? She was supposed to leave them at the office on my desk." Ginger's voice always rose an octave when she was mad and it was going up by the second. "I told her I'd pick them up on my way. All right, I'll go get them. Yes, now. I'll see you shortly." She hung up and went to the dresser, where she began pawing through the drawer. "Can you believe it? Donna took the flyers for the open house with her. She left them in her car and now I have to drive all the way over there and get them."

"Shouldn't Donna be responsible enough to bring them to the open house?" Elise asked, enjoying the view of Ginger's bottom as her muscles clenched and unclenched with each furious word.

"You'd think so, but no. Mallory doesn't trust her to be there on time. I don't blame her." She pulled on underwear then went to the closet for an outfit, leaving Elise to wonder when Ginger might find time for her.

Still in an obvious panic, Ginger dressed, rushed her hair and makeup then did a quick scan in the full-length mirror.

"What do you think? Would you buy a house from me?" Ginger struck a pose for Elise's approval.

"Definitely. You look very nice, sweetie. I love that pantsuit on you. Very classy." Elise sat crossed-legged, propped against the headboard, as she watched Ginger prepare for the day. "Next time we go out to dinner you should wear that."

"I can't think past today. You'll have to remind me, El." She came to the bed and gave Elise a quick kiss on the cheek. "I hope I remembered everything," she said with a flustered giggle and rushed downstairs.

"Drive carefully," Elise called after her. The front door slammed. Elise heard Ginger's car start and drive away. She leaned her head back against the headboard and closed her eyes. She didn't want a date with her vibrator. She wanted a date with her partner. An honest to God sweaty romp in the sack until her body could take no more. She wanted to be appreciated and adored and satisfied. Was that too much to ask?

"Wow," she said, putting her feet on the floor. "If I didn't know any better I'd think I was horny." She groaned and went to take a shower.

Afterword, she stripped the bed and stuffed the sheets in the washing machine. They weren't that dirty. Nothing had been done on them to need changing. No essence of lovemaking. But Sunday was the day she changed the sheets so she washed them anyway.

It was almost noon when Elise considered driving out to view the open house. She could surprise Ginger and get a guided tour of the expensive home. It might be fun. She didn't have anything else to do. At least nothing else she wanted to do. The project plans waiting in her briefcase could continue to wait.

Elise was still deciding if she would drive her own car or call a taxi when she realized she didn't know the address. She thought back to Ginger's description but all she could remember her mentioning was the price. No neighborhood. No street. Elise sat down at the computer and opened the real estate company's website. She clicked on the tab for open houses. There were four today that could possibly be Ginger and Mallory's. All four were in the two million dollar range but all were on different sides of town and she had no intention of driving all over Boston.

She pulled out her cell phone and tapped in a text. *Hiya. I hope all is going well. Have you had lots of lookers?*

She sent it on its way and went to pour another cup of coffee. It took a few minutes before Ginger replied. *A few. You were right. Gawkers. Not buyers. Oh, well.*

Elise checked the website again then entered another text. *Is it the house on Ellsbury Street? The white colonial with the circle drive?*

Ginger replied immediately. *Yes. Why?*

You didn't mention an address. I was just wondering which open house it was. There are four listed in that price range on the website.

Elise's phone rang.

"Are you spying on me?" Ginger asked with a playful snicker.

"No, I'm not spying on you. I was going to surprise you."

"It sure sounds like you were spying."

"I was going to come by and see the house. I even thought about driving out there. In my own car, strange as that sounds."

"You know you'd never drive all the way out here, El." Ginger laughed. "And why would you? You don't like open houses. You hated going to that one last month."

"It was an overpriced studio apartment. I have no idea why they scheduled an open house. You could see the whole place from the front door."

"El, I've got to go. We're getting busy. I need to answer some questions. I'll tell you all about it when I get home tonight. It might be late. We're taking the family out for pizza later. And El, do yourself and the other drivers a favor and stay off the roads." She laughed again and ended the call.

Elise closed the website. Ginger was right. Open houses weren't her thing. She'd end up criticizing closet placement or pointing out poorly thought-out traffic flow. She looked over at her car keys in the dish on the desk, wondering if she really could have or even would have driven out there.

"So I would have called a taxi," she muttered to herself and went to change the laundry load.

Elise spent the rest of the day looking over project plans and making notes for her trip to Springfield in the morning. She went to bed just after ten. Ginger wasn't home yet.

She didn't know how long she had been asleep when she heard the front door downstairs open and close.

"How did it go?" Elise asked when she heard the closet door squeak.

"Did I wake you, El? I'm sorry."

"I'm awake, sort of." She didn't open her eyes. "Did you sell it?"

"God no. We had a guy make an offer but it was ridiculous. Mallory isn't even sure she's going to submit it. It was about half the listing price. Go back to sleep, sweetie. I need to shower and wash my hair. I smell like cigarette smoke."

Elise tried to stay awake but couldn't. She didn't hear Ginger come to bed and Ginger was still sleeping when Elise climbed out of bed the next morning and went to shower. The weekend was over and Elise's brain was in work mode. She had a long list of details she had to accomplish today and everyday this week. Meetings. Visits to job sites. Conference calls to subcontractors. Everyone and everything that needed her attention would have a time slot in her busy schedule.

Sometime during her shower Ginger had crawled out of bed and gone downstairs. Elise could smell the coffee brewing. There was something about freshly ground coffee beans washed with steaming water that got Elise's day going. The four hundred dollar automated coffee machine she had given Ginger for her birthday guaranteed that delicious cup. Elise dressed in slacks, a shirt and sensible shoes for her trip to Springfield. She'd be tromping around the job site and wasn't about to ruin another pair of heels.

"Good morning, El. I brought you a present," Ginger said from her perch on a padded stool. She was still in pajamas and sipping coffee as she played with her cell phone. She pulled over a plate of pastry bites.

"Good morning," Elise replied cheerfully and kissed the top of Ginger's head as she went to fill a cup. "Wow. Your hair does smell a little like cigarette smoke."

"Didn't I get it out? Damn. I'm sorry." She ruffled her hair, broadcasting the smell across the kitchen.

"What's the occasion?" Elise asked and took a piece of cinnamon roll.

"Leftovers from the open house. Mallory said I could take some home. She over-bought."

"That was nice of her. These are good." She took another bite. "Instant breakfast."

"Try one of these." Ginger took one and popped it in her mouth. "They're little baby tiramisu. Aren't they cute?"

"There's a zillion calories on that plate and I'd love to have them all. However..." Elise opened the refridgerator and retrieved a cup of peach yogurt. "So no one signed on the dotted line for the big house?" She leaned against the counter as she ate her yogurt.

"Nope. Lots of people wishing they could afford it but nope." Her attention was on her phone and the texts she was sending. She laughed at an incoming message then tapped out a quick reply. "Where are you off to today? You're not dressed for the office."

"I'm going to Springfield, remember? The city doesn't want the street closure for the hospital expansion."

"I thought they already agreed to that."

"They did. But the new council members are recanting."

"Can they do that?"

"No." Elise dropped the yogurt cup in the trash. She checked the time on her cell phone then set it on the counter. It was nearly seven. Her driver would be there any minute, assuming she was punctual.

"Do you have a car picking you up?"

"Yes. She should be here at seven."

"She? Should I be jealous?" Ginger gave her a crooked smile.

"Yes, a she. And no, you shouldn't be jealous. This woman is not my type."

"What type is she?"

"Arrogant. Exasperating. Brash."

"Then why hire her?"

"She delivered me from Cambridge to Logan in twenty minutes without crashing the car. That's all I care about." Elise looked up from sorting through her briefcase. "And she doesn't smell like smoke and Brut."

"Speaking of smoke," Ginger said, climbing off the stool, "I'm going to wash my hair again. Have a good day." She trotted up the stairs.

Elise thought it unseemly to be honked for, so as instructed, Jan called Elise's cell phone when she pulled up out front.

"I'm leaving," she called and grabbed her jacket, purse, briefcase, phone, tube of diagrams and a plastic bag with her hard hat in it and then headed for the door.

"See you tonight, El," Ginger replied from somewhere upstairs.

Jan was standing next to the car, her black suit and white shirt looking fresh and clean. There was a stiff breeze blowing but like last week, Jan's blond hair was combed back on both sides in strict obedience but for one springy curl that refused to comply.

"How are you this morning, ma'am?" Jan took the tube and briefcase from her hands and waited for her to get settled in the backseat.

"I'm fine, thank you."

Jan set the briefcase and tube next to her. "Shall we get started then?" She repositioned the sleeve of Elise's jacket and closed the door.

The car had just pulled away from the curb when her cell phone chimed an incoming message. Elise checked it but was surprised at the message across the screen.

Yes, magical and it continues to be.

The text was from Mallory Jenkins.

Strange, Elise thought. Why was Mallory texting her and what was it that continued to be magical? She barely knew the woman. Elise read it again then tapped the home button and opened the settings.

"Driver, wait. Stop," she said.

"Ma'am?" Jan studied her in the rearview mirror. "Did you need something?"

"Yes. I need to go back home. I picked up the wrong phone."

"I'll go around the block."

"Thank you." Elise closed the case, mad at herself for not paying more attention. Their cell phones were alike. The cases were identical as well, both camel tan Italian leather. She opened the case and took one last look at the message. Was this spying? Probably.

Jan pulled to the curb. Elise trotted up the front steps, let herself in with the key and rushed into the kitchen. Ginger was still upstairs. Elise exchanged phones and left without a word, still trying to process what the text meant. She could only assume the open house had gone well and Mallory appreciated Ginger's help. What else could it be?

It was a quiet ride west on the Mass Pike. Jan had the addresses programmed into the car's GPS so there was no need for conversation. Like most professional chauffeurs, Jan didn't initiate conversation without an invitation to do so. She respected her client's privacy. She drove the car in silence unless Elise needed something. Elise appreciated it. She was battling her need to concentrate on work and her curiosity about the message on Ginger's phone. She tried not to read too much into it. That would be immature. But it was hard not to at least consider it.

Elise called the job foreman to let him know she was on the way. She was to meet the members of the city council planning board at the job site at nine. It was ninety miles to Springfield. An hour and a half, tops. But with the traffic and construction delays it was going to be tight.

"I'm supposed to meet the foreman onsite at nine. Do you think we'll make it?"

"I'll see what I can do," Jan replied, maneuvering in and out of traffic.

"When we get there you should park on the street. You'll see the reserved parking signs. Don't go inside the fence. You'll puncture a tire."

"Yes, ma'am." Jan tossed a worried look at her in the mirror. "Are you all right, Ms. Grayson? You look a little pale."

"I'm all right. Traffic makes me a little nervous is all."

Elise kept her gaze inside the car, mindlessly opening and closing her cell phone case as she looked over paperwork, forcing herself to stay on task. But it was hard not to return to the contents of the message. Ginger was a real estate agent. Mallory was the broker and her boss. It never occurred to Elise to question that relationship. She was being silly. She was looking for trouble where none existed. And she was demonstrating an ugly character flaw. Jealousy. She trusted Ginger. That was all there was to it.

"Ms. Grayson?" Jan said, standing outside the open passenger door.

Elise hadn't noticed them pull up and stop. Nor Jan open the door. It wasn't like her to drift off into a fog like that. It took a moment for her to gather her thoughts and come back to reality.

The construction site adjacent to the hospital was surrounded by portable fencing. The gate stood open and workers were busy with their duties. Jan held the tube and briefcase as Elise did a quick check in the mirror then climbed out.

"This should take about an hour, maybe two," Elise said, slinging the straps over her shoulder. Jan was watching the excavator move scoops of crushed stone. "Jan, did you hear me?" she demanded.

"Yes, ma'am. I'm sorry. I just like watching. It looks like fun."

"They can be."

"Can be? You mean you can drive those?" Jan pointed at the loader inside the fence with wide-eyed amazement.

"Not all of them. Not the big ones." She reached back in the car for the plastic bag, took out a white hard hat and settled it on her head.

"How about the little one over there scooping gravel? Can you drive that?"

"Yes." Elise was busy adjusting her belongings.

"Wow. I'm impressed, Ms. Grayson."

"Why? Aren't women supposed to operate heavy equipment?"

"That's not what I meant. I just assumed you were, I don't know, a desk jockey."

"I suppose I am now but I haven't always been. I worked my way up through the ranks. I like to think I can ride more than just a desk."

"Good for you." Jan looked up and chuckled at what was printed across the front of Elise's hard hat. "I like that. The Dirt Lady."

"It was a gift from one of the crew." Elise started for the gate then looked back. "You can go inside the hospital if you'd like. There's a coffee shop in the lobby. I'll call you when I'm ready."

Jan waited at the car while Elise crossed the lot and climbed the steps of the construction trailer. Elise could feel Jan's eyes watching her every step. It made her uncomfortable when any of the men did it. Jan Chase's eyes on her didn't seem as insulting or invasive. Almost protective.

CHAPTER SIX

Jan leaned against the side of the car and for a half hour watched the equipment scoop and grade until she needed to find a ladies' room. And a cup of coffee. She locked the car and headed around the corner to the hospital's main entrance. She had been there before, many times. It wasn't her favorite place to visit but she wasn't going beyond the lobby.

The coffee shop was busy. The patrons were a mix of hospital personnel and visitors in street clothes. She noticed that the woman ahead of her wearing blue scrubs had two rolls of white tape attached to her ID badge suspended on a lanyard around her neck, the kind of tape used to secure gauze or surgical dressings. They were just rolls of tape but Jan was transfixed by them.

"Jan Chase," a man exclaimed happily, his kind voice cutting into her fixation. He too was wearing blue scrubs. "Hi sweetie. How are you? How's your grandmother?" He gave Jan a hug then looked her up and down as if judging for himself.

"She's fine." It took a moment to process who the man was. She might not have remembered if not for his concerned smile and firm hug. "Julian, right?"

"Yes, you remembered." He seemed pleased. "You look all professional in your black suit and white shirt, pussycat. Sexy too." He winked and adjusted the lapels of her jacket, brushing away a speck of dust. "I like this look on you."

"It's my uniform, sort of."

"Doing…?"

"I work for an executive car service in Boston."

"You're a chauffeur?" he said. "Good for you. And Boston even."

"I needed a change."

"You needed to get away from your mother and grandmother, that's what you mean, God love 'em." He grinned knowingly. "I think it's great. I love Boston. If they don't have it, you don't need it."

"Definitely bigger than Springfield."

"What brings you to town and to the hospital?" He gasped, his eyes widening. "Don't tell me your grandmother had another stroke."

"No, Baci's fine. I'm here for work. It has to do with the hospital addition," Jan said, nodding in that direction.

"Isn't that a mess? Every time it rains there's mud everywhere. Well, I've got to run, pussycat. But you take care of yourself and tell your grandmother Julian says hi. She's the sweetest little thing." He hugged Jan again then hurried away.

She was next in line to order when she felt her cell phone vibrate.

"You can meet me at the car, Jan. We're finished. It didn't take as long as I thought."

"Yes, ma'am. I'll be right there." She stepped out of line and headed across the lobby. Maybe there would be time for coffee later. Or maybe lunch. She was hungry. The bowl of raisin bran she'd had six hours ago was fast losing its worth. She assumed Ms. Grayson planned on lunch, perhaps a luncheon meeting that would give Jan a few minutes for a drive-thru burger.

Elise carried a second blueprint tube and a cumbersome cardboard box as she descended the steps outside the trailer. Jan met her at the gate. She took the box and reached for the briefcase strap.

"I'll take this for you," Jan said as she guided the strap down Elise's arm.

"I'll carry the briefcase."

Like the awkward stumble at the airport with the suitcase, Jan nearly lost her balance. She quickly regained her composure, hoping Elise hadn't noticed, but she felt her eyes on her as she headed to the car, walking a few paces ahead.

"Are you all right?" Elise asked with a critical scowl. "You didn't add a little something to your coffee, did you?"

"I always add cream and sugar to my coffee. I like it light and sweet." If Elise meant alcohol she was going to have to say alcohol. Jan wasn't going to defend herself against a suggestive accusation.

"You feel you're able to drive?"

"Yes, absolutely. Do you have a problem with my driving, ma'am? Am I making you nervous? By the way, I didn't have coffee. The line in the coffee shop was too long. I'll have something later."

"No, your driving is fine." Elise seemed satisfied. She leaned in and placed her briefcase and purse on the backseat. She reached for the box in Jan's hands but her hard hat slid forward. Jan's quick reflexes caught it before it hit the ground. Distracted by the falling hat, Elise dumped the contents of the box on the sidewalk, scattering a dozen gray plastic rings.

"Dang it," Elise said angrily.

"I've got them. You hold the box." Jan perched the hard hat on her own head and gathered them up. "Liners for the hard hats?" She arranged them in the box so the lid would close.

"No. These are suspensions. Liners are the knit or quilted cap things that fit inside the hats in cold weather."

"Suspensions, huh? I always thought they were just called liners."

"Two different animals. And these are the wrong ones. They ordered swing suspensions."

"Uh huh," Jan said without a clue as to what that was.

"Some of the guys wear their helmets backward, depending on what they're doing. They need a swing suspension." Elise looked up at the hard hat on Jan's head. She gave a curious smile before claiming it. "You don't look at all like a dirt lady." She climbed in the back without another word about Jan's stumble or what might have caused it.

By the time Jan settled in the driver's seat Elise was on her phone. Jan tried not to eavesdrop but without a partition between them it was hard to tune out backseat conversations. She was apparently relaying highlights of her visit to the job site. The city had finally agreed to whatever they were requested to do. The plans needed tweaking before interior walls were finished. The electrical subs weren't happy with the access panels ordered. And the janitorial closets weren't adequate. But from what Jan could gather from Elise's side of the conversation none of it was particularly alarming. Just run-of-the-mill issues.

"We're heading over there now. I'll let you know what I think. Just so you know, Dad, I'm not interested in investing in upscale apartments in a slum neighborhood. We can't make any money with half the units sitting empty because no one wants to rent them. We've been down that road before."

Jan checked the GPS and headed for their next destination. She didn't recognize the exact address but knew the area, having briefly dated a woman from the neighborhood. It might be low-income but she wasn't sure she'd call it a slum neighborhood. Small homes, some older, some duplexes, many without garages, most in need of some minor repair or paint.

"Ms. Grayson, do you want me to park somewhere so you can walk, or just circle the block?"

"Is this it? Is this the address?"

"The next corner." She slowed as she approached the intersection. "The addresses you gave me start right here and run down the side street." She pointed to the cinder block single-story building on the corner, an insurance company sign over the door, a For Lease sign in the window. It looked empty. It needed painting.

"You don't need to stop but could you turn the corner and go slow?" Elise put her window down and took a few pictures with her cell phone.

"That next building used to be a great pizza place. Bobo's Pizza and Grinders." Jan pulled to the curb and stared out the window, remembering the night she and Cathy had ordered anchovy pizza just so they could say they tried it. The pizza building was empty too. A sheet of plywood nailed across one of the front windows suggested it had been vandalized. The beauty shop next door was still in business but looked like it was hanging on by a thread.

"You lived around here?"

"No, not here. I was born in Springfield but my parents live in Indian Orchard."

"Should I know where that is?"

"It's east of Springfield about eight miles."

"Is that a nice area?" Elise's interest seemed piqued.

"I think so. It's an older working class neighborhood but it's nice. People take care of their homes. At least they do better than this area."

"Would you drive around? I want to see the area a little bit more."

Jan circled the blocks, looping through the side streets and back onto Boston Road as Elise studied the other businesses, size of homes, even the traffic lights and fire station. She took several more pictures and made notes.

Jan couldn't resist. "Do you plan on building apartments in Pine Point?"

"Is that what this area is called? Pine Point?"

"Yes. Roughly speaking it's from the cemetery up to Five Mile Pond."

"Do you know how far we are from a shopping center?" Elise asked.

"Sure. There's a Wal-Mart about two miles east on Boston Road and the Eastfield Mall is another mile past that." Jan pointed in that direction.

"Show me."

Jan navigated the area so Elise could see the shopping center, restaurants and businesses within easy access to Pine Point. It was well past noon and Jan's stomach was beginning to grumble.

"Excuse me, Ms. Grayson?" Jan looked in her rearview mirror then waited for Elise to look up.

"Yes?" she replied absently.

"I have a question, or rather a small request. It's after one. Would you mind if I found a place to grab a quick bite? It can be anywhere but I need a little sustenance every so often. I'm sorry but breakfast isn't sufficient to carry me through to dinner." She didn't mean to be disrespectful to a client. She knew her response bordered on sarcasm but she was hungry. And sure enough, it brought Elise's eyes up to meet hers.

"So you are requesting a lunch break?"

"Yes, ma'am. If you don't mind."

"That's fine. Go ahead and find someplace." She went back to her notes.

"What are you hungry for, Ms Grayson?"

"It doesn't matter. I'm not familiar with what's available around here. I'm not big on fast food franchises."

"Then you probably don't want Chuck E. Cheese's," Jan said as she drove past the restaurant.

"Lord no. Not McDonald's, Burger King, Taco Bell or Rudy's Ribs either."

"I bet you expect tablecloths," Jan muttered to herself as she maneuvered a U-turn through the shopping center parking lot. She hadn't intended for Elise to hear her but she obviously did.

"Not always," she said without looking up. "Just find us a clean place to have lunch, please. It doesn't have to be fancy."

A few minutes later Jan climbed out and went to open Elise's door. Hanna's Diner wasn't a fancy restaurant but it was always clean and the food was good. Normally Jan didn't sit with the client during meals. Her job was to drive and remain inconspicuous. She hadn't been chauffeuring long but she knew how to keep out of the client's way during meals. She usually dined alone and ordered something simple and quick to prepare. It was all part of the job. So long as she didn't have to go hours and hours without a meal she didn't mind. She opened the door to Hanna's for Elise and waited for her to decide where she wanted to sit. As soon as Elise decided Jan would slip away and order something, allowing Elise Grayson her privacy.

"Shall we sit in a booth?" Elise finally asked, scanning the restaurant.

"You go right ahead, ma'am." Jan stepped out of the way but Elise looked back at her curiously. "Is there something wrong with sitting at a booth?"

"No, nothing. I just thought…"

"You thought I'd prefer to not have my chauffeur dine with me, is that it?"

"Something like that."

"Normally I'd agree but you've eaten here before. I haven't. I might need your advice on what to order."

"Hi. Nice to see you again." The woman working the cash register waved to Jan. "Sit anywhere you like. We'll find you."

Jan waited for Elise to decide then followed her down the row of booths.

As they closed their menus a waitress set glasses of water on the table and a basket of sliced bread. "Do you ladies know what you'd like?" she asked.

"I'll have a turkey club on toasted wheat," Elise said. "Mayonnaise on the side please. And coffee."

"I'll have the number four with potatoes. Spinach pierogi if you have them," Jan said. "And coffee."

Elise's phone made a strange muted sound from inside her purse. She rolled her eyes and pulled it out. "Not again," she grumbled.

"Still the wrong phone?"

"No. It's my phone but I think it's haunted. An app wants to update and I don't want it to."

"You can ignore it or even turn off the update setting. The app will continue to run with the existing version."

"That's the trouble. I don't want any version of it. I've tried to delete it but every time I do it updates instead."

"Sounds like an issue with the phone's settings," Jan suggested.

Elise set the phone on the table and slid it over in front of Jan. "Here. Make it go away."

"Jelly Bean Surprise?" Jan chuckled at the bouncing candy on the screen.

"Yes. I'm thinking about calling it Jelly Beans from Hell."

"It shouldn't be that tough." Jan closed the game and returned to the home screen. She touched a few icons then set the phone back in front of Elise. "There. I've performed a Jelly Bean-ectomy."

Elise grabbed it up and looked. "Are you sure it's gone for good? No surprise visits in the middle of the night?"

Jan reached over and touched the screen. "Looks gone to me."

"How did you do that? No, don't tell me. I'll just forget. I'll let you be responsible for my phone issues," Elise said.

"You have to delete from the home screen. That's the only way I know to do it. You really don't strike me as a Jelly Bean Surprise kind of woman."

"I'm not. My partner's niece put it on my phone thinking it was Ginger's phone. I've been trying to get rid of it ever since."

"So it's Ginger's phone you tried to run off with," Jan teased.

"Yes. Our phones and cases look alike. I grabbed the wrong one."

"Is that Ginger with you in the picture on your home screen?"

"Yes."

"Nice picture. Does she have the same picture on her phone's home screen?"

"No. She used to but I think she changes it from time to time."

"You can download anything for your screen. It's like wallpaper on your computer. If it's out there you can download it."

"I'm not all that tech savvy when it comes to these new smartphones. I was a lot smarter when all I had was a simple flip phone. Call people. Send a text. Maybe take a picture every now and then. No apps. No games. No emails. The only thing I had to worry about was losing it in the bottom of my purse."

"Ah, yes. The good old days when your phone actually fit in your jeans pocket," Jan said as she buttered a slice of bread.

"Not this phone and not my jeans." Elise laughed.

"You two don't strike me as jeans people."

"Sure. I wear jeans. They may be prosaic but I wear them, usually just around the house."

"Prosaic?" Jan asked curiously.

"It means ordinary. Commonplace."

"I know what prosaic means. And loquacious and idiosyncratic. I just never heard jeans described quite like that."

Before Elise could reply her phone chimed an incoming text. She studied it, frowned, and tapped out a reply.

"Is everything okay? Looks like bad news."

"Not bad news. Just disappointing." Elise heaved a sigh. She seemed distracted by whatever was in the text. Enough that she only ate a few bites of her sandwich.

"Is your sandwich okay?" Jan didn't want to intrude. It wasn't her place to ask what was wrong.

"Yes. It's fine. I just wasn't very hungry after all." She sat with her jaw muscles clenched while Jan hurriedly finished her lunch.

Jan placed cash on the table for the check but Elise argued about who should pay.

"It's my treat since it was my idea we stop," Jan insisted. "Consider it my way of apologizing."

"Apologizing for what?"

"Last week when I drove you to the airport and stuck my hand in your pants. I shouldn't have done that. It was rude and I'm sorry."

"Ah, yes. The bra incident. Apology accepted. But I suppose I should be appreciative you did."

"I considered it like toilet paper stuck on your shoe. It's better to have one person point it out than have a hundred people see it. But I think you would have noticed it as soon as you started walking."

"Maybe so but I appreciate your attention to detail. And thank you for lunch." Elise slid out of the booth and headed for the door. Jan followed and reached around to open the door. Elise stepped out on the sidewalk and was nearly hit by a teenager on a skateboard. Jan wasn't so lucky. She was halfway out the door when the boy veered and bumped into her.

"Oops, sorry," was all he said and continued up the sidewalk, swerving back and forth to keep up speed.

Jan tried to catch her balance. She staggered but there was nothing for her to grab onto and she fell back against the building.

Elise grabbed for her as she stumbled. "That was rude. Are you all right?" The words were barely out of her mouth when Elise gasped. Jan's left pant leg had slid up, revealing a shiny metal rod where her shin should be. It disappeared inside her black sock. She stood dumbfounded, staring at it with wide eyes. The realization Elise had seen her leg, or the absence of it, triggered an image Jan didn't expect. It wasn't Elise's face she saw staring down at her, but Allie's. Jan drew a quick breath as the image flashed across her mind then faded.

"I'm okay. Did he run into you? Hey, watch where you're going, dude," Jan shouted to the skateboarder as she scrambled to regain her balance.

"I'll get some help." Elise's eyes moved up to meet Jan's.

"No, wait. I don't need any help." Jan grabbed Elise's arm. "I'm fine. It was just a little bump. Don't worry about it. "

"Are you sure?" Elise stared down at Jan's leg.

"I'm fine, Ms. Grayson." Jan brushed the dust from her suit jacket. "A little klutzy sometimes but I'm fine. Shall we go?"

"Yes, yes. We should go." She hurried to the car and tried to open the passenger door but it was locked. She continued to pull at the handle until Jan caught up to her and took her arm.

"Ms. Grayson, are you all right?"

"Yes. I'm perfectly fine. We should go." She gave the handle another tug.

Jan pressed the button on her remote to unlock the door then pushed Elise's hand aside and opened it.

"Are you sure? Because you left this over there by the door." Jan held up Elise's purse.

"Thank you." Elise grabbed the purse strap and tried to pull it away but Jan held onto it.

"Ms. Grayson, have I embarrassed you? I certainly didn't mean to. Please accept my apology."

"No, I'm not embarrassed." Elise seemed to struggle to keep her gaze upward and not down on Jan's leg. "I wish I had known is all."

"Known that I have a prosthetic leg? I didn't think it made a difference so I chose not to mention it. Does it bother you? Are you concerned I can't do my job? Because if you are I can have another driver come pick you up and take you back to Boston. Not a problem."

"I don't want another driver. And no, it doesn't bother me." She climbed into the backseat and pulled the door shut instead of waiting for Jan to do it.

Jan started the car but didn't pull away from the curb. She sat silently staring out the window deciding what she could say to reassure Elise's concerns. She could see Elise in the rearview mirror busying herself with her purse so she didn't have to look at the back of Jan's head.

"Ms. Grayson?"

"Yes," she said without looking up.

"I'm very sorry to put you in an uncomfortable position like that. I take full responsibility for it."

"I wasn't uncomfortable. Surprised is a better word for it." She finally looked up, a stone cold sober expression on her face. "You have nothing to apologize for."

"I'll understand if you want a different driver in the future."

"May we get started please? I'd like to be back at the office by four o'clock."

"Yes, ma'am. I'll do my best." She took one last look in the rearview mirror. Elise was staring back at her, a mix of curiosity and pity. It was the pity that Jan didn't want to see. Not from anyone, and especially not from Elise Grayson. The attractive Elise Grayson.

They were six miles from Boston when Elise said, "I've changed my mind. I'd like to go home instead of the office."

"Wherever you'd like to go, ma'am."

Half an hour later Jan pulled up in front of Elise's townhouse. She quickly climbed out and circled the car but by the time she got there Elise had already opened the passenger door.

"I've got it," Elise said, stepping out.

"I'll open the door for you, Ms. Grayson. It's part of my job. Otherwise I'm just a glorified cab driver in a black suit." She smiled. "And that's a whole different animal." Jan retrieved the tubes and Elise's briefcase from the seat and handed them to her. She then picked up the cardboard box, ready to carry it up the steps for her.

"I can take that." Elise reached for the box

"I've got it. You can unlock your door."

Jan followed her up the six front steps, taking her time with each one so as not to stumble. Elise unlocked the door and turned back for the box but Jan stepped inside and set it on the floor.

"I'm not an invalid, Ms. Grayson."

"I didn't say you were."

"You don't have to say it. I've seen that look before. I don't need anyone's pity. I'm doing just fine."

"May I ask if you were a victim of the Boston Marathon bombing? You don't have to answer if you don't want to. I don't mean to pry." Her eyes softened ever so slightly.

"No, not the Marathon bombing. Nothing that newsworthy." Jan didn't want to relay the details of her accident. She couldn't. Some of them she didn't know herself. "Goodbye, Ms. Grayson. Have a nice evening."

Jan had a feeling this was the last time she'd be asked to chauffeur Elise Grayson. She descended the steps and climbed in the driver's seat. She resisted the urge to look up at Elise's front door, knowing she was probably watching, expecting her to stumble. Yes, that woman is definitely a different animal, she thought, and pulled away.

CHAPTER SEVEN

Elise had barely closed the front door when her cell phone rang. She dug it out of her purse and answered on the third ring.

"Hello Dad."

"Well, I've been waiting. What's the word on that property in Springfield? You were supposed to call me."

"I just got home two minutes ago," she said, stepping out of her shoes. "I didn't know it was that urgent." She dropped down in an over stuffed chair and propped her legs up over the arm.

"What did you think?"

"The property is okay but I'm not sure about the neighborhood. Some low-income units might rent pretty easily but not the kind you were describing."

"I'll agree the neighborhood was a little suspect. That's why I wanted another opinion." He heaved an exasperated groan. "Okay, we'll keep looking. There'll be other places. How were things at the hospital site? Did you get the city onboard with what we're doing? I'll tell you what. How about you and Ginger meet your mother and me at Hinton's for dinner? I'll buy us all a steak and you can catch me up. What do you say, honey? Seven thirty?"

"Thanks for the offer, Dad, but we can't. Ginger is working late at the office. She texted me it could be past nine. Why don't we do that another night? I can tell you about my meeting tomorrow at the office."

"I thought you were coming back to the office when you got back into town. Are you okay? You sound like something's wrong. Are you ill?"

"I'm fine. Just a little tired." She wasn't in the mood to talk and she wasn't sure what bothered her more: Ginger's disappointing text that she had to work late or the realization Jan Chase wasn't awkward, clumsy or drunk. She had an artificial leg. Elise already hated herself for suggesting Jan had been drinking.

"Open invitation. You two just let us know when."

"I will, and thank you. Dad, I've got to go. I've got an incoming call I need to take."

"Good night."

She answered the call. "Hi Ginger. Please tell me you're going to be home on time after all."

"Hi El. No, I can't. I wish I could but we've got a ton of stuff to get caught up on. I've got two closings tomorrow and I'm nowhere near ready. I was just checking to see what time you thought you'd be home."

"I just got home. I had the driver drop me off here."

"Oh, you're home?" She seemed surprised.

"Yes. I wish you didn't have to work. The folks invited us to Hinton's for dinner."

"I love Hinton's."

"You could meet us there. Seven thirty?"

"El, I can't. I won't be done by then. You go to Hinton's with your folks and think of me. I better get back to work or I'll be here until midnight."

"Ginger," Elise started but hesitated. She wanted to say they needed to talk but she also wanted to say they needed some time together when talking wasn't necessary. She said neither. "Have a good evening. I'll see you later, hon."

Elise poured herself a glass of wine and went upstairs to change out of her work clothes. She always felt dirty after a trip to a construction site, where excavators and graders kicked up clouds of dust. She seldom got two wearings out of clothes she wore on-site. She unzipped her slacks and let them fall, exposing her panties and the pale skin of her legs. She stared at her legs in the full-length mirror. She couldn't help but wonder how much of Jan's left leg was missing. Just the ankle and foot? All of it? If it wasn't blown off at the Boston Marathon bombing, how did she lose it? Cancer? Was she born without it? How painful was it? When her mind began to conjure up all the horrific accidents that could have hacked it off she turned away from the mirror. They were too gruesome to consider and they made her stomach turn. Still she wondered what the stump looked like. Why did macabre and grotesque things fascinate people? It was like picking a Band-Aid. Elise's curiosity had her contemplating what evil scar was hidden beneath Jan's black dress pants. And it was none of her business.

Elise finished her wine, dressed in jeans and an over-sized shirt and went downstairs to find something for dinner. She stood at the open refridgerator door, staring at the three take-out containers lined across the bottom shelf. Linguini with béarnaise sauce, vegetarian lasagna or teriyaki chicken. The doorbell rang, chiming out the melodic Westminster tones.

"Coming!" She opened the door expecting to see her neighbor for her weekly visit to complain about the streetlight that was out. Why Mrs. Phillips thought Elise needed that information was a mystery. But it wasn't her neighbor. It was Jan. She had Elise's jacket in her hand. The black car was double-parked, the motor still running.

"Hello, Ms. Grayson. I found this in the backseat. It got wedged under the fold-down armrest. I thought you might need it tomorrow. It's supposed to be chilly." Jan gave the jacket a shake then handed it to Elise and smiled. "I'm sorry I didn't notice it before."

"Thank you, Jan. I forgot all about it. Come in. I'll get my purse." Elise stepped back and motioned her in. She pondered how large a tip she owed her for delivering a jacket. Was twenty dollars enough? Thirty?

"No, I don't need to come in. I just wanted to bring your jacket back while I thought of it. I don't know where I'm scheduled tomorrow. I wasn't sure I'd have time to bring it by."

"That was very nice of you. I probably wouldn't have remembered where I left it. Today was a little crazy."

"I'm sorry about that."

"No, no. I didn't mean it was you," Elise stammered.

"Sure it was. How many chauffeurs have you had with a prosthetic leg? I didn't mean to frighten you or freak you out. That's the last thing I try to do." Jan smiled. "But I see you do wear jeans. No shoes but jeans. Good for you."

Elise laughed and looked down at her jeans and bare feet. "Occasionally I find my way into jeans."

Elise suddenly had a wild idea. "Jan, are you off for the day or could I still hire you for a couple hours this evening?"

"Hire me? Going where?"

"Malzetti's restaurant. I can call in an order and just run in and pick it up. Then I want to take it to Harbor View Real Estate offices on Tremont."

"I'm guessing you want to order take-out and surprise Ginger with it. Am I right?"

"Yes. I just need five minutes to get ready. Can you wait for me? Will your boss approve?"

"I'll call and let them know I'm still on the clock."

"Good. I'll be right down."

Elise hurried up the stairs, excited at her plans. She wasn't normally an impulsive person. Her job had taught her to be cautious and deliberate. A poor decision could cost the company thousands. But tonight, with Jan's services so accessible, why not? It took a little more than five minutes but Jan was waiting at the passenger door when she came down the front steps.

"We're all approved for this extension?" Elise asked before climbing in.

"Absolutely. My pleasure, ma'am." Jan waited for Elise to climb in and buckled her seatbelt. "Malzetti's on Essex Street?"

"Yes. I've already called. The order will be ready in twenty minutes."

When they reached the restaurant, Jan pulled up in front and waited in the car while Elise went inside. The food was packaged and waiting for her. She and Ginger were good customers so the owner included complimentary raspberry tarts for dessert.

Ten minutes later Jan pulled into the parking lot next to the real estate office. The only vehicle was a van with a sign on the side advertising a cleaning service.

"Is this the only parking lot?" Jan asked.

"Yes." Elise looked up and down the street for Ginger's car. "Sometimes she parks on the street."

"Would you like me to see if the building is locked?"

"No, no. I'm sure she's here. She's probably parked in the back."

Jan opened the car door and offered Elise a hand as she climbed out.

"Shall I wait?" Jan asked protectively as she scanned the darkened street.

"It isn't necessary. I'll text you when I'm ready." Elise headed for the front door of the building. She was almost there before she heard Jan close the passenger door as if she was in no big hurry to leave. The building was locked. A woman in gray scrubs was running a sweeper in the hall and saw Elise knocking.

"The office is closed," the woman said, opening the door a crack.

"I know but I'm here to see Ginger Lindquist. She's working late. I brought her dinner." Elise held up the bag. "I talked to her a little while ago."

"No one's here. The offices are closed." The woman seemed adamant.

"Look, miss, I know Ginger is here. Maybe you just haven't seen her yet. Her office is the second one past the conference room on the right."

"Miss Lindquist isn't here. No one is here. They all left."

"But I talked to her. She was here. She had a lot of work to do. Would you mind if I check? Please."

The woman shrugged and opened the door wide enough for Elise to enter then relocked it. She followed Elise down the hall, around the corner and into the darkened empty office. Elise snapped on the light as if she needed that clarity.

"I've already cleaned this room," the woman said.

Elise turned off the light and stood in the doorway, trying to make sense of it. Why would Ginger tell her she was working if she wasn't? Elise wasn't stupid or naïve. She suspected she knew the answer but she still searched for an excuse. Ginger had taken her advice and gone to have dinner someplace close by, and she'd be back to finish her work. But her desk was clear, everything in its place. No paperwork or folders awaiting urgent attention. Nothing out of place.

"No one is here," the woman exclaimed, as if she had proven herself right.

"I appreciate you letting me look." Elise headed back for the front door, her eyes darting in and out of each room she passed. She somehow hoped she'd find Ginger sitting at a different desk, buried in paperwork.

"I'm sorry, miss." The woman unlocked the door. Elise stepped out onto the sidewalk then looked back at her.

"Have you eaten yet? How would you like a couple Italian dinners?"

The woman's eyes widened expectantly.

"They're from Malzetti's." Elise handed her the paper bag. "They're still warm. Enjoy." She smiled and headed up the sidewalk. She expected the black car to be gone and she'd have to text Jan to come pick her up. But it was still in the parking lot. Jan was leaning against the passenger door with her hands in her pants pockets. Something about her expression told Elise she wasn't surprised to see her so soon.

"Home, ma'am?"

Elise reached in her purse and took out her cell phone. She stared at the contact list, ready to press Ginger's number. But she closed her phone and dropped it back in her purse instead. "Yes. Take me home, Jan."

Part of her wanted to call Ginger and ask where she was. But did it really matter? The truth was she had lied. She wasn't at work. Elise knew she should wait and hear Ginger's side of the story. She shouldn't jump to conclusions, but hard as she tried to convince herself otherwise, evidence suggested this wasn't the first time. Ginger's indifference toward their relationship and toward Elise had been growing for months. Jan Chase, a hired driver with a crusty sense of humor, had shown more compassion than her partner. Would Ginger have driven back across town in rush hour traffic to return a jacket? Would Ginger wait in an empty parking lot without being asked? Would Ginger apologize at the thought she had made Elise uncomfortable? Elise knew the answer and it wasn't a pretty thought.

The clock on the bedside table read eleven twenty-four when Elise heard the front door open and close. She had been reading and removed her glasses to wait for Ginger to come upstairs. It was another ten minutes before she heard the creak of the fourth step.

"El, what are you doing up?" Ginger looked surprised. She came to the bed and kissed Elise on the top of her head. "Can't sleep?"

"As a matter of fact no, I can't."

"Too much work or too much caffeine?" she asked, stepping out of her shoes.

"I thought you were only going to work until nine. It's past eleven."

"Yes, I know, honey. But I got so busy I lost track of time. You know how it is. Once you close the office door and lock into the zone you aren't aware of anything, even time."

"Did you take time to eat?"

"No, but I'm not hungry. I'm too tired to be hungry."

"Ginger, are you having an affair with Mallory?"

"What?" Ginger laughed out loud. "Where in the hell did that come from? Is this because I wouldn't cancel work to have dinner with you and your parents?"

"So you were working all evening?"

"Yes, I told you I was," she said with an exasperated snarl then went to the closet.

"Was it magical?" Elise asked.

"Magical? What are you talking about?"

"I'm asking you again, are you having an affair with Mallory?"

"I don't know where you've come up with this harebrained idea."

"Do I have to catch you with your mouth on her crotch before you'll admit it?"

Ginger turned, glaring daggers at Elise. "You don't trust me, do you? That's what this is all about. You just don't trust me."

"Ginger, I know you weren't at your office tonight because I was."

"You were spying on me?" she demanded.

"I went to Malzetti's and got us dinner. I brought it by your office and the only person there was the cleaning lady. She said you and everyone else left on time. No one was working late. I'm not spying on you. I'm asking you."

"Fuck you, El."

"So you are." Elise crossed her arms, braced for what was to come.

"All right. You want the truth? I'll tell you the truth. Yes, Mallory and I are seeing each other and yes, it's magical. She makes me feel alive and important and special. The sex is fantastic," Ginger gloated. "El, admit it. We haven't felt like that about each other in a long time. We haven't done anything together in months."

"How does that make it any less cheating?" Elise's voice cracked.

"I'm sorry, El."

"I think you're only sorry you were discovered."

"I thought you knew," Ginger said with a sneer.

"You actually thought I knew you were having sex with Mallory and I was okay with that? What do you take me for? An idiot?" Elise collected her composure. She didn't want to raise her voice but she wanted to know the whole truth. "When did this all start?"

"What difference does it make, El?"

"I want to know. How long? Two months? Three months?" Ginger lowered her eyes.

"When, Ginger?" she demanded.

"It's been a few months."

Elise had heard enough. She got up, grabbed some clothes and went downstairs. As painful as it was to accept, Ginger was right. It had been months since they'd shared a tender moment. She couldn't remember the last time she'd told Ginger she loved her. She couldn't remember the last time Ginger had said it either. Maybe she should have known. The signs were there and she hated herself for ignoring them.

"Where are you going?" Ginger asked from the stairs. "Don't we need to talk?"

"Don't you think we've talked enough, Ginger?" she said, rummaging in her briefcase. "We talked about you lying. We talked about you screwing your boss all the while you've been sleeping in my bed. I think we've talked about all we need to talk about. I'm going to work." Elise headed for the front door. She would sleep at the office.

"El," Ginger called.

"What?" She didn't look back.

"I'll be out by the end of the week."

Elise didn't reply. She only nodded then pulled the door shut behind her. She stood on the porch as tears welled up in her eyes. She didn't feel like it but she'd go to the office for the night and then bury herself in work. Meetings and conference calls and blueprints and emails. She'd find something to occupy every second so there wouldn't be time to cry.

CHAPTER EIGHT

Elise was standing at the window in her office sipping her second cup of coffee when Lorraine knocked and entered.

"Good morning, Elise," Lorraine said. "Would you like a bagel and cream cheese? I brought some from Maria's Bakery."

"No, thank you," she replied as she scanned Boston's skyline. She wasn't hungry. Ginger had taken away her appetite and her will to work.

"Elise?"

"Uh huh?"

"What's wrong?"

"What?" Elise turned, only half listening.

"What happened? Something obviously happened last night. What was it?"

"Nothing happened." She went back to scanning downtown Boston.

"Oh, so this is a fashion statement? I guess I could get used to it."

"Lorraine, what *are* you talking about? What fashion statement?" Elise went to her desk.

"I like the slacks and shirt but, Elise, you're wearing one black shoe and one brown shoe. Did you do that on purpose?"

"Oh, jeez." Elise checked her shoes then rolled her eyes. She stepped out of the mismatched shoes and retrieved from a shelf in her office closet a pair of loafers she kept for emergency trips to job sites. "Lorraine, do me a favor."

"Absolutely. What?"

"Keep me busy. For the next few days, keep me really busy."

"May I ask why? I'm a good listener." Lorraine came to the corner of the desk. "Is there a problem I should know about? Have I done something wrong?"

"No." Elise chuckled sarcastically. "You haven't done anything wrong. It's all my doing." Her phone rang. She answered it before it could ring again, relieved to have something to take her mind off Ginger and what had happened last night.

Whether it was Lorraine's doing or just the nature of the beast, the construction business kept Elise hovered over her desk and in meetings for two weeks, nonstop. Long hours, distractions and details helped block out the heartache. Just the way she wanted it.

Ginger had moved out, leaving Elise a half empty closet and four extra dresser drawers. She had taken her bed pillow, a stack of CDs and DVDs, her Ikea desk chair, as well as Elise's Kindle and blow-dryer. They weren't worth an argument. Neither were the muddy footprints tracked across the living room carpet. Elise had finally had the locks changed and could go home without fear of running into her. She wasn't afraid of her so much as she wasn't sure what she might say to her. What do you say to an ex-girlfriend who'd admitted to and justified her cheating? Ginger obviously didn't care what came out of her mouth. Elise did.

"Elise." Her father stormed into her office. "I'm getting tired of this. I'm a patient man but I've had about enough. This is costing me money."

"Good morning, Dad," she said, looking up from a blueprint. "You've had enough of what?"

"OSHA is fining us ten thousand dollars." He shoved a hand in his pants pocket and began nervously jingling his change.

"Fining us ten thousand for what?" She scowled.

"Some asshole working on scaffolding without a harness. Evidently the OSHA guy was standing right there. He even took pictures as evidence."

"Who was it? Somebody new? One of our temps?"

"No, it's that same guy from last year. Stan something or other."

"The one from the Woodside office building? He promised he wouldn't do that. We had him sign an official notification acknowledging he had been warned. I can't believe he did it again."

"He was four stories up without a lifeline. I'm not putting up with this crap. I want him gone."

"He's working at the hospital site in Springfield," she said, checking the employee schedule on her computer. "I was just there two weeks ago. Roy's the foreman. Have him do it." Elise didn't like firing people, even idiots.

"Roy's worried the other guys will take Stan's side. He's got a wife and a couple kids. He wants one of us to do it."

"Stan's lucky his wife isn't a widow."

"I should be glad we're not processing his life insurance policy. But dammit, Elise. I tell these guys and tell these guys. Some of them just don't listen."

"Dad, calm down. I'll take care of it. I'll need a copy of this OSHA letter and a copy of the letter Stan signed."

"Thank you, honey." He turned to leave then hesitated in the doorway. "Elise, you'd tell me if you had a problem, wouldn't you?"

"Sure, Dad. But I can handle this. I'll go out there tomorrow. It won't be my first time giving someone the ax."

"I mean a personal problem. If there was something going on at home I needed to know, you'd tell your old man? Something with you and Ginger."

"I'm guessing this is your not so delicate way of saying you've heard Ginger and I aren't together anymore."

"Then the rumors around the office are true. When did all this happen?"

"Two weeks ago. Actually, two weeks ago Monday."

"Why didn't you tell me?" he asked with a concerned frown.

"There's nothing yet to say. I just need a little time to come to terms with it."

"I'm sorry, honey. Have you told your mother yet? She'll want to know."

"No," Elise said with a chuckle. "Not yet. I'm not ready to hear her say I told you so."

"She only wants what's best for you. We both do. You'll have to tell her. It has to come from you."

"I will."

"Soon." He gave her an encouraging nod and left her to her work.

"Soon, but not today," she muttered under her breath.

Elise had just turned back to her computer when her cell phone rang. From the caller ID she knew it was one of her college friends, one she heard from once or twice a year just to catch up on things.

"Hello Linda," she said brightly. "How are things in Portsmouth?"

"I have no idea, Elise. We moved back to Boston." She groaned painfully. "My partner insisted we live in the city. So here we are."

"Portsmouth is a city."

"That's what I said. But she likes being where the action is, whatever the hell that means."

Elise removed her glasses and leaned back in her chair, ready to hear whatever news Linda wanted to share. She'd give her ten minutes.

"How are you, Elise? How's work? How's Ginger?"

Elise had hoped she wouldn't ask. "I'm great. Couldn't be better. Work is great. Busy, like always. How are you and Nan?"

"We're fine. Actually, that's why I called. It's Nan's birthday. We thought we'd have a little get-together. Some of the girls can't come so it'll just be you, Tammy, Luce, Brandy if she's in town and us. I know, I know. We're terrible to wait until the last minute. But we thought what the heck. We haven't gotten together in months. It's nothing fancy, Elise. Just drinks at Nodi's around seven. What do you say?"

"Sure. I'd love to." She found no reason to say no. Maybe drinks with friends would restore her perspective. She certainly wasn't doing it because she was feeling sorry for herself over a failed relationship.

"Bring Ginger if you'd like." The invitation almost sounded like an afterthought. Elise didn't reply. "See you this evening, Elise."

"I'll be there. I look forward to it. Thanks for the invite, Linda."

Elise picked up her coffee cup and headed to the break room for a refill. She stopped at Lorraine's desk to fill her in on the trip she needed to take but she seemed to already know.

"Would you like me to call the car service for tomorrow?" she asked, waiting for the printer to spit out documents.

"Yes. Is that the OSHA letter?"

"Yep, and I've already printed the safety notice Stanley Hebert signed last year."

"Jerk," she hissed. "By the way, I need a car and driver for this evening too. I'm meeting some friends at Nodi's at seven. It's a bar in Jamaica Plain. I'll go from here but it won't be a long evening. An hour, maybe two."

"Good for you." Lorraine smiled approval. "You need to get out and socialize. Should I ask for that woman driver you had before? Jan wasn't it?"

"Yes. Request Jan Chase for both trips."

"Did you ever find out why she limps? Sports injury? Bad knee?"

"I'm sure it's not a sports injury," Elise said and strode down the hall to her office.

Some hours later Elise had just finished revisions on a contract when Lorraine knocked on her door. "Your driver is downstairs in the lobby," she announced. "I told her you'd be down shortly."

Elise slipped the papers in a folder and shut down her computer. It had been a long day and she was ready for a little

R and R. If she was lucky no one would ask about Ginger. She could have a nice evening, a drink with friends and no questions.

"Hello, Ms. Grayson," Jan said cheerfully. She was dressed in her black suit and a white tuxedo shirt with narrow pleats down the front. She had a small black cross-tie at the neck accentuated with a rhinestone stud. "Nice to see you again." She pushed the revolving door to start it moving then stepped back and smiled.

"Good evening, Jan. Nice outfit by the way."

"Thank you. I think it goes well with the car."

Instead of the executive sedan Elise was used to seeing, a longer white limousine waited at the curb.

"What happened to the other car? The sensible black one."

"The Lincoln town car I usually drive is in the shop getting a tune-up, brakes and tires. We're still just charging you your normal rate." Jan opened the back door and like before, took an awkward step back.

"It's nice to know I could take half a dozen people with me if I chose." Elise chuckled then climbed in, feeling like a child in a king-size bed.

"Make yourself comfortable. The bar is stocked if you'd like a little refreshment."

"No, thank you. I'm on my way to have drinks with friends."

"Yes, at Nodi's." Jan closed the door and circled the car. The partition between the driver's seat and the passenger compartment was open. "I understand you need a driver tomorrow as well. You're headed back to Springfield."

"Yes. Are you available?"

"You bet." There was an unmistakable glint in her eye when she looked back. "I promise not to fall or embarrass you this time."

"I wasn't embarrassed. Just surprised, remember? Do you have the address for Nodi's Bar? It's in Jamaican Plain."

"I know the place."

"You've been there?"

"Yes. Several times. It's a…" Jan looked in the rearview mirror. "It's a gay bar. It's nothing fancy. It's not what you'd call trendy or chic."

"Good. I'm not feeling trendy or chic tonight." Elise turned her gaze out the window. "I'm just meeting some friends for a drink and to wish someone a happy birthday. It shouldn't take very long."

It was a quick ride through town south to Jamaican Plain. Jan pulled the big car to the curb and came around to open the door. She extended a hand to help Elise maneuver the step.

"I'm going to gas up the car. You can text or call when you're ready. Do you still have my card?"

"Yes." Elise straightened her blouse and slacks from the wrinkles of the day. "Do I look all right for Nodi's?" she asked, surprised she cared what a chauffer thought. But it was Jan. She had saved her from an embarrassing moment before. Why not ask?

"You look very nice. Nodi's patrons will be envious." Jan straightened Elise's collar. "Have fun. I'll be here when you need me."

Elise reached for the door to the bar but hesitated and looked back.

"After you put gas in the car you're welcome to come inside. I'll be with friends but you don't have to sit in the car."

"Thank you, ma'am. I'll see."

"Of course, I'd prefer you not imbibe. I don't think I could drive that big car."

"I never drink while I'm on the job, ma'am." She gave a silly salute.

"Good to know." Elise returned the salute and chuckled.

Elise hadn't been in Nodi's for nearly two years. Ginger didn't like the atmosphere. She preferred the more upscale bars downtown. Nodi's hadn't changed. It still smelled like citrus fruit and beer. Dimly lit, it had a seafaring motif and held surprisingly few customers even for mid-week.

"Elise," someone called from the far side of the room. "Over here."

Elise surveyed the group. Linda hadn't changed much except for her short gray hair. Her partner of a dozen years, Nan, was a plump woman with a 1980s mullet and big brown eyes. They had been and still were perfect for each other. Both were practical jokers and loved to laugh. Luce and Tammy were also at the table, both with brown hair yet to go gray. Luce was a legal aide and was dressed as if she had come right from work. Tammy worked in the mayor's office and dressed accordingly. They had come into the group as friends of a friend but were a good fit. Elise shared hugs all around and the normal chitchat of how everyone was, how good everyone looked and how long it had been since their last get-together. Elise ordered a Tom Collins. The others ordered their second round.

"I had an appointment with my allergist last week," Linda offered. "His new office is in the Chestnut Hill Physicians' Pavilion. It's gorgeous, Elise. You did a great job. I love the mosaic floors in the lobby and the garden in the atrium."

"Originally there was supposed to be a Koi pond in that atrium but that got changed when they learned how much perpetual maintenance that required."

"You built the Physicians Pavilion?" Luce asked.

"Yes, she did." Linda beamed with pride. "There's a plaque in the lobby that says Grayson Construction, Energy Star Award of Excellence."

"Wow, Elise."

She groaned. "You make it sound like I built it with my own two hands. I had help, you know."

"Whose idea was it to put handrails down the halls?" Tammy asked. "My mom's new knee replacement really appreciates that. Her orthopedic surgeon is in that building."

"We did that just for her," Elise said with a wink.

"I thought most medical facilities have those for safety," Nan said.

"Shh. Don't tell her that. I'm luxuriating in my fifteen seconds of fame here."

They laughed, ordered another drink and moved on to talk about their holiday plans.

"Speaking of gift giving," Tammy said behind her glass, "there's a woman at the bar I'd like to unwrap."

They all turned in unison to look.

"OMG!" Luce said with a lusty whisper. "The one at the end?"

"Yes. Nice, huh?"

"Put that under my tree, Santa."

Elise did a quick double take. It was Jan. She hadn't noticed her come in. She was perched on a stool, sipping from a coffee cup and reading something on her cell phone. The other bar stools obscured a full view of her prosthetic leg but Elise could see her tug at the side of her pant leg as if to make sure it was covered. Tammy and Luce were right. Bathed in the soft glow of the bar light, she was a good-looking woman.

"She looks like an escapee from a formal wear store," Nan offered then leaned into Linda. "Why don't you dress like that?"

"She looks like one of those women who use initials instead of a name. Like J.J. or T.C."

"No, I think she looks more like a Mattie or maybe a Frankie."

"Her name is Jan." Elise took another look in that direction.

"You know her?" Tammy asked eagerly.

"Yes. She's my chauffeur this evening."

"Good taste, Elise. Very good taste." She grinned at Elise then turned her smile toward the woman at the bar.

"You still don't drive in Boston?" Nan asked.

"Not if I can help it."

"Elise is a weenie behind the wheel," Linda said then patted Elise's hand. "We forgive you, sweetheart."

"It's like bumper cars out there. Why would I want to drive in that?"

"I don't blame you. I wouldn't drive in Boston either if I could afford a chauffeur like that," Tammy said. "What does Ginger think of that woman? I bet she is really jealous."

"Speaking of Ginger, where is your significant other? You should have brought her," Linda said nonchalantly.

Elise had hoped this topic wouldn't come up but she wasn't surprised. They had all met Ginger and as far as they knew she and Elise were still a couple.

"Ginger and I aren't together anymore," she replied, averting her eyes toward her glass.

"You're not? When did all this happen?"

"Two weeks ago." Elise took a deep breath, braced for their inevitable questions.

"Oh, sweetheart, I'm so sorry," was all Linda offered.

The four women looked at each other but said nothing. Elise frowned. It was as if they shared some secret they dare not divulge.

"What? No third degree? No demand for details? When Brandy broke up with that woman last year you didn't give up until you knew every detail, including the last time they had sex. I thought you'd at least want to know why Ginger Lindquist and I broke up."

"Tammy, isn't that the same Ginger you were seeing last year?" Luce asked.

"Luce!" Tammy scowled as if to silence the question. But Elise heard it and tossed her a puzzled look.

"Tammy, you went out with Ginger?" Elise asked. "My Ginger?"

"She said you two were separated. I swear, I thought you weren't together, Elise. I wouldn't have gone out with her if I thought otherwise."

"We weren't separated. We've been together for six years. All it would have taken was one simple phone call. You couldn't call to ask if it was okay to have a date with my girlfriend? I thought we were friends."

"I'm sorry. I didn't know." Tammy shrugged defensively. "Brandy said it was okay."

"What does Brandy have to do with it?" Elise asked.

"She went out with her a couple times too."

"What?" Elise demanded loudly. "You and Brandy both dated my girlfriend?" Elise looked up to see Jan peering curiously at her from across the bar.

"We all thought you knew," Linda said quietly.

"We? Who else thought it was okay to go out with my girlfriend?"

"We thought you had one of those open relationships. It works for some people."

"Well, it doesn't work for me. It's called cheating. And I can't believe my friends encouraged my girlfriend's infidelity."

"You're not together anymore. What difference does it make?" Luce said with a cavalier shrug of her shoulders.

"You're right. There's no difference. I'm being silly." Elise stood. "I should forgive and forget, right? That's what friends do."

"We're really sorry, Elise. No one meant to hurt you, I swear," Linda said with a pained expression. "We just assumed you knew."

"I feel really bad about this." Tammy sounded like she was on the verge of tears. "Please don't hate me."

"Don't leave, Elise." Linda reached for her arm. "Please stay."

As bad as her friends seemed to feel, it didn't lessen Elise's humiliation and embarrassment. Two weeks after the breakup and Ginger was causing fresh pain.

"Happy birthday, Nan. I wish you many more," she said, holding tight to her composure. She scanned the others at the table. There was nothing to say. Nothing she wouldn't regret later. She headed for the door, shoving chairs out of her way as she crossed the room. She didn't have to get Jan's attention. She was right behind her.

"This way, ma'am," she said, pointing up the sidewalk to where the car was parked.

The angrier Elise became the faster she walked. She stood at the passenger door, feeling her blood pressure escalate. As soon as Jan opened the door Elise threw her purse in the backseat and climbed in, ignoring Jan's offer for assistance.

"Where would you like to go?" Jan asked, looking in the open door.

"Just drive," she snapped.

Jan started the car then lowered the partition and looked back. "Any particular direction?"

"Just drive," she repeated, her voice cracking. "Anywhere away from here."

Jan raised the partition again, leaving Elise to her festering anger. Anger and overwhelming sense of betrayal. The group of friends she'd thought could mollify the pain of her breakup had only added to it. The temperature inside the car was comfortably warm against the chilly evening air but Elise was cold. Through and through, she was cold. Emotionally cold. She crossed her arms and stared out the window as they drove through Boston, meandering from one neighborhood to another. She couldn't make sense of it, any of it. Was she that terrible a person that her girlfriend felt obliged to cheat on her? Was she that terrible that her friends thought it okay to betray her?

Jan lowered the partition.

"Are you doing all right back there, Ms. Grayson?" She sat at a traffic light, staring at Elise in the rearview mirror.

"Sure. Just dandy."

"If you don't mind me saying so, you don't look just dandy."

"Would you answer a question for me, Jan? A personal question."

"If I can, ma'am."

"Do you have any friends you trust implicitly? I mean really trust."

"Wow. That sounds like a loaded question."

"You're right. It probably is." Elise turned her gaze back out the window.

"Although I'm sure I'd be mad if I knew they lied to me, if that's what you mean. And I think a deliberate omission of the truth is the same as a lie."

"So do I," Elise said softly as tears pooled in her eyes.

"There's tissue in the console, ma'am."

"Would you do me a favor, Jan? Just for tonight, would you not call me ma'am?"

"Would you prefer Ms. Grayson?"

"Could you call me Elise?"

There was a moment of silence before Jan answered. "I could. I like to keep things on a professional level but I could."

"I'm not asking for a friend. I'm just feeling a little betrayed right now and being called ma'am doesn't soften that."

"If you don't mind me asking, does this have something to do with Ginger?"

"You heard that?"

"Everyone in Nodi's heard that." Jan pulled a quirky grin. "But don't worry. It's not the worst thing shouted out in a bar. It doesn't even crack the top ten."

"I didn't mean to make a scene like that."

"I'm sure you didn't. You strike me as a very reserved and private person. The last thing you wanted to hear was your girlfriend's name flung out for all to hear."

"Exactly." Elise opened the cabinet. "Is there anything in here to drink? Bottled water perhaps? This evening has left a very bad taste in my mouth."

"I'm sorry but I don't think there's any water. I forgot to restock the bar. There might be something else in there though."

"Hennessy cognac," Elise said, reading the label on the only bottle in the cabinet.

"Would you like me to stop and get you something?"

"Nope, cognac it is," she said, retrieving a stemmed glass from the rack. Elise remembered her father insisted on serving cognac or brandy in a stemmed glass if a brandy snifter wasn't available. Something to do with swirl-ability. "It'll go well with the gin in the Tom Collins I've already had. Thanks to my friends, I left most of a nine dollar drink on the table." She poured a generous amount then took a sip, grimacing as she swallowed. "Wow. Strong stuff."

"Uh huh."

"Tell me about your significant other, or your partner. Since you've been to Nodi's I assume you don't have a husband." Elise felt the urge to chat. She wanted reassurance that there was something else besides her own screwed up love life in Boston.

"I'm sorry but I don't have anything to tell." Jan kept her hands on the steering wheel and her eyes on the road.

"I was just offering a little conversation. I didn't mean to pry." Elise felt she had crossed some kind of professional line. Jan Chase could be one of those people who, above all else, wanted to keep her private life private. And she couldn't blame her.

"Actually," Jan finally said, "I don't have a partner or a wife or a significant other right now. And no, definitely not a husband." She turned the corner and headed up Commonwealth Avenue.

"Were you a nun in some past life?" Elise asked tongue in cheek, relieved the line of communication was once again open.

"No, although my grandmother would probably like it if I was."

"Are you Catholic?"

"I was. I like to say I'm a reformed Catholic. The church and I don't see eye to eye. I don't even like the kind of wine they serve. And you?" Jan asked nonchalantly.

"Catholic? No. I was raised in a secular household. My parents believed in the divine redemption of the dollar. The more they had, the further into heaven it would catapult them."

"A lot of people subscribe to that belief."

"You're lucky you don't have a girlfriend." Elise continued to sip as they talked, finishing one glass and pouring another.

"That sounds like someone who just broke up with one."

"That's me." Elise held up her glass as a toast. "What was your last girlfriend's name?"

"Allie."

"Short for Allison?"

"Short for Alexandra. She didn't like it."

"That's a lovely name. What was she like?"

Jan thought a moment, her concentration on the traffic and the road.

"I know. I'm being nosy again. But humor me. Please." Elise ignored her better judgment and refilled her glass again. She wasn't a heavy drinker. She hadn't consumed enough alcohol to get drunk since her misguided attempt at joining a sorority.

"Allie was a sweet girl."

"Pretty?"

"Very."

"How long were you two together?"

"About a year, give or take."

"How long have you been without a girlfriend?"

"I don't consider myself without." Jan looked both ways, waited for a fast-moving car then turned the corner. "I prefer to say I'm between girlfriends."

"That's a peculiar way of saying you're single, but whatever works, right?"

"I just think saying without implies some kind of deficiency."

"Are you between girlfriends because of…" Elise stopped herself before she asked the obvious question. It was none of her business why Jan didn't have a partner and it certainly was none of her business if her prosthetic leg had anything to do with it.

"Because of what? Because I'm a limousine driver?"

"Never mind." Elise found the switch on the armrest and raised the partition. She rode along in silence, mad at herself for nearly asking an insensitive question. It was the alcohol talking and she regretted it.

Jan steered around a delivery truck double-parked in front of a bodega then quickly pulled back into her lane to avoid oncoming traffic. The sudden maneuver made Elise's stomach do a flip-flop. The more they wound through traffic the more perspiration formed on Elise's upper lip. She dabbed a tissue across her mouth and forehead. When a car pulled out in front of them and Jan applied the brakes, she pressed the switch and lowered the partition.

"Ah, Jan." She swallowed back hard. "This is embarrassing but I need you to stop please."

"Where?"

"Here. Now!"

Elise opened the door and scrambled out, holding her stomach against the inevitable. Jan rounded the back of the car just as Elise leaned over and puked.

"Okay then." Jan took a step back to avoid splash-back.

Elise braced her hand against the car as her body began to shake. Jan stood behind her and wrapped her arms around her waist, supporting her as she retched again and again.

"I've got you. I won't let you fall," Jan whispered.

Jan's strong arms saved Elise from falling face first into a puddle of goo. Jan pulled a clean handkerchief from her pocket and wiped the drool from Elise's mouth. Elise clutched at Jan's arms as she heaved and retched again. When Elise finally emptied her stomach she leaned back against Jan and closed her eyes, waiting for her strength to return.

"Oh God. I haven't done this since college and I hated it then too," she gasped and sank into Jan's arms. "I'm so sorry."

"That's okay."

"No, it's not okay. It's embarrassing." She shuddered deeply. It was involuntary and seemed to mark the end of her need to vomit.

"It's not that bad. I'll survive and so will you. You just drank too much too quick."

"It was stupid." Elise kept her hands folded over Jan's. Her legs felt like rubber and she wasn't sure they'd support her.

Jan kept a hand around Elise's waist for support while she opened the door and helped her in.

"You're a very trusting soul. Aren't you worried I'll mess up your shiny clean car?"

"I think I'm safe. A little gal like you couldn't possibly have anything else left to give." Jan eyed the bottle of cognac. "I assume you'll abstain from anymore Hennessey." She dumped the small amount left in the glass out on the ground.

"Oh gross," Elise gasped and turned away.

"Is your tummy okay?"

"My tummy may never be the same again. I think I turned it completely inside out."

"Was she worth it?" Jan asked.

"No." Elise lowered her eyes. "If you want to know the truth of it, I think I was trying to drown the betrayal."

"I don't think there's enough booze in the entire world for that."

"Take me home, Jan. It's probably the one place I won't make a fool of myself this evening."

"I don't think you're a fool." She pulled away from the curb and headed up the street.

"I broke up with my girlfriend because I found out she was cheating on me with her boss and has been for some time. This evening I found out she's also been cheating on me with my friends. And it's been going on for years. Doesn't that sound like the perfect description of a fool to you?"

"No disrespect intended, but if it's been going on for years how could you not know?"

"I guess I assumed she was being faithful. I was. It never occurred to me to question her fidelity. At least not until recently."

"Sounds like you took the path of least resistance. It was easier to ignore the warning signs than confront them."

"Maybe so." Elise stared out the window. As much as it hurt to hear it, Jan was right.

"Ms. Grayson? For what it's worth, I think she was nuts to cheat on you."

Elise put the partition up. She just wanted to be home. She wanted this whole day to be over. She wanted to forget the pain and embarrassment. She leaned her head back against the seat, praying the ride home would be quick and smooth. It was.

Jan opened the passenger door and extended a hand.

"You're home, Ms. Grayson." She smiled her professional smile.

Elise sat for a moment, collecting her thoughts and her composure. Her head was spinning. She didn't want to fall as she climbed out, adding to her embarrassment. She finally looked up at Jan.

"You're a good chauffeur, Ms. Chase," she said, slurring her words.

"Thank you." She continued to stand at the door with her hand out.

"Yep, a darn good chauffeur. And I ought to know. I've had my share of crappy ones." She swung her legs out and reached for Jan's hand wildly. Jan grabbed her hand and pulled, helping her to her feet. Elise wobbled, her legs unsteady at best. "Oops. I think I had a little too much cognac. What do you think?" She giggled and stumbled into Jan.

"Perhaps."

"Did I apologize for puking on your shoes?"

"Yes, ma'am. You did. But you didn't puke on my shoes. You puked on your own shoes."

Elise looked down, squinting at her shoes.

"You're right. I did. I'm probably going to be really mad about that in the morning, huh?" She pushed Jan away and started for the front steps.

"Can you make it by yourself?" Jan asked, retrieving Elise's purse and briefcase from the backseat and draping the straps over her shoulder.

"I sincerely hope so." She took the steps one at a time, pulling herself along by the railing. She suddenly felt an arm around her waist, holding and supporting her as she climbed up the steps. Jan stood beside her and waited while Elise fumbled in her purse for her keys.

"May I?" She took the keys from her hand and unlocked the door. She reached inside and snapped on a light. "You're home at last."

"Thank you."

"Are you sure you still want to go to Springfield tomorrow?"

"Springfield? Oh, right." Elise closed her eyes tight, forcing herself to concentrate. But it was fruitless. "Whatever I decide, it won't be until the morning. I'm in no condition tonight to do anything. Good night, Jan."

She waved Jan out the door then closed and locked it. "That woman must think I'm looney tunes. Through and through, looney tunes." She heaved a disgusted sigh then headed upstairs to bed, hoping the room would stop spinning by the time her head hit the pillow.

CHAPTER NINE

Jan crossed the lot toward the black Lincoln town car. Repairs finished, it was ready to return to service. Like all mornings before she had a pickup, she wiped down the seats, checked the compartments for trash and replaced the under-seat air freshener. She ran the hand held vacuum over the floorboards and checked the windows for smudges. Ensuring the car was clean and presentable was part of the job and something she took pride in, especially for Elise Grayson. In spite of the woman's inability to hold her liquor, she seemed to appreciate the service and Jan's attention to detail. They would be safe today. There was no bar in the town car.

Jan checked to see if anyone was watching, then smoothed her hands down her left leg and adjusted the socket of her prosthesis. It didn't feel quite right and hadn't for a few weeks. If it was just phantom pain, it was different from what she usually felt. Perhaps she'd put on a couple pounds. That could explain the tight fit. But her pants still fit the same.

"Good morning, Ma." She cradled her cell phone against her shoulder as she climbed in the driver's seat.

"Jannie, you didn't call last night. I was worried." Her mother's voice was a mix of concern and annoyance.

"I worked last night. I didn't get home until after eleven. Did you want me to call then?" She settled in the seat and waited for the car's Bluetooth to pick up the call.

"You could have called this morning."

"I was going to but you already did."

"When you come over today be sure and take home the timer. Your father said it's here at the house."

"I don't know yet if I can make it. I may be working all day."

"You said you were going to ask for the day off so you could come watch the twins' soccer game."

"Ma, I said if I didn't have to work I'd try to come, but I can't. We've been really busy."

"I already told your sister you'd be there."

"So un-tell her. Ma, I have to go. I've got to pick up a client."

"You'll call me later?"

"Yes, I'll call you later. Love you, Ma."

"I love you too, sweetheart."

Whatever arguments or discussions they had, they always ended the same. Above all else, Jan loved her mother and her mother loved her back unconditionally. The grief and stress over Jan's accident seemed to accentuate that fact.

Jan headed across town to Elise's home in Back Bay. She would have bet money that the trip would have been cancelled but no, according to the dispatcher she was to pick up Ms. Grayson at eight and drive her to the hospital construction site in Springfield. The trip had been confirmed with her secretary. She pulled up out front and called Elise's cell phone.

"Good morning, Ms. Grayson. Whenever you're ready I'll be waiting out front. Take your time."

"Thank you, Jan. I'll be out shortly." Elise sounded chipper enough. Or she was good at disguising a hangover.

Jan settled back in the seat, getting comfortable for what she assumed would be a twenty minute wait, as she had learned to expect from clients who said they'd be out shortly. She had a few clients who thought ignoring a waiting chauffeur altogether was acceptable as well. Jan didn't mind. Boring as it was to wait, the company was paid from the time she arrived and notified the customer she was waiting, regardless of when they climbed in the back of the car. Some car services charged from lot to lot, billing the customer for the driving time across town and back again. Jan agreed that billing from the time of pick up to drop off seemed more equitable. But she had barely gotten comfortable when Elise came out her front door and bounded down the steps, purse in one hand and briefcase in the other. Jan scrambled out of the car and hurried around to open the door.

"Good morning," she said, arriving at the passenger door at the same moment as Elise did.

"Good morning," Elise said dryly. She wore a dark blue pantsuit and a blouse with ruffles at the neck. She also had on a pair of dark sunglasses in spite of the overcast skies. She stepped into the backseat without expression.

"Hospital construction site in Springfield, correct?" Jan knew where they were going. It was already confirmed. But she wanted to test the waters. Was Elise in a good mood or was she on the verge of biting someone's head off? If Jan had crossed the line last night she wanted to know.

"Correct." Elise kept her gaze straight ahead and didn't offer further conversation. No instructions on where to park or how long she'd be at the site. And no comment about last night, at least not yet. Not even a groan of disgust over being sick.

The ride west on the Mass Pike was ninety miles of painful silence. At least in the white stretch limo the partition provided a barrier. But the black sedan didn't have one. Jan wasn't usually given to paranoia but Elise's rigid expression behind large sunglasses glaring back at her in the rearview mirror was enough to make her wonder what she had done wrong.

Jan stopped at the gate to the construction site and hurried around to open Elise's door. Usually she was ready and climbed out immediately, but this time she sat stone-faced, seemingly unaware the door was open.

"Ms. Grayson?" Jan held out her hand.

"This is my least favorite part of my job," Elise said, but made no move to exit the car.

"Visiting construction sites?" Jan scanned the lot, wondering what made it so objectionable this time. It looked the same as when they were there before.

"It's the reason for the visit I hate." Elise took a deep breath then reached for Jan's hand and stepped out. "How do you fire someone and allow them to retain their dignity?"

"That's a rhetorical question I assume." Jan closed the car door and rested her hand on the roof.

"Probably." Elise slung her briefcase strap over her shoulder and headed for the foreman's trailer with a determined stride.

"Shall I wait or will this be an extended visit?" Jan called after her.

"Short and sweet," she replied without turning around.

Jan leaned against the car with her arms crossed and watched. She didn't need to hear any dialog to know what was happening. Elise went into the trailer. A minute later a man in a white hard hat came out, a concerned look on his face. He crossed the lot and entered the building under construction. He returned to the trailer, followed by a younger looking man in a yellow hard hat who seemed unaware of what was about to happen.

"There goes the Christian to the lions," Jan muttered as the trailer door closed.

The meeting was indeed short if not necessarily sweet. Three minutes later the young man stepped out of the trailer with a scowl on his face and his yellow hard hat in his hand.

"Lions one, Christians zero," she said under her breath.

Elise came out of the trailer, followed by the man in the white hard hat. He shook her hand, patted her on the back like she was one of the boys, then went back inside. Elise wore a contented, almost victorious smile on her face as she descended the steps. Why not? She was the boss and had just exercised her authority to fire a worker. She headed for the car, her sunglasses still firmly in place.

"All finished?" Jan asked, opening the door for her.

"Yes. I hope so."

Jan was dying to know what had led up to the firing, what transgressions the man had committed. If he'd had nothing to lose, she could just imagine what nasty insults and colorful language he'd used. But she knew better than to ask.

"Am I returning you to your office or your house?"

"Office. I've got three days' worth of work that all needs attention today."

Clearly Elise was in a hurry to get back to Boston. Requesting a quick detour to pick up a package didn't seem likely. But it was worth a try. She climbed in the driver's seat.

"Ms. Grayson," she began, turning in the seat to face her. Elise was digging in her purse.

"Uh huh?" she said without looking up.

"I know you're in a hurry to get back to Boston."

Elise's digging became more frantic.

"Did you lose something?"

"Yes." Elise gave her purse a shake then went back to digging. "I could have sworn it was in here somewhere." She grabbed her briefcase and dug through it as well.

"Can I help?"

"Aspirin. I'd trade my iPad for some aspirin right now."

Jan opened the glove compartment and took out a small bottle of Advil.

"Here you go."

"Thank you, but I can't take ibuprofen. It has to be aspirin. For me it's worse than taking syrup of ipecac." She wrinkled her nose.

"No Advil for you then." Jan tossed it back in the compartment and closed the lid. "Sorry. That's the sum total of my medicine cabinet."

"That's okay. I've got some at the office I think. I hope." She closed her purse. "Now, what was it you said? Something about Boston?"

"Yes. I know you're in a hurry to get back to work but I was wondering if we could make a quick stop on the way out of town. But only if it's not inconvenient. I need to pick up a set of remote switches and a timer. It's all paid for and waiting. All I have to do is run in and grab it."

"Here in Springfield?"

"Yes. Well, in Indian Orchard. Not that far from where we ate the other day. We can jump on the Mass Pike at Ludlow. All I need is three minutes, tops," she added hopefully. Her mother wasn't going to like a quick three minute stop but she'd explain later.

"Sure. Why not? We'll call it even for you helping me last night."

"Thanks. It'll save me a trip back to get it." She headed across town.

"Which supplier are you using? Grainger? Most of them will ship directly to your house if you ask them. Shipping can't be that much."

"It was a special order. The frequencies had to be modified so they didn't interfere with ones I already have."

"That's way beyond my scope, that's for sure."

"Mine too. I just let him do it and tell me when it's ready."

"Then you trust the guy at the store to know what he's doing? That's a long ride back if it needs tweaking."

"I trust him." Jan smiled.

"This looks more like a residential area than a commercial one."

"It is." She rounded the corner and stopped in front of the third house. "I'll be right back."

"This is where you bought electronics? What did you do? Buy them on Craigslist? Buying used electronics online sounds like a place ripe for fraud."

"They're not used and I didn't buy them on Craigslist. This is my parents' house. My dad owns an electronics and plumbing supply store. He ordered them for me." She opened the driver's door and swung her legs out.

"This is where your parents live?" Elise leaned toward the window and studied the two-story home.

"Yes." Jan looked into the backseat. "Would you like to come in? I bet we could rustle up some aspirin for you."

"Are your parents home?"

"My mother probably is. And my grandmother. She lives with them now. Dad's truck isn't here so he's probably at the store."

"Would I be intruding?"

"Not at all." She happily opened the back door for Elise.

"Shouldn't you ask first?"

"No need. Mom loves company." She extended a hand.

"Unannounced company isn't always appreciated though."

"It'll be fine."

Elise left the sunglasses on the seat and stepped out of the car. Jan knocked on the mudroom door then opened it.

"Ma, we're here." She led the way into the kitchen. It was empty but a saucepan on the stove was boiling robustly. "Ma, something's going to boil over."

Jan had just reached for the burner knob when her mother hurried into the kitchen wearing a snap-front cotton robe.

"Don't turn it off. They need to cook for another ten minutes," she said, checking the flame as if to make sure Jan hadn't turned it down.

"They're going to boil over."

"No, they're not." She adjusted the flame slightly and put a lid on the pan then turned to Jan for a hug. "Hello Jannie. The soccer game got cancelled. The coach for the other team had to work overtime. They're going to make it up on Sunday."

"Hi Ma." Jan gave her mother a quick kiss on the cheek.

"And who is this?" she asked with a congenial smile in Elise's direction.

"Ma, this is Elise Grayson. Elise, this is my mother. Harriet Chase."

"Nice to meet you, Mrs. Chase."

"Oh, honey. Call me Ma or Mom. Everybody else does." Elise extended her hand but Harriet ignored it and gave her a hug instead, one that seemed to take Elise by surprise.

"Ma, where would I find aspirin? Downstairs bathroom?"

"There's a bottle on the shelf with the glasses." She pointed to the cabinet next to the sink. Jan opened it and took out the bottle, read it then put it back.

"Aspirin, Ma. Not ibuprofen."

"What's the difference? Are you sick, Jannie? Do you need to stop at Urgent Care?"

"No, Ma. I'm not sick. Ms. Grayson can't take ibuprofen. She needs aspirin. You've got plain old aspirin, don't you?"

"That's okay," Elise said. "I can wait."

"I'm sure we've got aspirin. Let me look." Harriet went down the hall.

"I don't want to make a big deal out of it," Elise called after her.

"No problem, honey."

"We could just stop at a convenience store and buy some," Elise said to Jan.

"Don't tell my mother that. You'll get a lecture on how overpriced those stores are and how it's always better to accept help from friends."

"But I'm not your mother's friend. She barely knows me."

"Don't tell her that either." Jan chuckled.

"I hope I'm not being rude, but does your mother's kitchen always smell like this?" She wrinkled her nose.

"No." Jan lifted the lid to the boiling saucepan and peeked inside. "I suspect it's whatever died in here."

"I found it." Harriet returned to the kitchen with her hands full of medicine bottles. "Don't touch that, Jannie."

"What is it? It smells gross."

"Chicken livers. Baci's stewing them with onions and garlic."

"Why?"

"For Ruby." Harriet grimaced.

"She's cooking chicken livers in onions and garlic for her dog?"

"Yes. The vet said she was anemic."

"The dog is older than dirt. Sure, it's anemic."

"I know, but you can't tell Baci not to do it. Okay, I've got Walgreens brand aspirin, Bayer chewable baby aspirin, Excedrin PM. I think it's aspirin. And some of this." She set the bottles on the kitchen table. Jan snatched up the brown prescription bottle with her name on it.

"What are you doing with this?"

"You left it here so I put it in the medicine cabinet. There's still a bunch of pills in the bottle."

"You shouldn't keep this around the house. What if the twins got a hold of it?" Jan dumped the pills down the garbage disposal.

"That's wasteful. What if you need to take them again?"

"I won't." She stood at the sink, running water down the drain as a painful memory overtook her.

"I'll just take two of these." Elise picked up the bottle of aspirin but her eyes were on Jan. "Thank you, Mrs. Chase."

"Tell my daughter she needs to be practical. You have to plan for the future. A penny saved."

"Is a penny earned," Elise added. "Yes, you're right. I agree. I'll be sure and tell her that." She raised a mocking eyebrow at Jan.

"My mother saves Cool Whip tubs and aluminum pie pans. She usually has a Ziploc baggie hanging over the faucet to dry after she's washed it out. She's the queen of penny saved, penny earned."

"What's wrong with that?" Harriet demanded. "So your mother found a use for otherwise discarded materials. It's called green living."

"There's at least two dozen rubber bands around the doorknob to the pantry." Jan pointed.

"They're from bunches of asparagus," Harriet explained.

"Ma, I don't have a problem with you saving and recycling but saving dangerous and out-of-date prescriptions is a bad idea."

"How dangerous?" Elise asked cautiously.

"It was just Jannie's pain medicine. She never used it all so I saved it just in case."

"It's three years old. It's expired, Ma."

The saucepan boiled over and sizzled on the burner.

"I'm turning this down." Jan lifted the pan as she adjusted the knob. "It smells bad enough without slopping out all over the stove. Where is Baci, by the way? She must be able to smell this."

"Napping, I think. Her sinuses are bothering her."

"Your grandmother's name is Baci?" Elise asked, accepting the glass of water Jan handed her for the aspirin.

"Baci is Polish for grandmother. Well, actually, Babci is. When we were little kids we pronounced it Baci and it stuck. She was born in Poland. Her married name is pronounced No-vatch but it's spelled Novak."

While Elise took her aspirin and visited with Jan about family heritage, Harriet busied herself in the kitchen, heating something in the microwave and refilling the coffeemaker.

"Thank you for the aspirin, Harriet. It was a lifesaver."

"You're welcome. Why don't you take a couple more with you for later?"

"That's kind but I've had all I'll need, I'm sure. But before we go could I use your restroom?"

"Absolutely," Jan replied before her mother could agree.

"Use the one at the top of the stairs. I've already cleaned it today. The pink towels are fresh."

"Thank you." She started down the hall.

"You might have to jiggle the handle on the toilet. It keeps running sometimes," Harriet called after her.

"Ma!" Jan gasped.

"Well, it does."

"You don't tell guests that."

"Why not? The toilet handle needs jiggling. What's the big deal?" She shrugged.

"First of all, Elise is smart enough to know if the toilet handle needs jiggling without you mentioning it. She's a building contractor. I'm sure she knows how a toilet works."

"She builds houses?"

"She builds office buildings and apartment complexes. They're doing the addition on the Baystate Medical Center downtown. She's one of the Graysons in Grayson Construction."

"Is she a customer of yours? Is that why you're all dressed up in your spiffy black suit?"

"Yes, she's a client." Jan felt a twinge of pain in her stump and shifted her weight, hoping to relieve the pressure without her mother noticing. But she did.

"Are you all right, sweetie pie?" Harriet looked down at Jan's leg, as if she had x-ray vision. "Is everything okay with your…"

"Leg, Ma. It's okay to just call it my leg. And yes, I'm fine. I just stepped wrong."

"You'd tell me if there was a problem, wouldn't you?" She touched her daughter's face tenderly.

"Yes, I would tell you, Ma. When have I ever been able to keep a secret from you?"

"How about the year you and your sister got tattoos? You kept that from me. If I hadn't seen you at the beach I would have never known."

"Pop has a tattoo on his shoulder and I've never heard you complain about that."

"Your father got that when he was in the army. I didn't even know him then. If he had asked me I would have said no."

"Well, good news. That tattoo on my leg is gone." She grinned. "I found a surefire way to remove it."

Harriet closed her eyes and cupped her hands over her ears. "Don't say it, Jannie. I know what you're going to say and don't say it."

"Okay, Ma. I won't." Jan wrapped her mother in a bear hug and swayed her back and forth. "I'm sorry."

"Maybe you should give your body a rest, sweetheart. You know, take a break."

"What are you talking about?"

"I've seen you lately. You make faces when you walk. You stumble. You know what I mean. Give your leg a rest. Stay off it for a while is all I'm saying."

"And what? Use a wheelchair? No, thank you."

"Not forever but for a few months. Long enough to give your body time to adjust."

"No."

"If it's bothering you, what's the harm? The doctor said not everyone heals at the same rate."

"Ma, for the last time, I'm not using a wheelchair. I'm fine. I'm still working on balance but I'm fine. Don't worry about it." She gave her mother a kiss on the forehead just as Elise walked back into the kitchen.

"I love the little teddy bear guest towels," Elise said brightly. "And no, I didn't have to jiggle the toilet handle." She offered a little smile in Jan's direction.

"Come to the table, girls." Harriet carried the coffeepot and a plate of sliced banana bread into the dining room.

"I think it's time for us to go." Elise moved toward the mudroom door. "Thank you again, Harriet."

"Where are you going?"

"Ma, Ms. Grayson needs to get back to Boston."

"Come sit down, both of you. Have a bite to eat first. Do you like banana bread, Elise?"

"Yes, I do. Banana bread is one of my favorites. My mother has it out during the holidays."

"Jannie, grab the tub of cream cheese from the fridge."

"Ma." Jan was ready to defend Elise's request to head back to Boston.

"It's all right, Jan. Your mother has made us coffee and banana bread. We can spare a few minutes. I don't mind. To be honest, I didn't have breakfast this morning and I'm hungry. A little nosh wouldn't hurt."

"Why didn't you say something? We could have stopped to get you breakfast."

"Food wasn't uppermost on my mind this morning." Elise cocked an eyebrow.

"Come sit down, you two." Harriet herded them into the dining room.

She had prepared more than just coffee and banana bread. There was also a bowl of strawberries and melon balls and a pitcher of orange juice on the table. The place settings were next to each other on the far side of the large table. There was enough space between them so elbows wouldn't touch but they were still close enough to be intimate. Jan chuckled to herself. She knew what her mother was doing. Every time she saw Jan with a woman she made the assumption there was romance in the air. She didn't ask. She just assumed. Even though Jan had told her Elise was a client, she would be sowing the seeds anyway.

"This is lovely, Harriet. It looks delicious." Elise took a seat. She could have moved her chair down a little if she felt uncomfortable with the spacing, but she didn't.

Jan took off her suit jacket and draped it over the back of the chair. She waited for Elise to get settled and took a seat.

"We could have eaten in the kitchen," Elise said as she poured juice for both of them. "Harriet, come join us."

"No, no. I'm going to rinse the livers and get them in a refrigerator dish before the neighbors complain about the smell. You two enjoy. Take your time." She giggled.

"Ma, go clean the kitchen."

"She's a sweetheart," Elise said after Harriet had left the room and closed the swinging door to the kitchen.

"She means well." Jan poured creamer into her coffee and stirred in a spoonful of sugar.

"You're very lucky to have a caring mother." Elise took a sip of her coffee. "And thank you, by the way."

"For?"

"Not mentioning last night and the probable cause for needing aspirin today."

"That's none of my mother's business. I consider it driver-client confidentiality."

"I appreciate that. I must say, you looked surprised to see me this morning."

"Given what happened with the cognac I wasn't sure you'd be up to this today."

"Absolutely. Work always comes first."

"Even with a killer hangover?"

"Yes," she said quietly, spreading a thin layer of cream cheese on a slice of banana bread. "Besides, if I stayed home I'd just sulk and that would accomplish nothing. It was easier to go to work and let last night be last night. I want you to know I don't make a habit of doing that. Drinking myself into a stupor is ridiculous. It won't happen again. I promised myself that when I couldn't get up the stairs to my bed."

"It happens. Breaking up can be devastating. Everybody has girlfriend woes sometime or other."

"Even you?"

"Even me." Jan studied Elise for a moment. "I get the feeling you want to ask me something about Allie. Go ahead. Ask away."

"Did losing your girlfriend have anything to do with losing your leg?"

It wasn't exactly what Jan had expected her to ask but it was close.

"Wait. Don't answer. I'm sorry. I shouldn't have asked. That's prying."

"That's okay. Lots of people ask about my leg but no one ever asked it quite like that."

"But she didn't cheat on you, right?"

"No." Jan chuckled softly. "At least, I don't think she did. She was too busy mothering me."

"It must have been comforting to have someone take care of you. Someone to make you feel special."

"That's not exactly what it was. After the accident I lost a girlfriend and gained a second mother. That's not what I needed from a girlfriend. My own mother does a fine job of that without any help. Allie was constantly hovering and worrying and protecting me."

Just as Jan lifted her cup to her lips for a drink she felt a stabbing pain in her leg. It didn't last long and it wasn't bad enough to send her to tears but it was enough to make her wince and spill some of her coffee.

"Are you okay?" Elise asked, quickly taking the cup from her hand. She dabbed her napkin over the spill.

"Yes. I'm fine. A klutz but I'm fine."

"No, you're not. I saw you grimace like something was definitely wrong. Shall I get your mother?"

"NO!"

"Are you sure? You look pale." She glanced at the kitchen door but Jan grabbed her arm before she could call for Harriet.

"I'm okay," she declared. "Please, don't call her." Jan pushed her chair back and stood up to prove she was indeed okay and didn't need help.

"Sit down, Jan, before you fall down."

"I'm not going to fall down. My leg is fine. It doesn't hurt. There's nothing wrong with it."

"I didn't say there was." Elise scowled up at her.

"I don't need someone else telling me to take it easy. I can do my job without any help."

"Whoa, whoa, whoa. I don't want to tell you what to do. You just seemed to be in pain so I asked if you were all right. I'm not your overly protective girlfriend. Now sit down and eat your banana bread or I will call your mother." Elise pointed to the chair.

"I thought you didn't want to tell me what to do."

"I'm not." She patted the cushion then went back to spreading cream cheese.

Trying not to look like a petulant child, Jan sat back down. She checked her coffee cup to see how much was left after the mishap.

"Here. Fill mine too." Elise placed her cup next to Jan's. "While you're up, that is."

"Sit down but go fill your coffee cup?" Jan muttered as she stood, a cup in each hand.

"Yes, please. I assume you'd like to prove your independence and mobility so I'll let you march off into the kitchen and refill our cups." Elise offered a wry smile.

Jan carried the cups to the kitchen.

"You could have called me. I'd have brought the pot," Harriet said from the doorway to the pantry.

"I got it, Ma."

"She's sure a cutie, Jannie. No, Allie was a cutie. Ms. Grayson is lovely. Don't you think so?"

"I didn't notice." Jan wasn't going to start this conversation with her mother. Of course Elise Grayson was lovely. She was classy and elegant. She had a refined sophistication that Jan recognized that first evening and she was also human. But her mother didn't need fuel for her curiosity. She finished refilling the cups and headed for the door.

"Jannie?" she said softly. "Don't let the good ones get away. You'll be sorry."

"Ma! Stop it. She's a client. That's all."

"I'm just saying."

Jan returned to the table, where Elise was reading a text on her phone.

"I'm not coming back over there, Roy. You handle the paperwork. That's what we pay you for," she muttered as she keyed in a reply.

"Everything okay?"

"The foreman wants me to come back to the site and handle some paperwork."

"Do you need me to take you back downtown?"

"Lord no." She sent the text and put away the phone. "He can do it. Filling out two forms is not that big a deal."

"Is this about that person you wanted to fire without wounding his dignity?"

"Yes."

"It's hard enough to find a good job these days without having that on your résumé."

"I agree. We vet our employees pretty thoroughly so hopefully this kind of thing doesn't happen. But you never know who'll fail to measure up. And before that frown on your face gets any deeper let me say I didn't fire him."

"But you said that's what you were going to do. And I saw the guy come out of the trailer carrying his hard hat and looking like he'd been sent to the woodshed."

"Oh, he was devastated all right. But I let him choose his punishment. I was prepared to fire him for repeated safety violations, which we documented. But I gave him a choice. Ground crew with a cut in pay or out the door."

"So he still has a job?"

"Yes. He's on probation and can't work above ground level but he'll have a paycheck. I did it for his family. His wife is expecting their third child. They need the insurance. But he knows I'll fire his keister in a red-hot second if he screws up again. What are you grinning at?" Elise fixed her with a suspicious glare. "Are you surprised?"

"A little."

"We're not monsters. We realize our employees have families. My dad might not agree with me but Stan is a good worker, when he remembers the rules. We need good workers."

"Would your dad have fired him?"

"Yes. He's more no-nonsense. Always has been."

"I'm glad you were the one sent to handle it then."

"How long have you been a chauffeur?"

"Not that long. Five months. But I've been driving since I was sixteen."

"What did you do before?"

"Delivery service." Jan took a sip of coffee, waiting for Elise's next question.

"You were a UPS driver?"

"No. Not that kind of delivery. I delivered body parts."

Elise had just taken a bite and nearly choked on it. "Body parts? That sounds a little morbid."

"I carried other things too, but sometimes I transported organs for transplant."

"That's sort of like a chauffeur. You just didn't have a person in the backseat telling you what to do."

"And I didn't use a car. I flew a single engine plane. A Cessna Skyhawk."

"You're a pilot?"

"Now *you* look surprised. Yes. I have a pilot's license. Or I did. I haven't taken my flight review in three years, but yes, I'm a pilot." Jan drank the last swig then stood up. "When you're ready I'll get you back to Boston."

"You don't fly anymore?"

"No." She carried her cup and plate to the kitchen. She wanted no more talk about flying or airplanes. She was a chauffeur now.

Elise followed, carrying her dishes. Jan could tell she wanted to ask something else but was glad she didn't.

"Thank you again for the refreshments, Harriet. It was delicious."

"You're welcome, honey. Anytime." She gave Elise a hug then one to Jan. "Call me, sweetheart, and let me know how you're doing, okay?"

"I will, Ma." Jan picked up the box of electronics with her name on it and headed for the back door, expecting Elise to follow. But Elise was looking at a photograph taped to the refridgerator, the one of Jan and Allie in shorts and tank tops at the beach. She suspected Elise was looking at her legs in the picture. "That was taken four years ago."

"Is that Allie?"

"Yes."

"Cute." Elise smiled at the picture then followed Jan out the door.

CHAPTER TEN

Elise set her cup of coffee on a coaster and sat down, ready to tackle the stack of work on her desk. It had been two weeks since her trip to Springfield and to Jan's parents' house for banana bread. There were several projects she knew needed her attention but the handwritten note on the yellow legal pad on top of the stack wasn't one of them.

"There you are." She carried the pad into an open office where her father and one of the draftsmen were studying a set of blueprints. "Hi, Ben. Dad, can I have a word with you?"

"Oh, you found my note," he said then went back to the blueprint.

"I found it but I'm not sure what I'm supposed to do with it. Brighton Hollow remodel and a long string of question marks is a little vague. And who is C T?"

"Charlie Tuttle. You remember him."

"The one with the bowtie and sweater vests?"

"Yes. Brighton Hollow is his property on Lake Winnipe-saukee. He'd like us to take a look and see if it's structurally sound to be remodeled. He wants to convert it to a three or four bedroom vacation house. Add a couple bathrooms. Modernize the kitchen. Add a hot tub. You get the idea. He bought it as an investment and wants to revamp it for his grandkids."

Puzzled, Elise shook her head. "I thought we don't do residential."

"We do for clients who build three hundred million dollar office complexes."

"I'm almost afraid to ask why this is on my desk when he's your buddy."

He handed the pad back to Elise with a blank expression that spoke volumes.

"Oh, come on, Dad." She scowled. "You do it. I don't want to go look at a cabin on Lake Winnipesaukee. You go to New Hampshire. You know the place."

"I don't know anything about it. I've never set eyes on it. He hasn't been up there in months but he's open to ideas. Remember convenience, efficiency and comfort. Oh, and resale. I think that last one is the most important. Submit a bill for time and travel." He lifted the pages of the legal pad to reveal a white envelope tucked in the back. "The key and photographs of the cabin are in there. The address and directions are in there too. Take a look. Draw up some sketches. Give him an estimate."

Elise pulled the photographs from the envelope. "It's a rock and beam A-frame? And it's at the bottom of a hill. How are you supposed to expand that? We'd have to start from scratch," she concluded, squinting at the pictures.

"Elise, between you and me, I think Charlie's looking for an excuse to bail on this vacation home idea. Don't stress yourself on details. The construction materials, delivery fees and labor alone will probably price him above what he wants to spend. Take some measurements and see what you can come up with. We'll do a cost plus but he'll want an estimate."

"Why doesn't he use it the way it is? It's small but it's right on the lake. What more do you need?"

"His wife hates it. Need I say more?"

Elise slipped the photographs back in the envelope, resigned to a waste of time accommodating her father's request.

"Take Ginger with you. Make a day of it."

"Dad, Ginger and I aren't together anymore. I told you that."

"Just checking. I probably should tell you to expect a call from your mother."

"About?"

"I might have mentioned Ginger isn't in the picture anymore."

"Dad!"

"I told you to let her know. I thought you did."

"I wasn't ready."

"Now you don't have to." He grinned mischievously.

Elise had no sooner returned to her desk than her cell phone rang. If she didn't answer it her mother would call her desk phone and if that wasn't answered, her father would be stomping down the hall wanting to know why Suzanne was bugging him.

"Hello Mother."

"Hello dear. What is this silly business about you and Ginger?" It was more of an accusation than a question.

"Mother, Ginger and I are old news. Can we not talk about it?"

"You should have come to me. Not your father. He isn't someone you consult for relationship advice."

"I didn't consult him. He happened to ask and I mentioned she and I are no longer together." Her mother and Ginger had had a contentious relationship at best. Why did she care if they were still together or not?

"What happened? Did Ginger object to your long hours at the office? You and your father spend way too much time staring at blueprints."

"That wasn't it, Mother."

"Are you sure? You can't expect someone to play second fiddle all the time."

It was clear Elise was going to have to confess why she'd ended things with Ginger. And why not? Maybe her mother would let the subject drop if she knew.

"She was cheating on me, Mother."

There was a moment of silence. Elise hoped her mother was preparing a suitable sympathetic response. Something compassionate and supportive.

"Are you sure?"

"Yes, I'm sure."

"Elise, there are worse things than that."

"Maybe so, but cheating ranks right up there."

"You need to forgive and forget, dear. You can work things out if you just set your mind to it. Sure, you wish it didn't happen, but some things you have to ignore. No one's perfect."

"You make it sound like being in a bad relationship is better than being in no relationship."

"Do you want to be single all your life?"

Elise chuckled. "Mother, it's been a few weeks. That's not a lifetime."

"The holidays are coming up. Don't you want someone to celebrate with?"

"I don't need a girlfriend to enjoy Thanksgiving and Christmas."

"Well, it will be awkward if you come to my harvest buffet alone."

"Are you doing that again? Why don't you just wait until Thanksgiving?"

"Heavens no. Most of our friends aren't available on Thanksgiving. Anyway, it's tradition that I do the buffet. It's expected. And your father and I will be in New York Thanksgiving week. We have tickets to see *Madame Butterfly* at the Met. Call Ginger. Invite her to lunch and see if you can't work things out, dear."

"Mother, I'll come to your harvest buffet but I'm not having lunch with Ginger to work things out." Elise heard a small exasperated sigh, the kind her mother uttered before sticking her nose in her daughter's business. "Mother, it'll be fine. I promise I won't show up at your dinner party with a neon S on my chest announcing I'm single."

"Wear your little black dress. The Vera Wang. The one with the mesh sleeves. And those strappy heels with the gold buckle on the toe."

"Are you dressing me now?" It suddenly occurred to Elise this dinner party might be her mother's opportunity to meddle. It wouldn't be the first time. She didn't want or need her to supply a surprise dinner partner. Not now, not ever. The problem had always been how to stop her. "Mother, I'm not saying I will, but there is a possibility I might be bringing someone to your harvest buffet. I'll let you know when I get a firm response." As soon as it came out of her mouth Elise knew it was a mistake. Trying to divert the conversation by suggesting she was seeing someone else backfired almost immediately.

"Who is it? Do I know her?"

"I said might. Nothing is definite."

"What's her name, dear? I might know her family."

"I have to go, Mother. I've got a meeting with a contractor."

"Bring your friend. I'm anxious to meet her." Her mother's voice held a fresh bubbling enthusiasm at the mere mention of a date. "Bye bye," she added and hung up.

Elise looked over at Lorraine sorting through a stack of folders on a nearby table.

"Your father needs the corrections for the Reed warehouse," she said. "He's certain you have them."

Elise closed the folder she was working on and handed it to Lorraine. "Tell him the corrections have been made but if they add restrooms again we'll have to refigure." She removed her glasses and rocked back in her chair. "Lorraine, I need a date. Who do we know?"

"Pardon me?"

"I need a woman willing to attend my parents' harvest buffet, so probably someone who hasn't met my mother but whom she'll approve of."

"You can't go alone?"

"I could."

"But you'd rather not."

"My mother would rather I not. I don't need a wife. I just need a dinner companion or I'll never hear the end of it."

"How about Betty Wheeler? The interior designer from Plymouth?" Lorraine offered hopefully. "I heard she's single again. Her ex goes to our church."

"I don't think so." Elise did her best to hide a disparaging chuckle. An attractive woman, Betty Wheeler would likely earn the approval of Elise's mother. But Betty was a superficial social climber, not the kind of person Elise wanted to invite as a dinner companion.

"How about Rita whatshername? The condo developer. Or that investment counselor, Joyce or Jocelyn something? The redhead."

"No," Elise said, discounting those suggestions as well, also not the kind of women she wanted as a dinner date.

She turned her chair to face the window. Someone else's name kept popping into her head, someone as unlike any of the women Lorraine suggested as she could be. It was crazy to consider but there was a strange attraction she couldn't deny. Jan Chase wasn't married or in a relationship, at least not that she knew of. She was the right age, intelligent, attractive and personable. She was also kind, unpretentious and polite. Elise had never been to dinner with a woman willing to offer her a hand as she climbed out of the car. It might be normal chauffeur behavior, but Jan had a certain measure of chivalry about her— down-to-earth, adorable chivalry, and Elise enjoyed it.

Elise scanned the Boston skyline as she considered the possibility. Was it ludicrous to invite Jan to dinner? Would she think it forward of Elise for asking?

"If I think of anyone I'll let you know," Lorraine said and headed for the door.

"Oh, in case you haven't heard, I'll be working up a proposal for a remodel." She spun her chair back around from the view. "My father has offered our services to remodel Charlie Tuttle's cabin on Lake Winnipesaukee."

"Bowtie Tuttle?"

"Yes. I'll need a car and driver to take me up there."

"I didn't think we did cabin remodeling."

"Well, evidently my father thinks we do."

"Would you like me to request Jan as your driver?"

"Yes."

"Hey, how about…," Lorraine started.

"How about what?"

"Never mind." Lorraine smiled and headed out the door. She returned a few minutes later with a disappointed look on her face. "I called the car service. Jan is already scheduled for the next five days. I guess she's pretty popular. Would you consider an alternative driver?"

Elise looked up from her work. "So I'll go to Lake Winnipesaukee in six days."

"Okay." Lorraine turned to leave then looked back. "Shall I have her pick you up here at the office?"

"Yes, around nine. I can do a quick perusal and be back by mid-afternoon." She went back to work.

"Are you going to ask her?"

"Ask who what?" she said without looking up.

"Nothing."

Lorraine was out the door and down the hall when Elise looked up and smiled to herself. If she meant ask Jan to be her dinner date, yes, she was going to ask her. Maybe.

Those next six days passed slowly. Elise wasn't in a huge hurry to look at Charlie Tuttle's cabin in New Hampshire but she was anxious to ask Jan if she'd accompany her for an evening at her parents'. There was always the possibility she'd decline the invitation. Attending a dinner party with a client could be the last thing she'd want to do. She might have her own plans.

"Good morning, Ms. Grayson." Jan carried Elise's tote bag and briefcase to the curb, and opened the passenger door to the black Lincoln town car. "I understand we're going to New Hampshire today?"

"Yes. Lake Winnipesaukee to take a look at a vacation house for remodel. What is it? Two hours? Three?"

"For the address I was given, around two and a half hours. It's on the northern shore. Pretty country this time of year."

Elise had just settled in and buckled her seat belt when her cell phone rang. It was a foreman needing permission to rent an excavator to replace one being repaired. When the call ended she began preparing what she would say to Jan in the way of an invitation. But another call interrupted her train of thought. Then another and another, each one demanding her immediate and undivided attention. Business came first. But that didn't mean she couldn't enjoy the enchanting cluster of blond curls at the back of Jan's head or her long fingers curled around the steering wheel.

They stopped once for a bathroom break and so Elise could buy a replacement phone charger. They also stopped at a roadside produce stand. Elise bought a jar of maple syrup. Jan bought syrup and some apples.

"If I buy your mother some maple syrup would you take it to her?" Elise asked, adding another jar to her basket.

"Sure, but you don't have to do that."

"But I want to."

"Then she'll love it."

"Look. Banana bread." She picked up a plastic wrapped loaf and sniffed it then put it back. "Nope. It can't possibly be as good as your mother's."

"I'll tell her you think so. She'll be pleased. I bet my grandmother made it though. She hates to see food wasted. She probably saw the bananas were overripe in the bowl and decided to make it."

"Then she gets a jar of maple syrup too." Elise placed a third jar in her basket.

"That's not necessary. They can share."

"I want to. So hush."

"You're the boss." Grinning, Jan followed her around the stand, carrying their baskets of goodies.

They each paid for their purchases. Jan loaded their bags in the trunk and waited at the passenger door while Elise made one more pass through the stand before climbing back in the car.

"How far are we from the cabin?" Elise asked as they pulled out onto the highway.

"GPS indicates we'll be there in twelve minutes."

"According to the directions, you turn off the road and follow a gravel drive. There should be a sign in the shape of a bear that says Brighton Hollow."

"Like that?" Jan pointed to the wooden carved bear holding an arrow. She slowed as she turned off the highway onto the narrow winding road.

"This isn't going to be easy," Elise muttered.

"We'll be okay. I'll go slowly."

"I didn't mean the car. I meant getting trucks and equipment up here."

"Oh, yeah. That'll be a challenge. You might have to widen the road."

Elise snapped some photographs and made notes as they wound through the woods.

"You should find a circular area at the end of the drive. That's where you park."

"According to the GPS this is it." Jan climbed out and opened the door for Elise. A crisp autumn breeze whistled in the treetops and stirred their hair.

"This is gorgeous." Elise drank in the heady smell of pine and fresh air. "Green as far as you can see. No wonder Charlie invested in this property."

"I don't see a cabin though. I thought you were here to check out a house for remodel."

"I am. The directions say follow the path next to the stump that's painted red. It goes down the hill. It says we can't miss it." Elise slung her briefcase strap over her shoulder and was ready to hoist the tote bag over the other when Jan took it from her hand.

"I'll carry this one for you. If we're going hiking we'll each need a free hand to keep from falling off the side of the mountain."

It sounded like a joke but Elise could hear trepidation in her voice.

"Do you want to wait here while I look around?"

Jan took a deep breath and tightened her grip on the bag. "Nope. I'm ready. You go ahead. I'll follow."

"Are you sure?"

Jan tossed her a caustic scowl. "Yes. I'm sure. I can do my job."

"Okay. Lake house, here we come." She snapped a couple more photographs then started down the path.

The narrow serpentine path was a combination of gravel, bark and pine needles between occasional flat stone steps. Elise never thought about Brighton Hollow being rustic. She should have known it would be. It was a lake house on the side of a hill. There were no handrails or tree branches for support. They were halfway down the path when she heard sirens in the distance.

"At least emergency services are nearby. The lake house isn't completely remote," Elise said, looking back at Jan working her way down the path one careful step at a time. She wanted to ask if she needed help but Jan had made it clear she was perfectly capable. Elise would respect that. Hopefully she wouldn't fall and break her neck.

Charlie Tuttle's lake house was just as advertised. As soon as Elise reached the clearing at the bottom of the path she saw the A-frame cabin with a salting of dried pine needles on the roof. The end wall that faced the hillside was randomly stacked field stone. A metal chimney pipe extended through the steep roof. The house was surrounded on three sides by a wooden deck that provided a spectacular view of the lake and the modest dock at the water's edge. Both the deck and the dock needed repair for broken and missing boards. Elise took a few pictures while she waited for Jan to catch up.

"Wow. Great view," Jan said from the railing overlooking the water. "Does that dock belong to the house?"

"Yes, I think so. It looks a little rickety though. I'm not sure I'd walk on it. Watch where you step." Elise straddled a loose board and unlocked the door. As soon as she opened the door she was greeted with a stale musty stench. "Phew. This place needs airing out."

Jan tried to open a window but it was stuck. The living space was one large room with tall windows facing the lake. A wood burning stove on a brick stage sat in the middle, its black chimney pipe extending up to the wood planked vaulted ceiling. A kitchen with out-of-date appliances and a few green painted cabinets occupied one corner of the room. A pair of red leather chairs faced the wall of windows and the view of the lake. A red and brown plaid love seat, a coffee table made from a paneled wooden door, a round dining room table with three chairs and a brass coat tree rounded out the cabin's furnishings. The building estimator in Elise was already evaluating the possibilities for expansion, limited as they were.

"This place looks built by hand." Jan stared up at the vaulted ceiling, smiling at the workmanship. "It must have taken months if not years to do all this on weekends and summer vacations. Nothing against you professional contractors but I love the homey touches. Like the random brick pattern under the wood stove. And the polished timber beams."

"If we remodel this like the owner wants, unfortunately all that will go away."

"That would be a shame. It's a great rustic retreat just as it stands."

"He wants a retreat with four bedrooms, three bathrooms, a hot tub and a modern kitchen. I can't squeeze all that into this footprint. It'll have to go up and out to meet his wishes. The load bearing walls aren't sufficient to support that kind of remodel."

"For a remodel like that, you're talking big bucks, right?"

"Uh huh." Elise made notes on a pad and took more pictures. She used a laser tape measure to calculate square footage and ceiling height then headed down a short hall for what she assumed was the bedroom and bathroom. "Oh yuck, yuck, yuck," she shrieked, swatting at a massive cobweb. The more she stomped and waved her arms the more ensnared she became. "I hate spiders. Hate 'em, hate 'em, hate 'em."

"Wait. Hold still." Jan pulled her hands down and swept away the sticky web. "Don't move. You've got it in your hair."

"Get it out, please." She closed her eyes and stood frozen while Jan combed her fingers through Elise's hair. She wiped threads of cobweb from her face, carefully picked pieces of it from her eyelids.

"There. It's all gone. You're good to go."

"Are you sure?" Elise brushed her hair back and gave a deliberate shiver.

"Yes, I'm sure." Jan swept a lock of hair behind Elise's ear and plucked a string of cobweb from her shoulder.

"Sorry about that but I really hate spiders and crawly things." She shuddered dramatically then turned for the bedroom door. "Would you mind going in there first, just in case?"

"No problem." Jan cleared the last remnants of the cobweb from the door frame then entered the bedroom. "No killer arachnids. You're safe." She found a hiking stick made from a tree branch standing behind the door and used it to sweep away a few minor cobwebs from the ceiling.

The bedroom was small, barely large enough for the double bed, dresser and bedside table. A fourth wooden chair with a missing back slat sat in the corner. There were no linens on the bed. The mattress looked old, lumpy and sunken on a bed frame with metal springs.

"That looks uncomfortable." Elise gave a careful look under the bed then moved on to the open door to the bathroom. The walls were cedar planks and Elise couldn't help but wonder if it had once been a closet. The toilet and sink were both 1960s avocado green. A white metal shower stall with a plastic shower curtain rounded out the bathroom amenities, all of them in need of a good scrubbing. She turned on the faucet but as she suspected, the water was shut off.

"What décor do you call that?" Jan asked, looking over Elise's shoulder at the small bathroom. "Backwoods rustic?"

"Functional but minimalistic."

"At least it isn't an outhouse."

Elise took more measurements and pictures. She checked the breaker box to get a general idea of how the cabin was wired. She also checked the electric meter. The red security seal meant the meter back had been booted and it would take a visit from the utility company to have it turned back on. A small hot water heater was mounted under the kitchen cabinet. One quick shower would probably exhaust the tank's supply of hot water.

"That's not much hot water," Jan said. "The range looks like it runs on the propane tank out back but the hot water heater is electric. I wonder what's up there?" She pointed to a wooden ladder mounted on the wall and leading to an open loft above the kitchen and bedroom end of the cabin.

"I'm guessing that's just for storage. The cross timbers are for structural support. There's not enough headroom for it to be a sleeping loft. And we're not going up there."

"Thank you. I can do a lot of things but climbing that ladder probably isn't one of them." Jan glared up at the ladder.

"That's okay. I can do a lot of things too but going up there where creepy crawly things might be definitely isn't one of them." Elise nodded reassuringly.

"I saw the little heater in the bedroom but I don't see one in here. The wood burning stove could be the only heat source. Of course, these things are pretty efficient." Jan opened the door to the wood stove to a rusty squeak. "Oops. Never mind," she gasped and closed it quickly.

"What? Is it full of ashes?"

"It's full all right but it's not just ashes."

"Let's see."

"You might not want to." Jan opened the door so Elise could see.

Nestled in a bed of silvery ashes was one adult squirrel and three babies, all dead and partially decomposed.

"Oh gross!" Elise wrinkled her nose and turned away.

"They must have come down the chimney and couldn't climb back out." Jan closed and latched the door. "At least it's not spiders."

"I'm finished in here. I don't need anymore surprises."

They wandered outside. Elise made notes and took pictures on the slope of the lot and the cabin foundation. She did a quick peek in the window of the wooden shed set back up in the trees.

"What's in there? Tools?" Jan asked but didn't climb the slope herself.

"They must have built this shed over the well. It looks like a pressure tank and control switch for the well. There's no water to the cabin so the tank is probably empty."

"Someone was ambitious and cut some firewood." Jan pointed to the dozen or so sticks of wood stacked between two trees.

"At least it's not stacked against the cabin."

"Termites, right?"

"Right." Elise packed her tote bag and relocked the door.

"Don't you want to go down and check out the dock?" Jan asked as Elise started up the path.

"No. I was just asked to submit a proposal for remodeling the house."

They climbed the path to the car. Jan tried to keep up but had trouble maneuvering the uneven steps, some more steep and slippery than others. Elise was waiting car side checking messages on her phone when Jan finally made it to the top. They retraced their route along the gravel drive onto the narrow road that led to the highway. Elise pulled out her notes while the details were still fresh in her mind. She had a good idea what even a simple remodel would entail and what it would cost. Since little of the cabin could be reused she also had an idea it would probably be more than Charlie wanted to spend.

"This doesn't look promising," Jan said as she pulled to a stop.

Elise looked up to see a sheriff's car blocking the highway. An officer in a tan uniform and brown wide-brimmed hat stepped out of the car. He was a short man with bushy eyebrows and a potbelly and first thought was he couldn't possibly keep up with a fleeing felon. Jan put her window down as the officer approached, his hand casually perched on his holster.

"Good afternoon." He looked past her to Elise in the backseat, as if checking the contents of the car.

"What's the problem, officer?" Jan asked. "Are you checking licenses and registration?" She reached in her back pocket for her wallet.

"No, ma'am. I'm sorry but the highway is closed ahead. There's been an accident at the bridge over Jennings Creek. A tanker truck overturned and took out the guardrail. Residents are asked to stay home until repairs can be made. Sorry for the inconvenience, miss."

"Couldn't we use the other side of the road? Have a flagman alternating the traffic?"

"The tank ruptured and spilled some kind of chemical all over the road. The EPA has to approve the cleanup. The only people allowed in the area are those in Hazmat suits."

"Is there an alternate route we can take?"

"Nope. There used to be a dirt road that cut across to Basin Road then back to 109 but a mudslide took it out last year and the county decided not to reopen it. Where are you ladies from?"

"Boston."

"What were you doing down there?" He nodded back up the road.

"We were inspecting the cabin at Brighton Hollow."

"I'm sorry, miss, but you'll have to go back."

Jan turned in the seat to face Elise. "I don't think we have a choice. We'll have to go back to the cabin. It's that or sit here until they open the highway."

"We'd prefer you go back inside. We're not sure how long it will take. They can't even move the truck until the EPA gives approval," the officer said.

"Officer?" Elise called. "You're absolutely positive there is no other way out of here? Couldn't we go north and around the lake?"

"Not unless you can fly," he said with a sarcastic chuckle.

"How are you getting out of here?" Elise gave him a stern look.

"Like I said, ma'am, I can't let you through. You can check the highway department website for updates. They'll post when it's open for traffic."

"We'll go back, but we don't have to like it," Elise muttered under her breath.

Jan had no sooner made a U-turn and headed back for the cabin than Elise was on her phone explaining her predicament to her father and letting Lorraine know she wouldn't be back in the office today. Possibly not tomorrow either.

"So you're spending the night in a cabin in the woods with Jan, the chauffeur? Nice." Lorraine had a wicked little snicker in her voice. "Did you ask her yet?"

"Ask what?"

"Oh Elise. You can't fool me. I've worked for Grayson Construction long enough to know when you're wrestling with a dilemma. I probably shouldn't tell you this, so don't quote me, but I overheard your father on the phone with your mother. It was pretty clear they were talking about you and their dinner party. I heard him say why don't you let Elise decide for herself. Then he said there's nothing wrong with her coming alone."

"Oh goody. Now they're both involved." Elise groaned.

"So, why don't you ask her? It won't kill you. And you know who I mean. If she's in the car you don't have to say her name."

"I have to go, Lorraine. Check my calendar. You'll need to reschedule my meetings with Julia Hibbard and with the Wesleyan University planning committee. If the soil tests come back on the Pittsfield site let Darcy know."

"I'll take care of it."

With Jan sitting just feet away and no doubt listening to her every word, Elise wasn't going to tell Lorraine she hadn't made up her mind when or even if she planned to ask Jan to the harvest buffet. She wasn't completely sure Jan wouldn't be offended by an invitation to cross the line from chauffeur to dinner companion just for the purpose of deceiving her mother over Elise's dating status. Jan was a smart woman. Surely she would be able to figure out why the invitation had been extended.

* * *

Jan parked the car but kept the engine running and the heat gently flowing into the backseat while Elise finished her phone conversation. She tried not to listen but she could tell Elise wasn't happy being stuck in the backwoods of New Hampshire, no happier than she was about it. The dispatcher at the car service would need to be told but there was nothing the company could do.

"How long do you think we can stay here in the car?" Elise asked. "It's clean and warm. And thankfully bug free."

"You're welcome to stay here as long as you want but eventually I'll need to turn off the engine so we'll have enough gas to at least find a filling station tomorrow. Maybe three hours, tops."

"That's all? It's going to get down in the twenties tonight. We'll freeze to death."

"Sorry. There's a V-eight engine under the hood. It doesn't sip gas ladylike. It guzzles it. Why don't you sit here for a few minutes while I go see if I can get a fire going in that wood stove?"

"You don't mind cleaning it out? It looked pretty nasty."

"Did you want to do it?" Jan mused. "You're the boss. I don't want to infringe on your enjoyment."

"No, no. Go right ahead. Please." She handed Jan the key.

"You might want to charge your phone while you're sitting here." Jan climbed out and started for the path.

Elise put her window down and called to her, "Should I be offering to come help? I don't want you to think this is part of your duties. It's not expected."

"Nope. I can handle it. We'll consider it auxiliary responsibilities."

"I really appreciate it." Elise hated the quiver in her voice. All of this was beyond her control and she hated it.

Jan leaned down and looked in the open window. "Ms. Grayson, this isn't your fault. It just happened. Don't beat yourself up about it. I don't blame you. You shouldn't either." She tapped her knuckles against the window. "Put your window up and keep warm. I'll be back shortly."

Elise plugged her phone in to charge while she checked a few emails. Immersing herself in work was the only way she knew to ignore the situation. She was ready to send a text when Jan opened the driver's side door and climbed in.

"All set."

"You got a fire started already? I bet that wasn't fun, considering what you had to clean out of the stove first."

"It wasn't too bad. I used some dried pine needles and a couple paper napkins for kindling. I found a key hanging on the coat tree that fit the padlock on the shed. The well pump has been wired to run off an auxiliary gasoline powered generator but there's no gasoline to run it. I wish I could tell you we had running water but we don't."

"I know what you're trying so delicately to tell me. No running water means no functioning bathroom."

"But we at least have heat." Jan retrieved a flashlight from the glove box and checked to see if it worked.

"I'm grateful for that. We'll be heathens in the wild but at least not frozen heathens." Elise stepped out of the car.

Jan collected the bag of apples from the trunk. She hoisted Elise's tote bag strap over her shoulder and followed her down the path.

* * *

Jan stoked the fire and brought a few more logs up onto the deck.

"I better call in and let my dispatcher know what happened. Do you need anything before I do?"

"No. I'm going to sit here and wish I'd brought my winter coat." Elise scooted her chair closer to the fire. "I noticed the weather app on my phone says there's a chance of snow flurries overnight."

"Yes, I saw that. Once the metal stove itself heats up it'll radiate more heat. You'll be backing that chair up."

"So long as I'm warm I don't care where I sit." Elise settled into the chair and folded her jacket tightly around her, locking her arms across her chest.

"Hi Glenda. You're not going to believe this," Jan said as she stepped out on the deck.

Jan explained their situation then listened to Glenda curse. She wasn't cursing at Jan, just at the unfortunate and unexpected turn of events. Glenda liked to curse. Four-letter words, hyphenated words, she used them all. Maybe it came from working in a predominately man's world of cars, driving and mechanics, but trying to cut her off only made it worse.

"So you'll be there in a freakin' cabin all damn night? Look at the bright side. You'll get paid for being stuck at the lake."

"That isn't what worries me." Jan suddenly wished she hadn't said that. She wasn't sure she wanted to confess her misgivings to Glenda. They were casual friends at best. But Glenda rescued her.

"Jan, I have to go. Lyle just brought back the white ten-passenger with a huge dent in the door. That's his second accident in three months. Shit is going to hit the fan, I just know it. Take care and let us know when you start back."

Jan was ready to go back inside when an incoming text from her sister chimed on her phone.

Baci's in the hospital. Dr. says it's pneumonia. As you can guess she's not happy about being admitted. I'll call you later. I'm trying to get her to cooperate with the nurses. She won't wear a hospital gown. Says they're drafty. Well DUH!!!

She tapped out a concerned reply and sent it then went inside to warm up.

"Is everything okay? Your company didn't blame you, did they?"

"No. They understand things like this happen."

"Then why the long face, if I may ask?"

"My sister just texted me that our grandmother is in the hospital."

"Oh Jan. I'm so sorry. What happened? Did she fall?"

"Pneumonia. Although she can't be that sick. She's arguing with the nurses about wearing a hospital gown."

"I'm sorry she's sick."

"Would you like an apple?" Jan took one from the bag and polished it against her sleeve. "Dinner, Ms. Grayson?" she offered comically.

"Thank you."

Jan polished another then stood by the fire eating it. "Not bad."

"At least we heathens won't starve. I'm very glad you bought these. I wasn't sure what we could do with maple syrup."

Whatever frustration Elise felt at being stuck in the woods was somehow mitigated by Jan's easygoing nature and kind smile. Elise couldn't remember any of the women she had dated in the past twenty years who would have accepted this predicament so cheerfully.

Jan finished and tossed her core into the fire. She closed the door then stepped back as a flash of light crossed her vision. It wasn't a new sensation but she hadn't experienced the phenomenon in several weeks, not since she walked through the lobby of the hospital while waiting for Elise to finish her meeting. Jan closed her eyes tightly and shook her head to clear it.

"Are you okay? You look a little pale."

"Yes. I stood a little too close to the fire. I told you it would get warm in here."

Jan's phone rang, instantly clearing her mind. It was her sister.

"Hey Lynette. How's Baci?"

"Baci's fine. She has a temperature of a hundred and two. She's wheezing and coughing and gasping for breath but she's fine. At least, that's her story." She groaned desperately. "She's finally in bed and on oxygen. They started an IV with fluids and antibiotics. The doctor said we should see some improvement in twenty-four to forty-eight hours. That's if she cooperates and doesn't pull the needle out. She *really* doesn't want to be here, Jan."

"I know she doesn't. Can't they give her something so she'll sleep and not fight the whole process?" Jan could see Elise's furrowed brow. Obviously she was listening to her side of the conversation. How could she not? She was standing a few feet away. "Lynette, tell Baci I'll be very disappointed if she doesn't do everything the doctor and nurses tell her. Remind her she has Medicare. It'll be covered. She's probably worried about that too."

"Can you come see her? Maybe she'd listen if it came directly from you."

"I wish I could but I'm stuck out of town."

"Stuck? Stuck how? Waiting for some schmuck whose flight is delayed?"

"No. We're in New Hampshire stuck in a cabin on Lake Winnipesaukee. There was a truck accident that closed the highway. We couldn't get through."

"We? You and some client you were driving around?"

"Yes."

"Man or woman?"

"Yes."

"Woman?"

"Yes." Jan tried to sound nonchalant as she kept up the word game.

"Jan, is this the same woman Ma said you had over at the house a couple weeks ago? The contractor or builder or something?"

"Yes. We've got a fire going in the wood stove so we won't freeze to death," she added to disguise the conversation.

"And she's standing right there?" Lynette chuckled. "Nice save, sis."

"How long does the doctor think Baci will be in the hospital?"

"He's not sure. It depends on how well she responds to the antibiotics. A week. Maybe more. But how about you, Jan? Are you going to be okay out there in the woods?"

"I think so. Which hospital is she in? I want to send her some flowers."

"Wing Hospital in Palmer. She wouldn't go to Mercy." Lynette hesitated. "Honey, is everything all right? You sound like there's a problem. Tell me what it is."

"I'm concerned about Baci too," Jan said as she walked out onto the deck. She stood at the railing and lowered her voice. "There's no big problem. I would just rather not do this."

"Why, honey? What are you afraid of? Is she being difficult?"

"No. She's very nice."

"Ma said she was gorgeous too. If she's nice and gorgeous what is the problem?"

"It's my leg. I have to take it off for at least a few hours sometime tonight. I can't wear it continuously for two days."

"Is it bothering you? Does your leg hurt?"

Jan hesitated long enough to raise her sister's concern.

"Jan? Is it phantom pain or is it real pain?"

"It's not the pain I'm worried about. I can handle that."

"Ah. You're afraid she'll see you take your leg off. Is that it?"

"Yeah."

"Jan, sweetheart, don't worry about it. If you have to take it off, so what? She's not your girlfriend. She's a client. You don't have to impress her. Maybe she won't even notice."

"I don't have my crutches. I'll look like a freak hopping around on one leg, using a chair for support."

"Does she know about your leg?"

"Of course she knows. She's not blind."

"Then why do you care what she sees? Oh my God, you do care. You're interested in her, aren't you?"

"Lynette, stop it. I'm not interested in Elise Grayson."

"It's been three years, Jan. If she's nice and gorgeous and you like her, it's okay. You're single. It's time to find someone again."

"Why does everyone think I need a woman in my life? I don't need to have sex with Elise or Allie or any other woman."

"Who said anything about sex?" Lynette laughed out loud. "I meant ask her out. Coffee at Starbucks. Dinner at Five Guys."

"I don't need to ask her out. I don't want to ask her out. I'm perfectly fine being single. Got it?"

"Yes, I got it. I'll say no more about it." Lynette sighed. "I don't have to like it but I got it."

"Five Guys? Is that Mike's idea of a romantic dinner for two?" They shared a sisterly chuckle.

"Honey, don't stress about your leg. No one will blame you for doing what you have to do. Be glad you have it. I better go. Baci's pushing the call button again. The nurses will be strangling her with the oxygen tubing before this night is over. I love you, sis. Take care of yourself. I'll talk with you later."

The last soft light of dusk had settled over the lake as Jan stepped back inside. Elise was working on her laptop, her face bathed in the soft glow of the screen.

"How's your grandmother?" she asked without looking up.

"Ornery. I love her to death but she can be a real pickle sometimes." Jan added another log then stood by the fire soaking in the warmth and trying not to favor her left leg. "They've got her on antibiotics and hope to see improvement in a couple days." She checked the fire and added another log.

"I'm sorry you're trapped here with me. You'd probably be on your way to see her if you weren't."

"Maybe. Although I can't do anything for her. She's exactly where she needs to be. They'll take good care of her."

"You're very lucky to have a big close family like that."

"Are your grandparents still living?"

"No. They've been gone a long time. I don't even remember my mother's parents."

"Do you have any brothers or sisters?"

"No. It's just me."

"There are times I'd lend you both of mine."

Elise looked at her over the top of her glasses and said, "No, you wouldn't. I can tell you have strong family ties." She removed her glasses and stared at Jan. "Turn around."

"What?"

"Turn around and back up over here. You've got bark or something on the back of your pants." She reached out her hand but Jan tried to see what it was for herself.

"Where?" She swept her hands over her seat.

"You're not getting it. Quit being stubborn and back up over here."

Jan finally relented and backed up, standing barely within reach. Elise brushed down the back of her right leg, sweeping away bits of bark. Jan was relieved it was her right leg, Elise's hand brushing only the contours of her muscles.

"There. My chauffeur looks all clean and distinguished again. Her black suit is all better." Elise gave another whisk of her hand down Jan's leg, as if tidying up. Then she gave one swipe down her left leg as well.

Jan quickly stepped away.

"Oh, I'm sorry. But there was a little on the other leg too."

"I'll get it." Jan brushed the back of both legs until there couldn't possibly be anything left sticking to them.

"You can stop now. They're clean," Elise said then turned her attention back to her laptop. "I'm sorry if I overstepped some sort of boundary."

"No. No boundary."

"No boundary but you'd prefer I don't touch your leg. I can understand." Elise still didn't look up. "It can be considered interpersonal space."

She answered two texts on her phone then typed feverishly, racing against the diminishing battery life on her computer. It was after nine when she finally removed her glasses and looked over at Jan sitting in the chair next to her. She studied her a moment then heaved a preparatory breath.

"I know this may not be the best time to ask this but would you be interested in working overtime?"

"Sure. I work whatever hours my clients need, within reason. Just let the dispatcher know and she'll take care of the booking."

"It's not exactly chauffeur work. How would you like to attend a dinner party with me? I need a dinner companion for my parents' harvest buffet. And I should warn you right up front it's as pretentious as it sounds."

"Dinner companion at a pretentious party." Jan gave her a puzzled look. "This sounds suspiciously like an attempt to hide the fact you're single, right?"

"It's a little complicated. My mother doesn't think I should show up at her annual hoo-ha alone. If I don't bring someone she's liable to supply a date for me."

"She accepts you bringing a woman?"

"Yes. She doesn't object. I've got a gay uncle somewhere in California. And it's suspected that my paternal grandmother married for convenience but had a thirty-year relationship with a woman."

"So your being a lesbian isn't an issue," Jan said appreciatively.

"No. But my showing up alone seems to be an embarrassment. You'd be doing me a great favor if you'd attend. We can find an excuse for you to duck out after a couple hours if you'd like. I'll pay you double-time for your services. It's on the sixteenth. Six thirty for drinks. Dinner at seven thirty."

"Are you sure there's no one else you'd rather ask?"

"There's no one else." Elise scowled deeply.

"If you're sure, then I'd be honored. It's a dress up affair I assume."

"Not formal but yes. Business professional attire. I'll understand if you don't want to wear a dress."

"I won't wear my uniform suit, if that's what you're thinking. But I don't wear dresses. It has nothing to do with my leg. I haven't worn a dress or a skirt since I was forced into wearing one under my high school graduation gown. I wouldn't wear one now even if I had two good legs. But I think I can manage something adequate to satisfy your mother." She fiddled with the seam of her pant leg then tossed a curious look at Elise. "I'm guessing you'd prefer your mother not know your dinner date is also your chauffeur."

"You're not my chauffeur. You're a chauffeur. You work for an executive car service."

"Okay. And how do you want me to handle..." Jan looked down at her left leg.

"That is completely up to you. Whatever you're comfortable saying, I'm comfortable with. Give details or smile politely and tell whoever asks it's none of their business. And in case you're wondering, my mother is far more likely to ask where you're from than any intimate questions about your leg or us or where we met. If she corners you and asks something you'd rather not confess, compliment her hair or her dress and she'll wander off onto another topic."

"And your father?"

"My father will spend the entire evening talking shop even though my mother will complain about it."

"And you?"

"I'll be wishing I didn't have to attend these boring dinner parties." Elise closed her laptop and slipped it back in her briefcase. She stretched her neck and heaved a tired sigh. "If you don't mind, I think I need to rest my eyes for a few minutes."

"Go ahead. I'll stand watch over the campfire and keep the hounds at bay." She added a log to the dwindling fire.

Elise leaned her head against the back of the chair and closed her eyes. Jan watched as she drifted off to sleep and heard the soft sounds of her snoring. She fidgeted with her leg, the long hours of wear starting to pinch and burn. She checked to see if Elise was still asleep then stood, ready to remove her pants and the leg, at least for a few minutes. She hated to do it but there was no place else to be that was warm enough for her to go pant-less. She had just unzipped and lowered her black pants when she heard rustling outside then footsteps on the deck. The bright beam of a flashlight swept across the wall of windows followed by the shadowy shape of a man.

"Hello!" he called. "Is anyone in there?"

Jan pulled up her pants and tucked in her shirt as Elise stirred and opened her eyes.

"Who's out there?" Jan shouted with as menacing a voice as she could muster. "What do you want?"

"Who is it?" Elise asked, squinting at the bright light.

"It's Deputy Wilkins. I came to tell you the highway is open."

Jan opened the door to the potbellied man in the wide-brimmed hat.

"The chemicals are cleaned up already?"

"Yes, ma'am. The tanker was carrying a soybean oil mixture. It smelled bad but it was harmless," he said, sweeping the flashlight around the room.

"So we can go?" Elise asked, not yet fully awake.

"Yes, ma'am. I thought I'd come tell you in person. It might be a couple hours before the website gets updated."

"Thank you. But we'll have to wait awhile. I don't want to leave the fire going in the stove. And we don't have water to put it out."

"I thought you might not." He handed Jan two bottles of water. "Can you use these?"

They each took a drink then Jan used the rest to soak and stir the fire until they were certain it was safe to leave. They followed the officer up the path, his flashlight leading the way,

Jan pulling up the rear. She was glad Elise couldn't see her grimace with every step.

They thanked him for his help and headed for Boston. Elise leaned into the corner of the backseat and faded off to sleep before they were out of New Hampshire. For Jan it was two hours of torture, her stump throbbing inside the socket, but she refused to give in to it. Or to take it off. It was after midnight when she delivered Elise to her front door and in agony carried her briefcase and tote bag up the steps, just as a helpful chauffeur would do.

"Good night, Ms. Grayson," she said and set the bags inside the door.

"I appreciate your help today. It was quite an experience. Thank you."

"You're welcome."

"And I appreciate you agreeing to be my plus one at the dinner. Saturday, the sixteenth. A little before six thirty?"

"I'll pick you up." Jan nodded politely.

She waited for Elise to close the door then grabbed the railing and staggered her way down the stairs, gasping with each step. She climbed in the car, helping her left leg over the running board. She pulled away from the curb and rounded the corner before coming to a stop under a streetlight. She pulled up her pant leg and released the locking bottom that held the socket to the liner then set the leg on the seat beside her. She rolled the gel liner down and pulled it off, groaning as she freed the stump from its confines. She could see it was red and swollen even in the muted light.

She leaned her head back against the headrest as she tried to massage away the pain. It was the first time she left the prosthetic lying on the seat as she drove home, but there was no way she could coax the liner back on, at least not yet. With luck, no one would see.

CHAPTER ELEVEN

Jan tossed and turned, waiting for the Tylenol to kick in. It had been a week since the adventure at Lake Winnipesaukee and since Elise's invitation to dinner. It was a date in name only but it was still a date. Her first since the accident. Her first since the topic of conversation would no longer be admiring questions such as what kind of airplane she flew. She was no longer a pilot for J and T Aviation. She was the woman with the artificial leg. She missed those days when the cuties in skintight jeans smiled at her and winked invitingly. Or when a dazzling woman moved down the bar and perched on a stool, close enough for Jan to see the unlimited possibilities in their eyes. Those days of encouraging looks and wishful sighs were gone. Now women smiled and held the door for her as if she needed assistance, a creature to be pitied.

Jan hadn't wrestled with her self-pity and lack of self-esteem for weeks. But here it was, barking at her heels. She wasn't a stupid woman. She knew it was undoubtedly because Elise Grayson, a dazzling woman in her own right, had invited her to be her dinner partner. That invitation would take her out from behind the wheel of a limousine, where she felt safe and confident, and into an evening of shared social graces.

She threw the covers back, swung her legs out and pulled herself up on her crutches. Her plaid boxer shorts and white T-shirt exposed more than they covered but she was alone in the darkness of her bedroom and if she stood just right and looked down, she could see her left leg to her knee and nothing more. The stump was hidden from view; the gnarly, scarred remnants of an accident she still couldn't remember.

She remembered having two legs then being in the hospital and having only one. Three days of her life were missing. Blank. The more she tried to remember, the more dark and empty the memory. Dissociative amnesia the doctors called it, caused by severe trauma or stress. Her mind had rejected thoughts and feelings too overwhelming to handle. It was protecting her from some enormous shock. But she wanted to know what had happened. She needed to know.

She stood at the window, leaning on the crutches as she watched early November snow glisten in the streetlights and blanket the street below. She could hear the rumble of a snowplow and see the flashing lights in the distance. The pristine snow-covered streets would be clear and open for traffic by morning. Tonight she stood and watched the big flakes dance in the breeze, wondering how different things might be if she had met Elise Grayson four or five years ago when she still had two good legs. But she'd never know. She'd agreed to be her dinner companion to please Elise's mother. And that's all it would be.

It rained the night before the sixteenth and continued throughout most of the day, stopping just after five o'clock. It was nearly dark as Jan pulled up in front of Elise's house. The shiny black sedan sparkled against the wet pavement. Jan checked her hair in the visor mirror. She plucked at the one obstinate curl falling over her forehead. It had always had a mind of its own.

"Fine. So stay there. Tonight I'll look like Elvis." She snapped the visor closed and climbed out. As soon as she knocked on the door the porch light came on and the door opened to Elise's smiling face.

"Good evening, Ms. Grayson," Jan said, her breath instantly catching in her throat.

Elise stood in the doorway in a form-fitting black dress with long lace sleeves. She had on black heels with a gold buckle on the toe. Her hair, artfully arranged, exposed one side of her neck completely. The heavenly scent of her perfume caressed Jan's senses. A single diamond pendant hung around her neck. She was gorgeous.

"Hello," Elise said, fumbling with one of her earrings. "Come in while I get my coat. How's your grandmother by the way?"

"She's home and doing well. Complaining about the hospital food but she's much better."

"I'm glad to hear it."

Jan followed her inside. She smoothed her hands down the sides of her jacket, her palms feeling suddenly very sweaty. She wore her silver pantsuit, the one with the matching vest and flared legs. She hoped the flared legs would thwart prying questions about her leg, for part of the evening anyway. It was the only suit in her closet that didn't remind her she was a chauffeur and she hoped it was satisfactory.

"You look very nice, Ms. Grayson."

"Thank you but my ear refuses to cooperate." Elise examined the French hook then tried again. "You look nice too. I like the color and the Edwardian-style jacket. They hang well on tall people." She continued to struggle with the earring.

"Excuse me, miss. But may I be of assistance?"

"Only if you promise to call me Elise for the rest of the evening."

"You're the boss. I guess I can do that." Jan held out her hand. Elise dropped the earring in it and cocked her head.

"You don't wear earrings do you?"

"Nope. But I'm familiar with the procedure for installation." Jan hooked the wire through her earlobe and checked the look. Elise was stunningly beautiful but she didn't need earrings for that. "Um, I might not be an expert on accessorizing but did you intend on wearing two different earrings?"

"They aren't the same?" Elise rushed to the mirror hanging by the front door, squinting at one ear then the other. "Oh heavens. That'll teach me to pick jewelry without my glasses. Be right back." She hurried up the stairs and returned with several earrings in her hand. "Which ones match? Pick something please. I'd never hear the end of it if I show up mismatched."

Jan stirred a finger through the choices in Elise's hand, looking for a pair.

"I don't see the mate to either of the ones you have on but I like these." She held up two delicate ear threads. From the size of the stone on the end she assumed they were rhinestones but they glistened nicely.

"Would you mind doing it for me?" Elise pulled the earrings out of her ears and stood waiting for Jan to replace them.

"You're sure?"

"Absolutely. I haven't worn those in months and months. Mother will appreciate your choice. She believes the bigger the diamond the more often you should show it off."

"These are the real thing?" Jan tried to sound nonchalant as she inserted the tiny chains through Elise's earlobes. She knew she was probably touching more than a month's salary.

"Yes."

Elise left the rest of the jewelry in a dish on the coffee table and picked up the coat draped over the back of a nearby chair.

"Don't you want to check the earrings?" Jan took the coat from her and held it open.

"I trust you."

Elise slipped it on and draped a scarf around her neck. Jan adjusted her dinner date's collar like she did for many of her clients. They descended the front steps to the car waiting at the curb, the motor running. Jan stepped ahead and opened the front passenger door. She was ready to explain that it might help the ruse Elise wanted to create if she didn't arrive in the backseat of a limousine. But without a second thought Elise climbed in the front seat and buckled her seat belt, a quiet confidence on her face.

It was a short drive to the Graysons' house. It sat at the end of a winding street of upscale colonial homes. Most of the lights in the house were on. Even from the street it was obvious whoever lived there was having a party. The curved driveway in front of the sprawling two-story brick home looked like a car dealership for Boston society. Two Mercedes-Benzes, a Land Rover, a BMW, a Volvo SUV and a Lexus were among the pricey stock. Jan parked at the end of the line and hurried around to open Elise's door.

"I guess we're ready to do this." Elise still had her seat belt buckled.

"I'm ready to do whatever you need me to do, Ms. Grayson. Elise," she quickly amended. She extended her hand and waited for Elise to take it and step out. "If you've changed your mind and rather I not attend just say so. I'll understand completely."

"Actually, you are the only reason I'm here. You don't know how close I came to cancelling." Elise took a quick look in the mirror then released her seat belt and took Jan's hand.

"Just for the record, you look stunning," Jan said and handed her the black satin clutch she'd left on the seat then closed the door.

"Thank you." Elise took her arm as they started up the driveway.

"By the way, I think this is the first time I've seen you without a briefcase."

"That doesn't mean business won't be discussed tonight, believe me. It always encroaches on these dinner parties."

Jan took a deep breath as they climbed the two front steps. She had picked up clients at houses this size before but she had never been inside as a dinner guest. Elise seemed to sense her apprehension and gave her arm a squeeze then rang the doorbell. They were greeted by a well-mannered gentleman in black slacks and vest.

"I have no idea who he is," Elise whispered to Jan as he took her coat. "I'm guessing supplied by the caterer."

"Elise, there's my beautiful daughter," her father said, a drink in his hand. He was the only man in the living room not wearing a suit. Instead he wore slacks with a dark plaid shirt and cranberry colored cardigan that made him look like a retired college professor. He gave Elise a kiss on the cheek then extended his hand to Jan with a curious smile. "Hello. I'm Forest Grayson."

"Dad, this is Jan Chase."

"Nice to meet you, sir." Jan shook his hand but he didn't let go.

"Nice to meet you too. You look familiar. Should I know you?"

"I don't think so, sir."

"Don't call me sir. That's for bank tellers and waiters. Call me Forest." He continued to shake her hand as he studied her. "The Boston Garden. Bruins and Flyers. Three weeks ago. We were in line at the snack bar waiting for calzones. Am I right? Huh?"

"Yes. Bruins won, five nothing. Bolden had a hat trick."

"Good game." He finally released her hand.

"Dad is a huge Bruins fan," Elise said, straightening his shirt collar.

"Elise!" a woman in a red evening gown called from across the room. "Where have you been? I expected you an hour ago, dear." She hurried to Elise's side and gave her a cursory hug, the kind meant to not smudge her makeup or spill her drink. She then turned her smile on Jan.

"Mother, this is—"

"Jan Chase," Suzanne interrupted. "Elise said you were coming. I'm so glad you could join us. Please, call me Suzanne." She took Jan's hand in hers and squeezed it.

"I'm pleased to meet you. Your home is magnificent. I love the Georgian architecture."

"Thank you, dear. Chase? Chase? Are you any relation to Arial Chase from Newport?" she asked with hopeful exuberance.

"I don't think so."

"Be careful, Jan," Forest said. "My wife may ask to see your family tree all the way back to the dawn of time. What would you girls like to drink?"

"I'm just making conversation." Suzanne frowned then noticed more guests arriving and went off to greet them.

"Elise, what will it be?" he asked.

"White wine."

"Jan? What will you have? Scotch on the rocks?"

"White wine is fine with me too."

"You don't have to be conservative," Elise said as he went to fill their order. "I guarantee my father's liquor cabinet can handle whatever you prefer."

"I'm the designated driver so white wine is fine, and probably only one glass."

"Dad, make ours champagne," Elise called after him then offered Jan a sheepish smile. "It's white wine, sorta."

"Your parents' home is really something. This living room is larger than my entire apartment. This is where you grew up?"

"Yes. And nicely done by the way."

"What was?"

"The comment about the Bruins and the Georgian architecture. Way to make points."

"It was true. I was at that game and I do like historic architecture."

"I know. That's what makes it special."

"Here you are, ladies." Forest handed them each a stemmed glass of champagne. "Elise, Robert needs to talk with you a minute. I suggest you do it before he's had his third drink." He nodded toward the tuxedoed man crossing the room toward them. "See you later, daughter," he said with a coy smile and walked away.

"Robert. So good to see you." Elise smiled and extended her hand to him. "I love that tie. You look right in season."

Jan sipped her champagne and scanned the room in an attempt to ignore what sounded like a private conversation between Elise and the distinguished looking man with a white goatee and horn-rimmed glasses. Something about window mullions and an obstructed view. Jan felt relatively certain she and Elise were the youngest dinner guests. Most were silver-haired. Some of the men were bald or nearly so. A few of the women, including Elise's mother, were bottle blondes but attractively coiffed.

Jan's gaze continued around the room as she sipped. A robust laugh from a group standing by the fireplace caught her attention. It was two couples all laughing as if they had heard an outrageous joke. The woman with her back to Jan had a unique tone to her laugh. High-pitched and staccato. She couldn't see the woman's face but Jan recognized the laugh and the distinctive hairdo.

"Oh damn," she muttered to herself and quickly turned her back.

"I'll check with our supplier, Robert." Elise patted his shoulder. "I'll take care of it personally. I promise."

He seemed satisfied and went to refill his drink. Elise took out her cell phone from her clutch and recorded a voice message to herself.

"How's the champagne?" Elise retrieved her glass from a nearby table and took a sip.

"It's good." Jan lowered her eyes, afraid to look for fear the laughing woman would see her.

"It makes my nose tickle." Elise sipped again. "Oh, look. Senator Kenmeyer."

"Who?"

"Senator Kenmeyer. State senator from somewhere up by Amherst." She smiled and nodded a greeting across the room. "Want to meet her?"

Jan had no idea who she meant so she looked in that direction. The woman with the strange laugh was smiling and waving.

"Come meet Reanna." Elise hooked her arm through Jan's. "Her husband is a little older but they are both nice people."

"Hello Elise. Your parents were so sweet to invite us." They exchanged small hugs.

"Reanna, I'd like you to meet a friend of mine, Jan Chase. Jan, this is Senator Kenmeyer."

"How do you do, Senator," Jan said politely. She hoped the woman didn't remember her but the curious squint in her eye suggested she might.

She offered a fractured smile then turned back to Elise. "I heard you're doing the library addition on the U Mass campus in Amherst," she said. "I love the projected design. The atrium looks magnificent. When do you plan to break ground?"

"Sometime in the spring, hopefully."

"It was nice to meet you, Senator, but I'm going to excuse myself." Jan looked at Elise as if to ask where the restroom was.

"There's one just past the kitchen on the left and there's one next to the coat closet in the hall," Elise said then went back to her conversation.

Jan really didn't have to go, but she didn't want to make the woman feel uncomfortable either. It was obvious she was struggling with where they had met. It seemed easier to walk away and go in search of a powder room.

Elise met her in the hall as she headed back for the living room. "Would you like to see the rest of the house?" she asked.

"Sure."

Elise took her by the arm and led her into the kitchen. She pressed a button on the wall and a pocket door slid open, revealing a small mirror-lined closet. She stepped in and waited for Jan to join her before pressing a button on the wall. The door closed and the sound of a motor began to hum.

"An elevator?" Jan chuckled. "What do you know!"

"I thought you might like this."

"I can do stairs, you know."

"I know you can. But riding in elevators is fun too. I used to ride up and down and up and down when I was a kid." The door opened to the upstairs hall. "It has great acoustics too. I used to listen to my portable stereo in there." Elise led the way down the hall, pointing out the various bedrooms and bathrooms.

"Which room was yours?" Jan asked.

"Last one on the right." She opened the door and snapped on the light. The walls were white with crown molding and high ceilings. It was decorated in mint green—everything from the floral drapes to the bedspread to the pile of accent pillows on the queen-size four-poster bed. "The bed is new but everything else looks the same."

"Very nice. Three closets?"

"Two closets. The door in the corner is a bathroom."

Jan circled the bed, drawing her fingers along the satin bedspread and admiring the elegant appointments.

"I know what you're thinking," Elise said. "Six bedrooms seems a little much for just the three of us."

"Not necessarily. You don't have to apologize for anything." Jan followed her back into the hall. "Although I'm not crazy about that color green. It looks like lime sherbet."

"You're right. It does. And I'm glad somebody agrees with me." Elise laughed and closed the door.

"I should apologize. I'm guessing Ginger didn't act like a gawking hillbilly when she came to your parents' dinners."

"You're right. She didn't. She tried real hard to fit in."

"Oh, ouch."

"That wasn't meant as a criticism. You're doing just fine. I think my parents truly like you. At least, my dad does."

"And your mother?"

"She seems to, superficially anyway. The acid test will come when she calls me at work and gives her full appraisal. But I think you'll pass."

"You're convinced she buys into your little deception."

"It doesn't matter if she buys into it. It matters that I didn't show up alone without a suitable dinner companion."

"But it's possible she may not completely approve of your choice, right?"

"I told you. They accept that I'm gay. That's a non-issue."

"That's not what I meant."

"I hope you don't mean your leg."

"I do my best not to advertise it, but it's hard to keep it from being a bone of contention, no pun intended."

"It would only bother them if it bothered me. And it doesn't." Elise pulled Jan to a stop. "I assure you I wouldn't have invited you here tonight if I thought you'd be subjected to ridicule and humiliation. Please believe me, I'd never do that to you. You're my date. And I'll treat you accordingly." She took Jan's arm as they continued down the hall. "Does this bother you?"

"Having arm candy? No. You're painting a picture. It's part of the illusion."

Elise gave her a strange look as if questioning her last statement.

"But no, Elise. I don't mind at all. Where else would your arm be but on mine?"

"Okay, now I have to ask. What was going on with you and Reanna? And don't tell me nothing. I saw the looks she was giving you. And you trying to crawl under the carpet. Do you know her from someplace?"

"Nothing personal, if that's what you mean."

"But you do know her."

"Let's just say she was a friend of a client I was hired to drive from Boston to Hartford and back. A *very close* friend of a client I was hired to drive from Boston to Hartford and back." Jan raised an eyebrow.

"I'm guessing a very close friend of a client who wasn't her husband."

Jan gave her a puzzled look.

"I understand client confidentiality. I promise whatever you tell me won't leave this hallway. And in case you're wondering, Reanna isn't my taste in a politician."

"I won't tell you the name of the person who hired me but I can say the woman was from Portland. And I think the Senator suited her taste just fine, if you know what I mean."

"In a limousine?"

"Yep. The long white one with the partition. The partition that runs off the button on the armrest. A very sensitive button on the armrest."

Elise chuckled softly.

"It wasn't funny. They kept accidentally leaning on that button and the partition would go down. I'd put it back up and they'd lean on it again. I heard bits and pieces of moaning and groaning all the way down highway eighty-four." She joined Elise in a good laugh. "I got a nice tip out of it though."

Elise laughed even harder.

"Did the Senator say if she recognized me?"

"I don't think so. She was sure you're one of the new adjunct professors at U Mass. If you want to be guaranteed total acceptance you should pull out the big guns."

"I'm not sure what you consider big guns."

"Mention you're a pilot. That'll impress these old fuddy-duddies."

"I'd rather not."

"But you are."

"I'd still rather not."

"Totally up to you." Elise led her to the elevator. "Shall we go back downstairs? Dinner should be ready soon."

"Let's take the stairs." Jan turned them toward the staircase. "They're impressive and should be descended."

"Okay." Elise held onto Jan's arm as they slowly descended the steps, like royalty attending a ball.

"See, I can do stairs. Of course, down is easier than up."

"It is for me too. It's a lot of steps. When I was a teenager I could trot up and down and never run out of breath."

"I can totally see you trotting up and down these steps. All kinds of energy and spunk, right?"

"P and V is the expression I think you're looking for." Elise squeezed her arm. "And thank you."

"For what?"

"No one has ever called me arm candy before. I take it as a compliment."

"It was intended that way."

"Elise and Jan, there you are," Forest said from the bottom of the stairs. "Dinner, girls."

"We're coming, Dad."

The dining room was set formally for the dinner guests. Tablecloths, centerpieces, stemmed goblets, china and silver all accented the table.

"Your mother sets a lovely table."

"Caterer probably did it," Elise said with a shrug. "I'd bet my new smartphone there are carts for the goblets and dishes in the garage." She picked up one of the place cards. "But this is my mother's handwriting. She did the place cards. And she probably spent two days deciding who should sit where." She put the card back on the table.

"Do they ever sit around the kitchen table and eat off paper plates?"

"I used to sit at the kitchen table and eat pb and j sandwiches," Elise mused. "But not on paper plates. I used a napkin."

As soon as the caterers arranged the last serving dishes on the buffet Suzanne ceremoniously announced dinner was ready. The guests meandered in that direction, raving over how wonderful it smelled and how festive the tables looked. A menu card, framed and sitting at the beginning of the buffet line, seemed to be just as Elise had warned: pretentious.

Shrimp Salad Endive Scoops
Romaine Salad with Cranberries and Apple Cider Vinaigrette
Butternut Squash Ravioli in White Wine Mornay
Steamed Asparagus Tips in Lemon Butter Sauce
Roasted Garlic and Fingerling Potatoes
Broiled Eggplant and Heirloom Tomatoes
Salmon Dijonnaise
Braised Pork Tenderloin Medallions with Grilled Portobello Mushrooms
Chocolate Crème Brûlée
Blackberry Cobbler with Vanilla Bean Sorbet

But Jan was hungry and everything looked good. She followed Elise down the line, serving herself foods she recognized. She also took small helpings of things she didn't recognize just to be polite. They joined the other guests already seated at the table. Waiters refilled coffee cups, water goblets and wine glasses. Suzanne sat at one end of the long table and Forest at the other. Since it was nearly impossible for guests at one end to hear guests at the other, conversations were isolated to those sitting nearby, creating a constant busy chatter in the room.

"May I ask what happened with the plans for the lake house remodel?" Jan inquired.

"Good question. I put together some sketches and a cost plus estimate but I haven't heard back."

"So no blueprints yet?"

"That won't happen until we're under contract."

"If you don't mind me asking, do you get paid for your time even if you don't actually build something?"

"Yes, of course. We submit an invoice for time and travel. But not for the time we were stranded."

"I bet you don't come cheap." Jan pulled a dimpled grin.

"I bet flying people around in a private plane isn't cheap either."

"I didn't own the planes I flew. I was just hired as a pilot. But you're right. Charter flights aren't cheap. Although some people have more money than time. They need to get to their destination ASAP."

"I was afraid you were going to say some people have more money than sense."

"Nope. I'd never say that. I don't question a client's motives. That's none of my business. I just transport them."

"Good, because I'm tired of explaining why I don't drive myself to job sites."

"It sounds like you're working yourself up to a confession. And for the record, I didn't ask."

"Okay, I'll tell you." Elise took a bite of salmon before offering her explanation. "I don't drive because I'm terrible at it. I can manage a multimillion dollar construction project but I can't parallel park to save my life. I can't back up or merge in traffic either."

"Lots of people can't parallel park. My mother can't."

"I panic in traffic and if there's one thing Boston has it's lots of traffic. If I don't want to kill myself on Commonwealth Avenue or the Mass Pike I hire a car and driver."

"But you said you could drive one of those little loaders like they use at your construction sites. I've seen all the levers and pedals in the cabs of those things. They look way more intimidating than a car."

"Au contraire. Much less intimidating. There are no semis cutting you off. No tight parking spaces in overcrowded parking garages. And no traffic cones pinching the lane down until it's barely wide enough to fit a tricycle through."

"Then you don't own a car."

"Oh, I own one. It's in the garage behind my house. I also have a pickup truck with the company logo on the side. I keep it parked at the equipment lot. I've driven it twice. The whole world is a better place with that thing parked. I've worked long and hard and I deserve to feel safe when I'm on the road."

"I'm not arguing with you. Your neuroses are my job security."

"Well, my neuroses want to try that chocolate crème brûlée." She folded her napkin next to her plate.

"I'll get it for you." Jan rested her hand on Elise's arm, keeping her at the table, then rose to go get it.

"A little one."

"How can you say that? Crème brûlée in any flavor is wonderful and should be gobbled down by the spoonful." Jan smiled, knowing all the guests had heard her and were probably thinking the same thing. She returned with Elise's dessert and set it in front of her then took her seat.

"Didn't you want one?"

"No, I'm full. But it was tempting."

"Here." Elise dipped a spoon into the dish and held it up for Jan to try. "Tell me if it's worth all the fuss." Jan leaned in and accepted the bite. They both seemed to know everyone at the table was watching and silently approving. "Good?"

"Excellent," Jan said, their eyes meeting over the spoon.

"More?"

"No. That was plenty." Jan felt her heart skip a beat. Elise's knee touched hers under the table. Whether accidental or not, it was surprisingly breathtaking.

"Damn, now I wish I'd taken that instead of cobbler," a man said from across the table.

The evening began to wind down just before ten. By then Elise had been cornered twice by clients wanting to talk details. She cordially obliged, visiting with each one as if they were the sole reason she was there. When they finally said their goodbyes, Jan received hugs and kisses from Elise's parents and promised to *do this again real soon.*

"Thank you for inviting me. I enjoyed meeting your parents." Jan held Elise's coat for her.

"You're welcome."

Lacy snowflakes fluttered through the night sky as they descended the front steps. Most of the cars had already left, leaving patches of dry pavement along the drive.

Elise said, "I'd like to stop at a Seven-Eleven on the way home if you don't mind. I need a loaf of bread so I can have toast with my morning coffee and I'd rather not go out if we get the four to six inches they're predicting for tonight." She flinched as she stepped on an icy spot. She quickly took Jan's arm. "These shoes are about the worst thing I could wear in snow."

"We'll go slow."

"Aren't you cold?" Elise hunched her shoulders as the wind ruffled her hair.

"A little, but I don't have cold air blowing up my skirt."

"I know. I should have worn a pantsuit."

"No. I should have brought the car up to the door so you didn't have to walk in this." She pointed her key fob and pressed remote start. The black sedan's engine roared to life.

Jan helped her into the front seat, holding onto her arm until she was settled.

"Do you need anything else other than bread?" Jan asked as she pulled into the convenience store's parking lot.

"No. That's all." Elise released her seat belt and reached for the door handle.

"You stay here. I'll get it. I don't want you falling in the snow."

"Thank you. I'd like wheat if they have it but I'm not sure I can be that picky." She opened her clutch, seemingly looking for money, but Jan reached over and closed it.

"Elise, I've got it."

She returned a few minutes later. "Here you go. A loaf of wheat bread. And this is for you too." She handed her a long-stemmed red rose. "It's my way of saying thank you." Jan couldn't look at her. She didn't want to see Elise's reaction if giving her a rose was inappropriate. Instead she backed out of the parking spot.

Elise rested the rose against her lips and they rode along but said nothing. Jan couldn't tell if that was good or bad. And she wasn't going to ask. The snow against the windshield and the accumulation on the pavement kept Jan's attention on her driving. It took twice as long to get back to Elise's house than it had to get to her parents'. Two inches covered the sidewalk as they pulled to the curb.

"I think we made it just in time. Another hour or two and it might be impossible." Jan climbed out and circled the car, taking care to not slip. She opened the door and held Elise's arm to help her out. "Be very careful."

"Walk me to my door, please," Elise said. "I don't feel confident in these shoes."

"Absolutely." They cautiously ascended the stairs, one step at a time, Jan supporting her all the way up.

Elise unlocked the door and pushed it open. "Would you like to come in?"

"I better get the car back before it gets any worse," Jan said regretfully. "Thanks again for a wonderful evening."

Elise looked up at her as if there was something she wanted to say. Instead she grabbed Jan's lapel and pulled her down, kissing her on the mouth.

"Thank you," Elise finally whispered then went inside and closed the door.

CHAPTER TWELVE

Elise stood at the kitchen counter in sock feet and flannel pajamas. She liked the warmth they provided against the cold Boston winters. Plans for the day included laundry, watching the Macy's Thanksgiving Day Parade on TV and working on the Framingham Library project, all of which she could do in her jammies. If she had the interest and energy later she might walk to Ithaca's Kitchen, a neighborhood eatery open on Thanksgiving. Being a fusion restaurant, they probably wouldn't serve a traditional turkey dinner but it would be a hot meal she didn't have to cook. There wasn't much in the refrigerator to cook. She had forgotten to go to the store. It wasn't the first time.

She carried her cup of coffee into the living room and turned on the TV. She stood sipping it while she flipped through the channels, looking for the parade. A high school band was playing "When the Saints Go Marching In" as they marched down the street in precise synchronicity. She watched and swayed in time to the music.

"No, no, no. Don't go to a commercial. Show the band or a balloon," she grumbled, and went to make a piece of toast. She sprinkled it with cinnamon and sugar, refilled her coffee cup and returned to the living room then curled up on the couch to enjoy it and whatever was next coming down Sixth Avenue. The huge Hello Kitty balloon had just come into view in the distance when her phone rang.

"Good morning, dear," her mother said cheerfully. "Happy Thanksgiving."

"Hello Mother. Happy Thanksgiving to you too. How's New York? How was the opera?"

"Oh, sweetheart," she sighed deeply. "It was magnificent. Such beautiful costumes, and the music!" She hummed a bit of an aria. "*Madame Butterfly* is by far my favorite opera. I thought it was *Aida* but no, it's definitely *Madame Butterfly*. When she sings that aria, you know the one, when she is waiting for her lover to return? I swear I had tears in my eyes, Elise."

"'Un Bel Di Vedremo,'" Elise said.

"Yes. It is simply gorgeous."

"I'm glad you enjoyed it. What did you wear?" She knew her mother enjoyed discussing such trivialities.

"The emerald green satin gown. It's not my favorite but your father likes it so I dug it out again."

"That dress looks lovely on you, Mother."

"Thank you, dear. What are your plans for today? Are you spending Thanksgiving with Jan Chase?"

"What? No, Mother. I'm not spending Thanksgiving with her. She'll be with her family." At least, Elise assumed she would.

"Where do they live?"

"Out by Springfield. And before you ask, I've met her mother. Harriet is a lovely woman."

"Harriet Chase? Do I know her?"

"No. I'm sure you don't. She's a middle-class housewife and an excellent cook. Her banana bread is better than Stowich's Bakery."

"You've been to their home?" Suzanne seemed pleased.

"Yes. We stopped by for a few minutes."

"Sweetheart, what happened to her leg? I didn't want to ask when you were at the house and draw attention to it."

"It was an accident, Mother."

"Was she one of the Marathon bombing victims? That was so tragic."

"No."

"It wasn't some disease though, right?"

"No, nothing contagious. It was an accident."

"Just checking. You can't be too careful these days. She seemed very pleasant. Lovely girl too. So tall, and I love the blond hair. Are those curls natural?"

Elise smiled to herself. There was something she and her mother agreed on: Jan's curls. They were adorable.

"Yes, Mother. I think so."

"I bet they're fun to play with." Suzanne giggled. "Your father is giving me the evil eye over his newspaper."

"Tell him Happy Thanksgiving for me."

"Wait, sweetheart. He's trying to tell me something." Elise heard muffled conversation in the background. "Oh, Forest. Here. You tell her yourself. I can't remember all that."

"Hi Elise. Happy Turkey Day."

"And to you too, Dad."

"I just wanted to let you know Charlie Tuttle called. He liked your ideas and sketches but he's decided not to remodel his place at Lake Winnipesaukee. He said the cost outweighs the benefits. I'm not surprised. He's just going to sell it and buy something turnkey. Something big enough for his whole family to use."

"I already heard the news but I agree. It was too small to easily convert to what he needed."

"What are your plans for today?" he asked, changing the subject.

Before she could answer she heard conversation in the background.

"Elise, honey, I've got to go. Room service is here with breakfast and your mother doesn't want to answer the door in her robe. Take care. Talk with you later."

Elise carried her dishes to the kitchen and loaded them into the dishwasher, humming the aria from *Madame Butterfly*. She hadn't been to the opera in several years. Ginger didn't enjoy it and it wasn't something Elise wanted to do alone. Ginger's idea of a musical outing was listening to a guitarist sing soulful ballads in some out of the way darkened bar where watered-down drinks and off-key renditions were commonplace. She wondered what kind of music Jan liked.

Elise started up the stairs to collect dirty laundry as the phone rang again.

It was Jan Chase. "I remember you said your parents weren't having a family Thanksgiving dinner, right?"

"That's right. They're in New York. Good morning, by the way," Elise replied, pleasantly surprised at Jan's call.

"Good morning. I don't know what kind of plans you have for today but my parents are having a family meal. I can't offer anything as big and as fancy as your parents' harvest buffet, but I'd like to invite you to join us. It'll just be the basic turkey dinner with enough side dishes to choke Godzilla. And a pair of screaming eight-year-olds running through the house. I have to warn you, it won't be at all pretentious."

"That's very sweet of you, Jan, but you don't have to do that. You don't have to invite me just because my parents aren't having a family gathering. I wasn't looking for an invitation when I said that."

"I know you weren't. I just thought if you didn't have plans maybe you'd like some pierogi with your turkey."

"Actually, I'd love to have turkey with your family. Is this a dressy affair?"

"I'm wearing Levi's and a slate blue sweater. And you never know—I might be overdressed."

"I've never seen you in jeans. You always look so professional."

"You can wear whatever you like. I'm on my way. Be there in a few minutes."

And just like that, Elise had an invitation to a home-cooked dinner at the Chases'. Unlike the tediously grandiose dinners at her parents' house, she looked forward to this one. Dinner with a down-to-earth, unpretentious family whose social status didn't define them. And dinner with Jan. She quickly showered and dressed in cream-colored slacks and a brown turtleneck sweater. She checked her appearance in the bathroom mirror, re-combing disobedient locks.

Moments later Elise stood on the sidewalk, pulling on her gloves as she looked up and down the block. She wasn't sure what she was looking for.

"Right here." Jan opened the passenger door to the blue Rav4 parked at the curb. "Sorry, but no stretch today."

"I love the color. I like blue cars." She climbed in. "Do we have time to stop someplace on the way?" she asked as Jan pulled into traffic. "I want to take something. I don't want to show up at your parents' house empty-handed."

"Then no, we're not stopping. If you do that then I'll feel guilty for not taking something to your parents'. That could start a whole ripple effect."

"Jan, I just want to take a little something. Maybe a couple bottles of nice wine. Or a box of pastries."

"Nope. All you need to do is enjoy the meal. My mother will consider that gift enough."

"Kind of bossy for a chauffeur, aren't you?" she mused.

"I'm not a chauffeur today. And you're not the client. You're just a dinner guest at the Chases'."

Elise's cell phone rang in her purse.

"Excuse me," she said and answered it. "Hello Margaret. Happy Thanksgiving." She didn't really want to talk shop with one of her subs but if someone was calling today she knew it needed attention. "How does the tile look? Did they deliver enough to finish all the bathrooms?" Elise tended to the call as Jan headed west on the Mass Pike. She tried twice to cut the call short and return to civilized conversation but there kept being one more detail to handle.

If it bothered Jan she didn't show it. She hung her wrist over the steering wheel and kept her eyes on the road. She did occasionally move her left leg as if it bothered her. Or maybe hurt. She tried to disguise it but Elise noticed her hand discreetly rubbing down her thigh as if to assuage the discomfort.

"Margaret, call me on Monday and let me know if the rest of the shipment arrives. If not I'll call the warehouse. We need the tile work finished before the first of the month." Elise finally ended the call and dropped her phone into her purse. "Sorry about that."

"You work even on holidays. You don't get much time off."

"For every job there seems to be a million details. Equipment breakdowns, weather delays, customers making changes. You name it, we'll hear about it. That's what they pay us to handle."

"Do you ever ignore the call or tell them to call someone else?"

"When you have a problem that has to be resolved you call the boss. I'm the boss. At least, one of them. Dad gets calls too. He has some of the detail-oriented calls redirected to me but I don't mind."

"Your phone is always within reach then?"

"Pretty much." Elise heaved a regretful sigh. She knew it sounded like her time wasn't her own but it was all part of the job and the success.

Jan exited the highway and wound through the neighborhoods. She found a parking spot down the street from her parents' and prepared to park.

"Did you want to try this?" she teased.

"Nooooo. Your fender doesn't want me to either." She covered her eyes and pretended not to look as Jan eased the car into the tight space. They hurried up the driveway, bundled against the chilly wind.

"Ma, we're here," Jan called as they came through the mudroom into the kitchen. The stove was covered with simmering pans. The kitchen smelled like sage and fresh bread. Serving dishes were poised on the counter, waiting for presentation. "Where is everyone?"

"I'm coming, I'm coming," Harriet said as she hurried down the hall. She was dressed in elastic-waist denim pants and a white top with autumn leaves on it, covered by her Grandma's Cooking apron.

"Hello Elise," Harriet said and gave her a warm hug. "We're so glad you could join us."

"It was a pleasant and quite unexpected invitation. It was sweet of you to allow me to crash your family dinner." Elise slipped out of her coat.

"You're not crashing. We love having whoever Jannie invites. My, don't you look nice. Jannie, you should have told her we don't dress up for this." She scowled at Jan.

"I did, Ma. I did. She wore that so you could pick on me." Jan kissed her mother's cheek and gave her a hug. "Where's Dad?"

"In Baci's room trying to hang a new ceiling fan. I told him to wait until Mike or Keith get here but you know your father. He insisted. Go see if you can convince him to wait until the boys get here, Jannie."

"I'll check it out," she said, patting her mother's arm reassuringly.

Jan hung their coats in the hall closet and led Elise to the only downstairs bedroom. The twin bed had been pushed to the side. Her father stood on a short step stool in the middle of the room working on the wiring protruding from the hole in the ceiling. "Hey Dad. Happy Thanksgiving."

"Hi. Can you hand me the wire cutters, Jan? They're on the dresser."

"Dad, this is Elise Grayson." She handed him the tool. "Elise, the man on the stool too stubborn to wait for help is my dad, John Chase."

"Hey Elise," he said without looking down. "Jan, I need the ones with the stripper teeth." He extended his hand like a surgeon waiting for an instrument.

"Hello, Mr. Chase. Do you need some help?"

"Not yet. I've got to rewire the hot leg. The wire isn't long enough to feed through the new mounting bracket." He tilted his head down and closed his eyes, grimacing as if his neck hurt.

"Hop down, Dad. Let me do that."

"It's almost done. I just need to strip these two." He groaned and stepped down, handing Jan the strippers. "I've got new wire nuts when you're ready." He handed the orange plastic nuts to Elise. "I'll go get the mounting bracket and motor."

Jan stepped up on the stool, carefully placing her feet for balance.

"Doing okay?" Elise asked as she watched her find a comfortable position to work.

"Yep." She reached up to finish stripping the wires. Her sweater rose slightly, exposing an inch of pale white skin above her jeans. "I'm sorry you got roped into this repair job."

"I don't mind. Your dad must be a very handy man to have around the house."

"Ma says it's like that old story of being married to a cobbler. Everybody has new shoes but her."

"Ah, like jiggling the toilet handle."

"Exactly. Although I think he finally fixed that." She held out her hand. Elise placed one of the wire nuts in it and Jan screwed it onto the ends of the wires.

"I must say, I'm impressed you know how to do this." She grinned up at her. "A woman of many talents."

"I was doing this stuff before I could drive."

"What were you going to do with those remote switches you picked up when we were here?"

"I was high-teching my apartment. I can turn on lights and the television and see who's at my door all from my cell phone."

"Wow. A cyber geek too?" Elise had trouble keeping her eyes off that intriguing strip of soft skin around Jan's middle.

"Not really. It just makes some things a little easier when I'm home."

"You mean easier when you're not wearing your prosthetic?" Elise asked carefully.

"Yep. Okay, Dad. Ready for the mounting bracket," she called.

"You want me to do it?" he offered, striding into the room with a mounting bracket in one hand and the ceiling fan motor in the other.

"I can do it. You save your shoulder."

"What do you do, Elise?" he asked while Jan attached the mounting bracket to the electrical box in the ceiling.

"I'm a general contractor."

"She's Grayson Construction, Dad."

"You're the ones doing the hospital addition downtown?" He looked impressed.

"Yes, we are."

Jan finished mounting the fan motor then attached the blades and light fixture while Elise visited with John about living in Boston.

"All done," Jan said, handing Elise the tools from her back pocket. She looked down, as if judging the step and how she would handle it.

"May I offer a hand?" Elise asked, but Jan had already stepped down.

"Thanks for the help, gals. I'll take it from here." He placed the tools back in a toolbox and collected the remnants of the job while Jan and Elise headed back into the kitchen, where the sound of voices meant more people had arrived.

"Sounds like my sister and her family," Jan said. "Lynette, Mike and the twins, Shawn and Shannon, and no, I can't tell them apart. No one can. Well, except Lynette. Maybe."

"Hi Jan," Lynette said happily, smiling at her, then at Elise. "You must be Elise. I'm Lynette. This is my husband, Mike." She pointed to the man helping one of the boys unstick a jacket zipper. He looked up, smiled and nodded. "That's Shannon, and the one who ran into the living room to lay dibs to the video game controller is Shawn," she said.

"Hello Lynette and Mike and Shawn and Shannon," Elise said, jumping out of the way as Shannon pushed past her, shouting it was his turn to be first.

"Mike," Lynette addressed her husband in a stern tone. Elise guessed it was his marching orders to keep the twins in line.

"Boys, I'm putting the controller in time-out if you can't share," Mike shouted. "Nice to meet you, Elise. Would you like a couple eight-year-olds?" he asked as he headed toward the living room.

"No, thanks. I don't think I could keep up with them."

"I love your sweater, Elise," Lynette said, hanging her coat on a hook in the mudroom before slipping on an apron. She wore jeans with scrolled embroidery up the side seams. "Jan should have told you we don't get all dressed up for Thanksgiving."

"I told Jannie that," Harriet said as she poked a fork into a pan.

"Ha!" Jan snorted. "Told you."

"Mike," Lynette called. "I need you to bring in the casseroles from the car."

"I'll get them," Jan volunteered and headed for the back door. "Backseat or trunk?"

"Trunk. There's two. They're in a box. Be careful with the sweet potatoes. They might slop out."

"Shall I come help?" Elise offered.

"Why don't you wait here and open the door for me?"

"I can do that."

"I hope she doesn't drop those." Lynette looked out the kitchen window.

"Should I have gone to help her anyway?" Elise asked.

"No," Harriet and Lynette said in unison.

"She can do it," Lynette said. "I just meant the hot casseroles might have compromised the integrity of the box. But she can figure it out." She put her arm around Elise's shoulders. "Don't try to overprotect her, honey. She can do more than you think she can. Sometimes I think she can do more than even she thinks she can."

"Did I hear voices?" An elderly lady came into the kitchen.

"Elise, this is our grandmother," Lynette said, hooking her arm through the woman's. "Baci, this is Jan's friend, Elise."

"Hello Louise," the woman said.

"Elise," Lynette enunciated more clearly.

"Hello Baci. I've heard so much about you. It's nice to meet you." Elise squeezed her hand softly. "I heard you were in the hospital. I hope you're feeling better."

"Door!" Jan shouted. Elise hurried to open it.

"Sorry. I was meeting your grandmother." She held the door as Jan took the steps one at a time.

"Hi Baci." Jan set the box on the counter then went to kiss her grandmother's cheek. "You met Elise?"

"Yes." Baci looked Elise up and down warily. "I didn't know we were getting all dressed up today."

"We're not, Baci. We're not." Jan winked at Elise.

"Where are Keith and Jefferson?" Lynette asked.

"On their way. They had to go back for Jefferson's inhaler." She had no sooner said it when they heard a car horn out front. "There they are."

A handsome man in black jeans and a black sweater, a turquoise scarf draped around his neck, came through the back door. His hair was short, spiked and gelled.

"Happy Thanksgiving, everyone," he announced.

"Hello, dear." Harriet gave him a hug and kiss. "Where's your coat?"

"In the car, Ma. I promise—I won't freeze to death." He turned a smile of curiosity to Elise. "And who is this creature in the gorgeous sweater?"

"Keith, this is Elise Grayson. Elise, my brother."

Elise reached out a hand to him but he ignored it and pulled her into a warm hug. "Hello Elise. Welcome to the house of horrors." Like Jan, he had a dimpled grin.

A taller man stood in the mudroom taking off his jacket. He looked well-toned and muscular under his tight fitting sweater, the sleeves pushed back to the elbow. His head was shaved and shiny.

"Jefferson, come meet Elise," Keith said, waving him over.

"Hello, Elise" he said in a deep but soft voice.

"Okay, everybody out," Harriet said, trying to get past the crowd in the middle of the kitchen. "I've got a meal to get on the table."

"Ma, should I call Uncle Leo and tell him to come on over?" Jan asked.

"I already did. I also told him to come to the back door but you know he won't."

"How about Beth? Is she coming?"

"No."

"Is Beth another sister?" Elise was doing her best to keep track of who was who.

"She's a cousin. And why isn't she here? I've never known her to pass up a family gathering."

"She has a new girlfriend." Lynette turned to Jan with a smirk. "The woman is a vegan. How are we supposed to feed a vegan?"

"I told Beth to bring her anyway but she said no," Harriet shared. "Couldn't she just eat the veggies like Beth does and leave the turkey?"

"Yeah, Ma. She could if you didn't put butter or milk or bacon drippings in them."

"How can you make mashed potatoes without milk and butter?"

"You're not putting butter in the potatoes?" Baci asked from the pantry, where she was choosing a jar of jelly.

"Yes, Baci, we're putting butter in the potatoes."

Amazingly the confusion in the kitchen eventually transformed into a semblance of order. John stood at the counter and carved the turkey. Lynette and Keith helped take up the rest of the dishes. Just as Harriet predicted, Uncle Leo came to the front door and complained he wasn't heard the first time he'd knocked. Jan introduced him to Elise but he seemed unimpressed despite Elise's cordial smile and handshake. He wandered off looking for a place to sit.

"Don't take it personally," Jan advised. "You've just met the sourpuss of the family. He's like that to everyone. He'll eat dinner and go home as soon as he finishes his second piece of pie. He lives across the street and we include him because he doesn't have anyone else."

"I think that's sweet. I'm sure he appreciates it. He probably just doesn't know how to show it."

"If you say so," she chuckled.

Jan excused herself and slipped away. She stopped and whispered something to her sister on the way out of the kitchen, something that brought a look of concern then a nod of agreement from Lynette.

"Come to the table," Harriet announced as she took up a second dish of gravy.

Elise wasn't sure where she was to sit so she stepped aside to wait for Jan.

"Come on, Elise," Lynette said as she carried two glasses of milk to the table. "Sit down, boys, and don't spill your milk." She looked back at Elise and waved her into the dining room.

"Come on. She'll be back shortly. I think she needed to adjust things."

"Is she okay? Does she need help?"

"No, no. She just said things were pinching a little so she needed to fix it. She jokes sometimes that her girdle is too tight."

"Jan doesn't wear a girdle. That isn't part of her apparatus, is it?"

"No, but that always makes everyone laugh and she'd rather hear you laugh than cry over it."

"I'll wait for her to get back."

"You shouldn't," Lynette said solemnly and pointed. "You two are sitting over there on the other side of the table. She'd be embarrassed if she thought you were just standing here waiting."

John grinned and smacked the chair cushion next to him. "Grandpa's got the pretty girl sitting by him," he announced playfully and winked at Elise.

"Watch him, Elise," Keith joked. "He may be old but he's still dangerous, right, Ma?"

Everyone laughed and joined in the teasing. He grumbled and complained but it all seemed in good fun.

"We'll protect you, sweetheart," Keith added.

"What are we protecting her from?" Jan asked as she made her way around the table.

The twins laughed and pointed at John. "Grandpa."

"In that case, absolutely. She can count on me. Hands off my date, Grandpa."

"Is everything okay?" Elise asked softly as she scooted her chair in and draped her napkin across her lap.

"Uh huh," Jan replied dismissively.

Finally the talking and commotion fell silent.

"As is our custom," Harriet began, scanning the others around the table, "Thanksgiving is a special time for our family. Shall we join hands, bow our heads and be thankful for our many blessings?" She joined hands with Keith on one side and Uncle Leo on the other. Everyone followed suit. Jan took Elise's hand to complete the circle. They all bowed their heads.

Elise's parents didn't say grace. Although this wasn't exactly saying grace, it was a moment of reflection. Elise had many things to be thankful for: her family, her success, the woman with the soft yet warm hold on her hand. After a few moments of silence Elise felt Jan gently squeeze her hand. She squeezed Jan's hand in return.

"Okay, shall we pass the turkey first?" Harriet said, handing the platter to Keith. The parade of food around the table began.

"Elise, when are you supposed to be finished with the hospital addition?" John asked then stuffed a big bite of turkey in his mouth.

"Hopefully July first."

"Do you build stuff?" one of the twins asked.

"Yes, I do."

"She builds big buildings," Jan explained. "Tall ones too."

"Did you build the Empire State Building?" the other twin asked with wide eyes.

"No. We didn't build that one." He seemed disappointed. "But we built the Chuck E. Cheese's in West Springfield. The big one."

"Really? Cool!"

"Speaking of building things," Jan said, "how are things going with the cabin on Lake Winnipesaukee? Have you started the remodel yet?"

"The owner decided not to remodel after all. The estimate was more than he wanted to commit to a renovation. He's going to sell it and buy a bigger place on the lake, which is what we think he wanted to do all along."

"It's a great cabin. I'd put in an on-demand hot water system and maybe wire the whole place to run on an emergency generator, but it's got potential."

"You can hook up a back-up generator to come on when the main power is tripped. Wire it right into the breaker box," John offered. "They've got some really nice two hundred amp units out there."

There was a knock at the back door. "I'll get it," Lynette said. "It's probably Beth."

"I knew she couldn't pass up Ma's cooking," Keith joked.

Lynette came back into the dining room carrying a refilled basket of bread. She had a suspicious look on her face. "Guess who's here," she said, tossing a quick look at Jan.

A woman in a leather jacket and knit beret stood in the doorway. She had red hair and freckles and a broad grin aimed directly at Jan. "Happy Thanksgiving," she announced.

"Allie," Harriet said then rose to meet her. "Hello, sweetheart." She gave her a friendly hug. "Look who's here." Like Lynette, Harriet turned her gaze to Jan.

Everyone at the table looked at Allie then over at Jan and Elise.

Elise thought she heard Jan whisper, *Oh shit.*

"Mike, get a chair for Allie," Harriet said, scooting her chair over to make room at the table. "Take off your coat, honey. We just started."

"No, no. I can't stay. I just stopped by to wish everyone a happy turkey day. I thought you all might be together for dinner."

So this was the woman in Jan's past, Elise thought. No wonder Jan had been attracted to her. She had a perky effervescence about her.

Sensing Jan's hesitation, Elise didn't wait to be introduced. "Hello Allie. I'm Elise. It's very nice to meet you. Please, join us."

"I wish I could but I'm having dinner with my mother." She looked over at Jan with a pained expression. "How are things with you, honey?"

Elise had no right to be jealous but somehow she was. Whether it was the woman's invasive stare or the fact she knew things about Jan Elise didn't, she felt razor-sharp pangs of jealousy. And it was a complete surprise. Every word the woman uttered was like nails on a chalkboard.

Finally Jan stood and excused herself. She walked Allie through the kitchen and out the back door. Elise was sitting in exactly the right spot to see through the dining room into the living room and out the front window where Jan stood on the sidewalk talking to Allie. She finally gave her a hug and headed back inside as the woman drove away.

"Sorry about that," Jan said as she took her seat.

They finished the meal and enjoyed dessert. The kids went off to play. Uncle Leo went home and Baci said her good nights and went to her room. Keith and Jefferson left as well. Throughout all the conversation and goodbye hugs Elise could tell something was bothering Jan. Her jovial mood and quick wit seemed muted.

"Are you okay?" Elise asked, helping carry dirty dishes to the kitchen.

"I'm really sorry about Allie. I didn't know she was coming by."

"What's to apologize about? She's a friend who wanted to wish you a happy Thanksgiving. I don't see anything wrong with that."

"It seemed a little awkward. I didn't want you to feel uncomfortable."

"It wasn't awkward for me." Elise took the plate from Jan's hand and carried it to the sink. "I'm your dinner guest. I'm sure there are lots of people you know that I don't. Don't worry about it."

Once the dining room table had been cleared and the leftovers packaged, Jan announced they were leaving. Harriet walked them to the back door. She hugged and kissed them both.

"Drive carefully, Jannie. And Elise, you come see us again real soon." She handed them each a refrigerator dish of leftovers, enough for dinner the next day.

"Thank you, Harriet. I had a wonderful time."

"You're welcome, dear," she said then looked up at Jan. "And just so you know, I did *not* invite her."

"I know, Ma. She told me."

"Is your leg doing okay, Jannie?"

"Ma!"

"I'm your mother. I can ask." Harriet turned to Elise and added, "She doesn't like me to ask in front of people. It's supposed to be a secret." She laughed and drew Jan into another hug.

"Yes, Ma. My leg is doing okay. There. Are you happy?"

"I am if you're telling me the truth. Is she telling me the truth, Elise?"

"Yes, she is. Her leg is doing okay." Elise looked up at Jan for approval. "Isn't it?"

"Goodbye, Ma." Jan opened the door and held it for Elise.

They headed back through town toward the Mass Pike and the ride east to Boston.

"What are you grinning at?" Jan finally said, taking the toll ticket.

"I had such a great time. Your family is so warm and engaging. I ate too much, of course, but I met some charming people. I even got a peek into your life. Thank you for inviting me."

"I don't know what kind of peek you got but you're welcome." They rode along in silence for several minutes, Jan occasionally drumming her fingers on the top of the steering wheel. "Okay, aren't you going to ask about Allie?"

"Why? Should I?"

"No. Not necessarily."

"Jan, you don't owe me an explanation about anything. You already told me about her and what happened. I don't need to know anything more." She thought a moment then asked, "Are you planning on dating her again? No, wait. Don't answer that. It's none of my business."

"Do you want an answer?"

As if generated by some unseen cosmic force, Elise's cell phone rang at that exact instant. It was another business call from a client who wasn't happy with the sub-contractor doing the plumbing work on his building. "Could this wait until tomorrow? I'll be in the office by eight. I need to be looking at the schedule we set up so we're on the same page." But he wasn't having it. He seemed to think catching her on a day off, even a national holiday, was better than waiting until Friday.

Jan turned into the Back Bay neighborhood and cruised the street, looking for a parking spot while Elise finished soothing the man's anger. Finally she was able to hang up.

"Don't get out," Elise said. "I can take it from here."

"I don't mind."

"I know you don't mind and that's sweet of you. But I'd feel better if you didn't. Your leg is bothering you and I'd prefer you just sit."

Jan opened her mouth to argue but Elise stopped her. "Don't say it. Don't say it isn't bothering you because we both know it is. We can just sit here while I thank you again for inviting me."

"You invited me on a date so I thought it was only fair if I reciprocated."

"So we're calling this a date?"

"I think I'd call it that. I invited you. You accepted. We went out. We ate. Now we're back. That sounds like a date to me."

"You're right, it does. And going by those standards this could be considered our second date."

"Yes, I suppose so."

"Then may I ask you something? Something personal?"

"Okay." Jan heaved a preparatory sigh.

"I'm not asking you this now, but someday is there any chance you'll tell me what happened to your leg? You talk about the prosthesis, and going up and down stairs and doing your job but you never talk about the accident and how it happened."

"Someday, maybe."

"It was bothering you today, wasn't it?"

"Just a little. Not bad. Sometimes the liner gets a little tight. But it's no big deal." Jan shifted in her seat, repeatedly rubbing her hand down the left leg of her jeans. She tried to hide a grimace with a benevolent smile but her wrinkled brow betrayed her.

"You were having trouble with it when we were stuck at the lake house too. You thought I was asleep and you were going to take it off, weren't you?"

"You saw that?"

"Yes. And I want you to know I wouldn't mind. I truly wouldn't."

"But I would. More than you know, I would." Jan's gaze turned out the side window for a brief moment as if something or someone had crossed her mind.

Elise ran her hand down the sleeve of Jan's sweater reassuringly. "Someday I hope you trust me enough to tell me about it. But I won't push you," she said softly, her eyes melting into Jan's. "I think it's time for me to go inside, but I have one more question."

"I'm listening."

"Most dates end with a good night kiss. I was just wondering if this one will?"

"I seem to remember our first date did. I guess it's only fair this one does too."

With that their lips met. It was a sweet kiss. Soft. Delicate. Warm. But it wasn't a fulfilling kiss. At least, it wasn't for Elise. She leaned in and kissed Jan again, parting her lips and pressing into the kiss. She felt Jan hesitate and stiffen as if she wasn't sure but then her fingers laced through Elise's hair to pull her closer. It was a complete kiss, full of emotion and expression. It went well until Elise inadvertently touched Jan's left knee. For a fleeting moment she could feel the hard plastic rim of the socket. But Jan pulled her hand away as if Elise had touched forbidden territory.

"I'm sorry," Elise whispered breathlessly. She was still lost in the wonderfulness of the kiss. She closed her eyes and leaned her forehead against Jan's. "I think I better go inside."

"Can I walk you to your door?" Jan drew her fingers down Elise's cheek.

"Only if you'll come inside with me and stay."

Jan took a deep breath as she considered her reply, a reply that seemed to take forever in coming.

"I can't do that," she finally said, a noticeable tremor in her voice.

"Are you sure?"

"Yes. I'm sure." She reached over and opened the passenger door. "Good night, Elise."

"Good night." Elise climbed out and trotted up the steps without looking back. She felt embarrassed. She had just propositioned her chauffeur and there was no denying she was disappointed that Jan had declined.

CHAPTER THIRTEEN

Lorraine stood in the doorway to Elise's office. Elise continued to type on her laptop assuming she'd speak if she had something to say.

"It's been two weeks and you haven't once asked me to book a car and driver for you. You've been to meetings and job sites around the area. I was just wondering if you weren't happy with me doing your scheduling. Or maybe you weren't happy with the car service I selected."

"If you must know, I've been using a taxi service to get around. I have chewing gum stuck to the back of a very nice pair of brown wool slacks to prove it."

"Would you like me to find a different car service? I'm sure we can find one you're happy with."

Elise placed her glasses on the desk and leaned back in her chair. "Lorraine, it's not the car service that's the problem. It's me. I've made it impossible for you to call a car and driver for me."

"What have I done? Just tell me and I'll fix it. I promise." Lorraine came to the corner of Elise's desk, a worried look on her face.

"You didn't do anything. But when I tell you I need a car and driver you're going to ask if I want Jan Chase and I'm going to say no. Then you'll want to know why and I'll have to confess I did something stupid."

"How stupid?" She cocked an eyebrow suspiciously.

"Really stupid. Something an employer should never do to an employee."

"Is this something the lawyer you keep on retainer needs to know about?" Lorraine pulled up a chair and sat on the edge, waiting to hear the details.

"I had dinner with Jan and her family on Thanksgiving. She said it was reciprocation for me inviting her to my parents' harvest buffet."

"I'm not a legal expert but that doesn't sound felonious to me."

Elise chewed on her lip a moment, deciding how to proceed. "What I'm about to tell you can't leave this office. Understand?"

"Absolutely. It never does." Lorraine sat up straight and gave an emphatic nod.

"When Jan brought me home I sort of propositioned her." She closed her eyes and grimaced.

"You mean you…"

"We kissed in the car. I should have left it at that. A good night kiss. But when she offered to walk me to my door, I said only if she'd come inside and stay."

"All right. You go, girl!"

"Lorraine, this wasn't a go-girl moment. It was awkward and embarrassing. I propositioned my chauffeur. And I think I embarrassed her more than myself."

"Okay, technically she wasn't your chauffeur when you just went to dinner with her. But what happened next?"

"Nothing. She said no and I went inside with my tail between my legs." Elise groaned. "I can't believe I did that. I don't proposition women. I've never done that in my life. Why did I think it was all right?"

"I'm going to step over the line here and say just because you don't normally do it doesn't mean it's wrong. Do you like her?"

"She's a very good chauffeur. She's very efficient and attentive. I feel implicitly safe when I'm with her."

"That's not what I meant and you know it."

"I know it isn't." Elise put her glasses back on and turned to her computer screen, ready to bury herself in work. She had drawn Lorraine into a conversation she didn't need to be having with her secretary.

"Okeydokey. I guess we're going back to work now," Lorraine mumbled and got up and headed for the door. She stopped and looked back. "Elise, I have a rhetorical question for you. Were you embarrassed because you propositioned your chauffeur or because she said no?"

Elise stopped typing but didn't look up, and didn't reply. Lorraine had just asked the same question she had been asking herself every day since Thanksgiving.

Just after one o'clock Elise pulled on her coat and carried some estimates she had been working on to Lorraine's desk. "I'll be back," she said and headed for the elevator.

"FYI, they are shipping the stained glass panel for the Calhoun building. It leaves Seattle tomorrow and should be at the Cape Monday." Lorraine covered the phone receiver with her hand. "Do you still want to be there or is your dad going down?"

"Yes. I want to be there. For that kind of investment I definitely want to be there. Keep me up-to-date on the shipping progress. They are not to uncrate it unless I'm there."

"Then I should schedule a car and driver?" Lorraine asked expectantly.

Elise wrapped her scarf around her neck and tucked it neatly into her coat as she thought. "Yes. I'll need a car and driver."

"The same company you've been using or would you like a different one?"

"The same company will be fine." She looked down at Lorraine. "Same company. Same driver."

"I'll take care of it," her secretary replied with an approving nod.

Elise stepped out of the elevator and into the building lobby. She had no regrets. Just a contented smile on her face as she headed to lunch. She liked it when destiny took a hand. She needed to be at the Cape next week for business. Jan would get her there. Business, nothing more.

It was a brisk ten minute walk to her favorite deli. "A bowl of clam chowder please. Crackers on the side," she said to the woman behind the counter. "And coffee—black." She found a spot to stand at the narrow counter along the front window. She wasn't the only customer relegated to eating lunch standing up. Those along the window were the first to notice the flakes of snow filling the air and covering the sidewalk. It was a pretty snow but it meant she'd have to walk back to the office in it. She dropped the last few oyster crackers into the bowl and stirred them through the remaining half inch of rich chowder.

She had just taken a bite when a white limousine drove by. It had tinted windows, but for all she knew it was Jan behind the wheel transporting a client through downtown. If it was Jan she wondered if the passenger appreciated the curls clustered at the back of her head or the way her long fingers caressed the steering wheel. Elise transported herself to an imaginary place where Jan offered her hand and she accepted it.

"Hello Elise," a familiar voice said.

"Hello," she replied, still lost in her imaginary dream world. When she turned around her smile immediately vanished. It was Ginger, dressed in a quilted parka with a fur-trimmed hood bunched at the back of her neck. "Oh, hello Ginger."

"Hi. I've been meaning to call. How have you been?" Ginger's smile seemed forced, even apprehensive.

"I'm fine. And you?" Elise wiped her mouth with a paper napkin and crumpled it into the bowl.

"I've had a cold but I guess that goes with the season. I wanted to call and let you know I think your car insurance cards got into my stuff somehow. I can bring them by when I know you're going to be home."

"That's okay. I can get new ones."

"I'd feel better if I returned them to you."

"Ginger, just shred them. I don't need you to bring them back." Elise carried her tray to the rack. Ginger followed right behind.

"I don't mind."

"Ginger, what is it you want?"

"I was just trying to be nice. I know you're a stickler for details."

"Insurance cards are replaceable. You know that. You also probably know I haven't driven my car in months. I'll call Allstate this afternoon and have them generate new cards. Moot subject."

She headed for the door but Ginger grabbed her arm. "Elise, what's wrong? Why are you being like this?"

"I'm not being like anything. I need to get back to work."

"Do you hate me now?" Ginger asked, tightening her grip.

Elise straightened her posture and smiled politely, pulling Ginger's hand off her arm.

"No. I don't hate you, Ginger." She slipped her fingers into her gloves and stepped out onto the sidewalk.

Ginger hurried after her. "If you don't hate me why won't you talk to me?"

"You want to talk. We've done this before, but okay. How would you like me to start? I know—let's begin with how you cheated on me. And as I recently learned, not with just your boss. That's a good topic. Or how about how you used me. That's another good one. There was a time I thought it was somehow my fault. But I didn't push you into other women's beds. You took that leap all by yourself, Ginger."

"So you do hate me," she said.

"No, the opposite of love isn't hate."

"What is it then?" There was an unmistakable glimmer of expectation in Ginger's eyes as if she hoped Elise would take her back or at the very least forgive her for what she had done.

"The opposite of love is indifference. And that's what I feel."

Elise turned and strode up the sidewalk, leaving footprints in the freshly fallen snow. She hadn't seen or spoken to Ginger in weeks and whatever fear she'd had over just such a chance meeting were now resolved. She felt no regrets. She wished Ginger well but felt no love for her. She wondered if she ever did.

"How was lunch?" Lorraine asked as Elise passed her desk.

"Satisfying."

"Well, just so you know, your car and driver have been reserved for next week. I scheduled them tentatively for Monday but told them it may need to be changed depending on a shipment's arrival date."

"Good. Thank you," Elise replied. She headed down the hall toward her office but looked back before entering.

"Before you ask, yes," Lorraine said with a smile. "Same driver."

Elise nodded and stepped into her office. She closed the door and leaned against it, smiling contentedly. She could spend the afternoon rethinking her run-in with Ginger and whether she'd handled it maturely. Or she could spend it in anticipation of seeing Jan again. She had contracts and estimates to work on but she knew they would get only part of her attention. Jan Chase would get the lion's share.

"Hello, dear," Suzanne said, walking into the office without a courtesy knock or an invitation.

"Mother, what a pleasant surprise. Come in and keep me company while I finish this email." She stood and greeted her mother with a hug. "What are you doing in town? Shopping? Dinner with Dad?"

"I stopped by Neiman Marcus and found a gorgeous pair of boots for our trip. And yes I'm meeting your father at Marliaves after his meeting, but I thought I'd stop in and see my daughter."

"I'm glad you did." She quickly typed the last line of the email before she lost her train of thought and sent it on its way. "You haven't been in to visit since last summer."

"It was last May. I was splashed by that idiot taxi driver as I was crossing State Street. He ruined a gorgeous pantsuit."

"Couldn't you have it cleaned?"

"It wasn't worth it. I'd always know what disgusting things were festering in that gutter water. I'd never wear it again."

"You're right. You probably wouldn't." Elise chuckled, knowing it was useless to argue with her mother about clothing.

Suzanne checked her watch and sighed noticeably. It was meant as a signal.

"It's after five, Mother. Would you like a little glass of sherry while you're waiting?"

"Yes, dear. That would be wonderful. I'm chilled to the bone."

Elise opened the cabinet where she kept a few essential bottles of liquid refreshment for those guests who expected such amenities. Her father had suggested it when she'd equipped her first office to receive high-end clients. She poured her mother an appropriate stemmed glass full of her favorite brand of sherry.

"Thank you, dear. Aren't you having any?"

"I better not. I've got to call a client later and I'll need a clear head to discuss the changes he wants to make."

"I told Forest he shouldn't allow changes after a project starts. Once a shovel goes in the ground, that's it. Subject closed." She sipped.

"I don't think we've ever had a project that didn't involve at least some changes. Clients change their minds. It's human nature."

"I know." She sipped again. "Speaking of human nature, how are things going with you and Jan Chase?"

"How are they going? Fine, I guess."

"Elise, I have to be honest with you. I did some checking." She set her glass on the desk as if preparing for some ominous declaration.

"Checking about what?"

"Sweetheart, this Jan Chase woman you are seeing is nothing more than a chauffeur. She drives limousines. I thought you needed to know before you became too deeply involved. She picks people up at the airport and takes them to hotels and back again."

"I know that, Mother. She has driven me to job sites several times."

"You knew she was a chauffeur before you started dating her?"

"That's how I met her. And we aren't dating. I simply invited her to be my dinner companion so you wouldn't invite someone for me. And she's not just a chauffeur. She happens to be a pilot as well. Or was before her accident. And she's a very intelligent and personable woman."

"Then you aren't dating her?"

"No. Well, she invited me to her parents' for Thanksgiving. But we aren't dating." Elise smiled to herself. Jan had said accepting a dinner invitation and returning afterward did constitute a date, but her mother didn't need the details. She especially didn't need the embarrassing ones.

"Do you plan to go out with her again?" There were judgmental overtones to her question.

"To be honest, Mother, I have no idea. She's unlike any woman I've ever met. And I don't mean because of her leg."

"Elise, I hope you don't think I'm so shallow that I'd judge her on that alone." She tightened a scowl at her daughter.

"Are you judging her on her job?"

"I'm judging her because I didn't think she was being honest with you."

"I'm sorry, Mother. That was my fault. I didn't think you'd approve if I told you I was bringing my chauffeur to your harvest buffet."

"Do you approve of her, Elise?"

"Yes, Mother. I do."

"Do you like her? As more than just a chauffeur?" she asked in a softer voice.

"Yes. It surprised me when I realized it, but yes. She comes from a blue-collar middle-class background and isn't consumed with acquiring possessions or climbing Boston's social ladder. She doesn't try to put on airs." Elise leaned back in her chair and smiled. "I don't know why but she makes me feel good when I'm around her. She has a down-to-earth practicality I find very charming. I hope we can be friends."

"I remember when your father and I were first friends. We were in our early twenties when we started dating. I had no idea who he was or who Grayson Construction was. He was just this handsome young man with an incredible smile. Just like yours, Elise. He wasn't president of the company back then. He was just a bricklayer." She smiled as if reliving the past. "Our dates were usually spent walking through the Public Garden. Sometimes, when he could afford it, we'd ride the Swan Boats. But most of the time we'd just walk all over Boston. I don't know how many times we walked the Freedom Trail. He loved to point out the historic buildings and their unique architecture."

"I think he still does." Elise was listening closely. This was new information about her parents and she was happy to hear it.

"Sometimes we ate in Quincy Market. Sometimes we shared a picnic on the Boston Common. He never complained when I made fried chicken." Suzanne laughed then leaned forward as if to confess a secret. "It was terrible. But he never said a word."

"I never heard that story," Elise told her with affection.

"Couples often have little memories that are important only to them."

"What made you think of it now?"

"I was worried Jan was deceiving you." She took a slow, pensive sip from her glass and leaned back in the chair. She lowered her gaze and traced her fingertip around the rim of the glass as she seemed to prepare her next admission. "Forest and I had been dating for almost a year. I still had no real concept of what his father's company did. All I knew was Forest's work clothes were filthy and his hands were rough. Well, I got a phone call from a boy I used to date before I met your father. He asked me to dinner, sort of a for-old-time's-sake thing. Forest was out of town for a few days for work, so I thought why not. We went to dinner and talked about all our friends we hadn't seen since we graduated. And I went home."

"That was nice."

"He called the next day and asked me out again." She closed her eyes and drew a stoic posture. "He asked me to spend the weekend with him at his parents' summer house at the Cape."

Elise saw a pained expression overtake her mother's face. "Did you go?"

"Yes," she whispered. "I was young and stupid and naïve. It didn't take long for me to realize he was just using me. I never saw him again after that weekend. But I was so ashamed."

"Does Dad know?" Elise asked as delicately as possible, knowing her mother was reliving a painful memory.

"Yes. I didn't tell him right away. But he seemed to know. He finally asked if I had something to tell him. I confessed that I had cheated. I was certain he would want nothing more to do with me. He said he loved me. But he said we were friends first and our friendship was strong enough to survive it. He asked me to marry him on our first anniversary."

"He told me he asked you to marry him over a lobster dinner."

"That's right. He saved his money and we had dinner at the Union Oyster House. And he got down on one knee and proposed right there in the restaurant. He's made me feel like a princess ever since. And we have learned to tell each other everything. Everything, Elise." She took the last sip then set the glass on the desk and stood. "And now, my dear, I'm going to dinner. I don't want to be late for your father." She gave Elise a hug. "If you want a word of advice from your mother, be honest, Elise. Wherever you find love, be honest with it. Accept it. Embrace it. Let it make you happy."

"I'll remember that. I'm glad you stopped by. We don't chat often enough." She helped her on with her coat.

"No, we don't. I'll miss you at Christmas, sweetheart."

"Where are you off to this year? Dad hasn't mentioned anything."

"We wanted to do Paris and Geneva but with all the terror alerts I told Forest I'd be a nervous wreck. We decided to do a Mediterranean cruise. We don't have to get off the boat if we don't want to."

"I hope you and Dad enjoy yourselves."

"We won't be on the moon. I'm sure we'll talk. You know your father wouldn't go anywhere that didn't have Wi-Fi. He has to be able to keep in touch." She laughed and kissed her daughter on the cheek then strode off to her dinner engagement, waving playfully over her shoulder.

Elise stood in the hall and watched until she was in the elevator. Her mother's visit had been another surprisingly satisfying revelation of her day. She was happy for her parents, even envious. They had a strong, healthy relationship. They loved each other in spite of their idiosyncrasies. And honesty seemed to be the foundation that love was built on. Elise wondered if she should be just as honest with Jan. Should she confess her feelings? Would a trip to the Cape be the perfect place for that? Given the wide gap in their life experience, maybe friendship was the most she could ever hope for. Could there be more? Could those blond curls and long fingers be hers to adore? She hoped so. She prayed so.

CHAPTER FOURTEEN

Jan nudged the throttle forward and listened to the roar of the engine. RPM's good. Oil pressure good. Checklist completed and awaiting tower clearance for takeoff. The windshield wipers swatted back and forth against the drizzle as the single engine Piper Arrow began its roll down the runway. Within five minutes she'd be above the afternoon shower and on her way west to Ithaca, where skies were blue with unlimited visibility. She'd have Dr. and Mrs. Ling back in Boston by dinnertime.

She eased back on the yoke and rose over the end of the runway. As per instructions from the tower she headed north to clear the airspace before banking to the left at three thousand feet. It was a little out of the way but it took her over the beautiful rolling Berkshires. She had just turned the yoke when everything went black. She could no longer see out the windshield. There was no windshield. No cockpit. No instrument panel. No airplane. The sound of the engine was replaced by a rhythmic beeping and a strong stench. A burning stench. Vinegar. No, stronger. Ammonia.

Jan sat up in bed, sweat drenching her pajamas and sheets. She felt like she was suffocating and gasped for breath. Her heart pounded in her chest. It was the same dream. The same nightmare she had had several times since the accident. She was powerless to prevent it, had no warning when or if it would grip her and rob her of sleep. She sat in the darkness, waiting for her breathing to return to normal. She finally lay back on the pillow, staring up at the ceiling and the light reflecting from the window. She was almost afraid to go back to sleep. Would the dream be there waiting for her, waiting to tease and terrorize her? She knew it held the secret to what she couldn't remember. But did she really want to know what was on the other side of the nightmare, what had happened to her leg? Maybe it was better she didn't know. Dissociative amnesia. That was the doctor's explanation for it. Her brain was protecting her from some profound trauma. But if she didn't need to know, why didn't the nightmare leave her alone?

Jan tossed and turned for the rest of the night as her mind jumped from one thought to the next. Wherever it went it kept coming back to the same thing: Elise's kiss. Elise's soft, supple and satisfying kiss. Days had passed since that kiss but it was as if she'd just felt it. And there was no mistaking her invitation to come inside. Even though Jan had declined, it had her thinking. What if?

Jan's alarm clock finally buzzed on the nightstand.

She showered and dressed for work. It took an extra few minutes to coax the gel liner over her stump. It was red and sore and had been for several weeks. She attributed it to long days and extra hours sitting behind the wheel. She planned to spend her next days off without it, relying on her crutches to get around the apartment. She'd give the stump a good long massage and she'd be back to normal in no time.

"I've got a last minute run for you today," Glenda said as soon as Jan came through the door of the car service.

"Okay, but I thought I was taking Elise Grayson to the Cape."

"Her secretary called and cancelled. Something about weather causing shipment delays. They'll let us know when they want to reschedule."

Jan felt a twinge of disappointment. She was looking forward to the drive along the coast and the forecast for a few days of mild December weather. She was, she admitted, also looking forward to seeing Elise again.

"When?"

"They didn't say. But in the meantime…" She handed Jan a piece of paper with a name, address and information on it. "You're picking up some dignitary and his entourage at the Hyatt Regency and taking them to meet his plane. He wants the stretch Escalade, Grey Goose in the bar and ice."

"So I'm taking them to Logan?"

"No. The guy's private jet is parked at Chaffey Airport. It's on the other side of Bedford."

Jan stared at her, as if the air had suddenly been sucked out of the room.

"The address is on the paper. It's not hard to find," Glenda added, noticing the surprised look on Jan's face.

"I know how to get there."

"Then what's the problem?"

Jan read the paper to be sure she'd heard what she thought she heard.

"No problem," she said and went to the cabinet to claim the keys for the Escalade. She had work to do before she left to collect her passengers. She had a limousine to clean and stock. She also had to come to grips with where she was taking the clients.

Chaffey was a small airport used by private customers, flight schools and charter companies, namely J and T Aviation, the aviation company where she used to work. She hadn't been to the airfield since the accident. She had no need to go there. She'd considered driving by last summer. But the closer she got the more she'd regretted it. And the more anxious she became and had abandoned the idea. She could refuse the assignment, give some excuse Glenda would probably understand, but she didn't want to do that. This was her job and she was determined to do it.

Jan was halfway out the door when she turned back to Glenda. "You'll let me know when they reschedule Elise Grayson's trip?"

"Yes, I'll let you know," she replied without looking up from whatever she was reading.

Jan sent the car through the car wash then wiped down the windows and seats and stocked the minibar.

"I'm heading out," Jan called to Glenda through the pass-through window next to her desk.

"Okay." She was busy eating a bologna and cheese sandwich. "By the way, show your ID and a guard will let you drive through the gate at the airport. You can pull on through and drop them plane side."

"Any word yet on that trip to the Cape?"

"No, Jan. I told you I'd let you know."

Jan didn't expect there to be word yet. It had only been an hour but she had to ask anyway. She headed across town to the hotel. It would take twenty minutes in normal traffic but she allowed extra time just in case. She pulled into the loading area in front of the hotel and notified the party in suite 720 she was there to take them to the airport. They weren't finished packing and needed an additional half hour. She reassured them it was no problem and she'd be waiting out front when they were ready. Thirty minutes came and went. After forty-five minutes a woman called to say they'd be down in a half hour. Jan agreed politely then called Glenda to let her know about the delay.

"Let me guess. You called to ask if Grayson's secretary called to schedule that trip to the Cape," Glenda said.

"No. I didn't ask, now did I?"

"But you were going to before you hung up. Get your mind out of your pants, Jan."

"Since when is doing your job well considered sexual?"

"Since you started hauling Elise Grayson all over creation."

"Not true. She's just another client."

"So if I schedule another driver for that trip to the Cape you wouldn't mind?"

"No, I wouldn't." Jan hesitated. "But you're not going to, are you?"

Glenda laughed.

"I've got to go, Glenda. Here they come, finally."

Jan held the back door while the five women, somewhere in their mid-fifties, climbed in and got settled. With the doorman's help she loaded their luggage in the back of the Escalade, all of it designer bags. The women's clothes, hairdos, jewelry and large sunglasses suggested affluence. A somewhat more garish style of affluence than Elise Grayson's tasteful and refined style. But conspicuous excess nonetheless. Once the luggage was loaded Jan leaned in the open back door.

"Is Mr. Ziegler on his way down?" Jan asked, since his was the name on the paper she'd been given.

"That's me," the woman in a mink coat and stiletto heels said from her spot in the middle of the backseat. At least, Jan thought it was a woman. But the deep voice and Adam's apple had her rethinking that assumption.

"Then we're all present and accounted for?" Jan said with a smile, hoping her faux pas was forgiven. "By the way, you ladies will find Grey Goose in the minibar if you'd like a little refreshment on the way to the airport. It should take about forty minutes. And you girls might like to know there's a box of chocolates in the cabinet. Help yourselves." Jan heard laughing and giggling even before she closed the door.

The ride to Chaffey Airport was a nightmare of snarled traffic and road construction. It took over an hour but her passengers didn't seem to mind. As soon as she turned off the highway and headed for the airport Jan felt her stomach tighten. She forced her thoughts to safely delivering her passengers plane side. She pulled up to the gate and waited for the guard to step out of the guard shack. Jan displayed her ID. So did Mr. Ziegler. After a quick call to the airport security office they were cleared to enter.

"It's the white plane with a blue feather painted on the side and twin engines on the tail," Mr. Ziegler said after lowering the partition partway. He pointed to a plane with an open door. A man in a pilot's uniform stood next to the extended steps.

"The Gulfstream G150?" Jan said, heading for the jet on the far side of the taxiway.

"Yes." He seemed pleased she knew what it was.

Jan opened the back door and offered each passenger a hand out, even though she suspected all the women were actually men. Mr. Ziegler's coat slipped off his shoulders as he stepped out, balancing precariously on his narrow heels. Jan took his arm as he regained his balance then helped him replace his coat over his shoulders. He was tall, a few inches taller than Jan. But he carried the femme look gracefully.

"Thank you, dear," he said, gathering the coat around himself. "Wearing these shoes is a bitch."

"They look good on you though."

Jan went to unload the luggage. The pilot and a young man she assumed was the flight attendant placed the bags in the hold. Jan tried to keep her eyes on the luggage or on the ground but curiosity brought her gaze up the steps and inside the plane. She couldn't see the cockpit or the instrument panel. It made her palms sweat to think about them. The other ladies had climbed the stairs into the plane. Mr. Ziegler stood at the bottom of the steps waiting for Jan to finish.

"All eight pieces are loaded," Jan said.

"Thank you, dear," Mr. Ziegler said. "I'm a pretty good judge of character and I appreciate your kindness."

"Anytime, ma'am. Anytime at all." She gave a small salute. "I hope you have a pleasant flight."

He offered Jan a delicate handshake. Jan accepted it warmly and found two folded one hundred dollar bills in her hand when he released her. He smiled and climbed the steps into the plane.

Jan moved the car and sat watching until the plane taxied to the end of the runway and took off. She lowered her window and listened to the sweet hum of the jet engines as it rose elegantly into the afternoon sky. Once the plane was out of sight the object of her focus was gone and she was left staring at a row of private planes parked in front of several metal hangars. The hangar at the end had a sign over the large door that read J and T Aviation, a new sign, freshly painted. The overhead door was closed but a man in white coveralls and a cap with earflaps stood on a ladder working on the engine of a bright red Piper Cherokee. That plane belonged to Jess Jones, the owner. She recognized the numbers on the side and the contrasting white landing gear and rudder. She didn't see his pickup truck parked next to the building but that was his plane.

Jan ought to know. She had flown it many times. It was a sweet ride, smooth and agile, effortless to control. It wasn't the plane she was flying three years ago. Maybe if it had been things would have been different. She wasn't even sure what plane she had flown. She had been told, but she had no independent memory of climbing into the cockpit. She had also been told Canada geese were found at the crash site, or rather parts of Canada geese. It was assumed a flock of migratory geese had crossed her flight path and were sucked into the engine, causing her to crash. Those details were also blocked from her memory. As many times as she had heard those stories, hoping to unlock the secrets to her amnesia, she still couldn't resurrect cognitive memory of it.

She parked the Escalade next to the hangar and sat staring at the little red plane. It wasn't until the mechanic noticed her and tapped on the driver's side window that she came out of whatever dream had clouded her thinking.

"Jan?" he said, squinting through the open window. "What the hell are you doing out here?" He grinned and shook her hand enthusiastically.

"Hi Vern."

"Long time, no see." His grin slowly turned to awareness and then to anguish. His gaze drifted down her leg, as if he knew what was there or not there. "I heard what happened. Shit, I'm sorry, Jan."

"Thanks. What's up with Jess's plane? Engine trouble?"

"No, just replacing the fuel pump. I heard you were working for a limo service." He looked the car up and down. "Nice ride. Bar in the back?"

"Yep. Bar, mini fridge, TV, stereo, DVD player."

All the while Vern drooled over the extravagant amenities in the stretch Escalade limousine Jan was remembering the amenities in Jess's airplane.

"You want to sit in the cockpit?" he offered, nodding toward the plane. "Jess won't mind."

"No, but thanks anyway."

"You sure? I have to start it up and drive down to the end of the runway to check the pressure. You want to ride along? It'll just take a couple minutes." He wiped his hands on the rag in his back pocket and nodded again. "Come on. Keep me company."

Jan meant to say no. She swore she did. But she found herself scrambling up onto the wing and stepping into the cockpit after Vern slipped into the left-hand pilot's seat. She lowered herself into the right-hand seat, struggling to get her leg into place. She didn't remember it being so hard to settle into the seat. She didn't remember the space being so tight. She also didn't remember the seat belt fitting across the chest and making it hard to breathe.

"How do you like the new upholstery? Jess's wife picked it out. Nice, huh?"

"Yes, nice." Jan hadn't noticed. She was more concerned with the fresh nausea turning her stomach into cement mixer.

Vern hurried through the checklist, reading gauges and flipping switches until the propeller began to spin and the engine chugged into service. He seemed to be listening to the engine. She was listening to her heart pounding in her ears. She'd made a mistake. As soon as the door closed she knew she'd made a big mistake.

"Ah, Vern," she said, the words catching in her throat.

"Tower, this is PA five five six," he said into his headset. "Permission to taxi and test."

"Vern," she gasped and released the top button of her shirt as she felt her throat tighten.

He didn't hear. He was talking to the control tower about his planned route around the taxiway. The plane began to roll. He steered down the center of the paved taxiway, heading toward the far end of the runway. Jan clenched her fists until her knuckles went white. She wanted to grab the yoke and turn the plane back to the hangar, back to the safety of the Escalade. Vern wasn't going to take off. He was just going to taxi to check his repairs, but it didn't matter. She wanted out. She needed out. She needed out or she was going to die in this plane.

"Vern, stop the plane," she shouted, gasping for breath. "Stop." She braced her hands against the dashboard. "Let me out."

"Don't open that door," he demanded and cut the engine. "What are you doing?"

"I've got to get out. I can't do this. I can't. I can't."

"Relax. I'll take you back."

"No. Just let me out." The propeller had barely stopped spinning and the plane had just come to a halt when she opened the door and slithered out of the seat. She climbed onto the wing and slid down onto the ground, quickly stepping away from the plane.

Vern climbed out as well, a concerned look on his face. "Are you okay, Jan?"

"Vern, I'm sorry. I can't do this. I thought I could but I can't. You go ahead. I'll walk back."

"Are you sure?" He looked back toward the hangar and the limousine she'd left parked next to it. It wasn't that far but he seemed to feel responsible. "I can go get the car for you."

"No. I can walk. You go ahead."

"Did I do something wrong?"

"No. I'm just not ready." She looked over at the plane, its door standing open and welcoming. "I used to love it but I can't..."

"When you're ready, you come see me, okay?" He placed his hand on her shoulder. "Even if you just want to sit in it, you come see me."

"Maybe someday." She took a last look at the plane and started for the car and the drive back to Boston.

Jan sent Glenda a text that she'd completed her delivery and was on her way in. With luck and an hour of driving time her panic attack would fade into just an embarrassing memory. She pulled into the lot and stopped at the gas pump. Glenda called to her through the window.

"Jan, tomorrow morning, seven a.m."

"Okay. Which car and where?"

"The black town car to Chatham."

"On the Cape?" Jan's ears perked.

"Yes. Grayson's secretary called about an hour ago. Word of warning, it may be an overnight trip. You should pack a change of clothes just in case."

"Where are we staying?"

"I don't know. They're making reservations someplace."

Jan assumed she'd have her own room, but she'd get into that later. Maybe they wouldn't be staying overnight. She didn't mind driving back late at night if Elise didn't mind. If not, she wanted a closed door between her stump and Elise's curious stare.

CHAPTER FIFTEEN

Jan packed what she would need for an overnight on Cape Cod, all the while wishing she wouldn't need any of it. Underwear, pajamas, clean shirt and suit, toiletries, collapsible set of crutches, spare gel liner and assortment of sock liners if she would need them and a large bottle of Tums. Even the thought of an overnight sent her stomach into a rage.

She was twenty minutes early when she pulled up in front of Elise's house. She was prepared to sit there and wait until straight up seven o'clock before she knocked on the door. Jan was staring out the side window watching a woman and her dog jogging down the sidewalk when Elise tapped on the passenger window.

"Are you waiting for spring?" she said with a grin. She was dressed in slacks and a sweater but no coat and she had her arms folded tightly over her chest.

Jan quickly climbed out and circled the car. "I'm sorry. I was told seven o'clock so I was waiting. I didn't want to rush you."

"I've been ready since six. Insomnia refused to take a day off." She trotted up the steps to her house. "Even if I wasn't ready you could have come inside to wait."

Jan followed her inside. Elise's briefcase, suitcase and small tote bag were lined up just inside the door.

"Did they tell you we'd be spending the night at the Cape?" Elise checked her purse for her cell phone, charger and other essentials.

"I was told we might." Jan swallowed hard at the reality of it and picked up the suitcase.

"Did you bring a toothbrush?" Elise asked with an impish grin.

"Yes. My Mickey Mouse toothbrush and sparkly toothpaste." She carried the suitcase and tote bag to the car while Elise finished getting ready and locked the door.

"By the way, I forgot. We need to drive down the alley to my garage. I need to get my car registration and vehicle numbers to email them to my insurance agent so he'll renew my auto coverage."

"He should have that stuff already if you're just renewing, shouldn't he?" Jan opened the back door for Elise.

"I thought so but, hey. It's no big deal. I was busy with a client when they called so I'll just do it and not argue." Elise pulled a set of keys from her purse and a remote door opener. "I'm not even sure what I'm looking for. I'm supposed to make sure the VIN number on the registration is the same as on the car. That's the number on the tag in the windshield, right?"

"Yes. The long number. Would you like me to get them for you?"

"That would be great. Thank you." She handed Jan the remote and the keys.

"There's just one car in the garage?"

"Yes. There's a bunch of junk in there but just one car. You have to stand by the corner of the garage to get the door to go up. It's finicky."

The pearl white Lexus SUV was parked in the middle but, as Elise had said, the garage was also home to stacks of boxes, a canoe, two expensive looking recumbent bicycles, a treadmill, an antique dresser, an assortment of picnic coolers, a small spinet piano and a stack of winter snow tires. She worked her way along the passenger side of the car, moving objects aside so she could open the door and reach into the glove compartment. It took some doing but she finally found what she was looking for. But the windshield tag was on the driver's side. As soon as she began working her way down the driver's side of the car she saw a scrape that quickly grew into a wide dent. It ran from the back door to the front fender. The front headlight was protruding from the socket like a bulging eyeball. The front tire wasn't flat but it was low.

"Yes, I know," Elise called from the backseat of the limo, the door open partially.

"Was anyone hurt?"

"Just my pride." She closed the door.

Jan quickly checked the numbers on the registration paper against those on the tag under the windshield. Then she backed out of the garage, closed the overhead door and handed the paperwork to Elise.

"I know what you're thinking. Why didn't I have the dent fixed? It's a nice car and I shouldn't ignore the damage. It'll just rust."

"How did it happen?"

"I have no idea. I was turning left onto Commonwealth. Next thing I know I hear this hideous scraping sound and some guy in a delivery truck is cussing at me."

"Were you on the phone?"

"No."

"Did you have your eyes closed?" Jan pulled a quirky grin.

"No." Elise scowled up at her. "I told you, I'm not a good driver. It scares me. I decided not to fix it. If I drive it again I'll just wreck it again. So I let it sit here so I won't."

"But you're going to renew the insurance on it?"

"Well, yes. I own it. I'll insure it." She began composing an email to her agent on her cell phone.

As Jan headed for the highway south out of Boston, Elise explained what she would be doing in Chatham. She expected to be tied up at the site for a couple hours at least. Probably more. The threat of sleet overnight meant they would accomplish as much as possible before dark.

As soon as they arrived at the construction site Elise became embroiled in work. Jan ran an errand for her but stayed out of the way for the most part.

She watched as a crane lifted a huge crate from a flatbed truck and lowered it to crew members at the ready to ease it to the ground. The crate and its contents seemed to be the object of everyone's attention from the moment the truck pulled into the parking lot and the crane cozied up alongside. Once the crate was removed from the truck it was transferred inside the building and Jan lost sight of it. According to Elise it was a stained glass panel of a lighthouse overlooking the seashore commissioned by a wealthy donor in memory of those lost at sea during Hurricane Sandy. It was to be on permanent display in the lobby of the new medical office building.

Elise was also right about the time. It was well after sunset when she emerged from the building still wearing her hard hat. Jan hopped out when she saw her coming, a tired look on her face.

"How's it going, boss?"

"I thought they'd never get the framing attached. I wasn't leaving until the panel was installed and secure. I could just imagine it toppling over during the night and ending up a pile of glass chips all over the floor." She removed her hard hat, giving her hair a ruffle and a toss. "I'm exhausted. What time is it?"

"Six fifty-four."

Elise climbed in the front seat and closed the door, settling in as if that's where she intended to sit all along. "Is it okay if I ride up here?"

"Sure."

"Don't worry. I won't ask to drive," she teased.

"Don't worry. I won't let you."

"Now, where is Grayson Construction taking us to dinner?"

"There are several places along the highway back to Boston if you can wait about twenty minutes."

"We're not going back to Boston tonight," Elise said. "We're staying at the Chatham Harbor View Inn."

"I thought you finished installing the panel."

"The panel, yes. But tomorrow is the case and trim around it. I want to be here to sign off on it. It's too important to pass it off to a bunch of guys who think stained glass is what's left on the bar after you drink a Bloody Mary."

"I could drive you back down in the morning." Even Jan knew that sounded ridiculous.

"I've already made our reservations. You have a room on the ground floor that overlooks the ocean. It has a luxurious bathroom and a king-size bed. Breakfast is included in the morning from six to nine."

"And you?" Jan was suddenly very curious about how far away she would be.

"My room is down the hall." She turned to Jan as if seeking approval. "Is that okay?"

"Sounds fantastic. Ocean view, huh?"

"I wanted you to have a nice room. And I didn't want you to worry about privacy. Once you close your door you won't see anyone until the morning, I promise."

Elise's words were reassuring. But they were also disappointing and Jan had no idea why. She didn't expect anything to happen between them tonight. In fact, she was worried Elise might expect that and she wasn't sure how to diplomatically tell her no without seeming hostile or aloof.

"Shall we head for the inn and see what we find along the way?" Elise turned to Jan with a concerned frown. "If I say I'm hungry for pizza am I going to get looks?"

"Depends," Jan said, checking both ways then pulling into traffic. "Thick crust or thin? Red sauce or white? Veggie or meat lover's?"

"Choices. Hmmm." She thought a moment. "Thin crust, definitely thin crust. White sauce with spinach, mushrooms, mozzarella, sliced tomatoes and fresh basil leaves."

"That's a Margherita pizza. You sound very adamant. Seems like a reasonable request."

"And root beer. I like root beer with my pizza."

"That part I like."

"You don't like thin crust spinach pizza?" Elise asked.

"I agree with the thin crust part. But not the white sauce."

"You're a red sauce lover then."

"Yes, on pizza and pasta." Jan slowed as they approached a café. "Blue Fin Pizza. What do you think?"

"Let's try it. We can always walk out if we don't like it."

"You've actually done that? Walked out of a restaurant because you didn't like the looks of it?" Jan pulled into a parking spot under the lighted sign.

"Yes. Absolutely. Haven't you?" Elise unbuckled and climbed out without waiting for Jan.

"Once, but it was because the wait would have been over an hour."

Jan opened the door to the café and waited for Elise to enter.

"Mmmm, smells good in here. Like bread dough," Elise said, unbuttoning her coat and scanning the room. "Looks like a popular place to eat too."

"I think we place our order up here. Is that booth by the window okay? It seems to be the only one cleared off."

"I'll snag the booth, you order the pizza." She handed Jan her Visa card and gave her a stern look. "Use this. It's my Grayson expense account and I need receipts to show I was here."

Jan stood in line to order the pizza and drinks while Elise claimed their table. It was a noisy café full of families and couples enjoying dinner. A retro-vintage pinball machine and a skeeball table were both in use, apparently paid for by customer tokens.

"Root beer for the boss lady," Jan said and set two foam-topped mugs on the table. "And here's your tokens for skeeball." She placed the Visa card and four tokens in Elise's hand.

"Since I don't know how to play, here." She opened Jan's hand and gave them back.

"You roll the wooden ball up the table and make it hop into one of the rings. The middle rings are worth more. Not exactly a game that requires a lot of skill. You should try it sometime."

"Are you insinuating I have no athletic talent?" Elise took a drink of her root beer, leaving a foam moustache on her lip.

"No. Not at all."

"Well, I don't. I can't even swim." Elise dabbed a napkin across her lip.

"You live in a coastal state and you don't swim?"

"Nope. Never learned. My parents didn't think it was important. I don't think they can swim either. Do you swim?"

"Yes. At least, I used to. No wonder you didn't want to check out the dock up at that cabin on the lake."

"Correct."

"Number sixty-two," someone announced. "Order number sixty-two."

Jan slid out of the booth and went to collect their order.

"One thin crust with white sauce for you. One thin crust with red sauce for me." She placed the pizzas on the table along with a shaker of cheese and one of pepper flakes.

Elise pulled the slices apart and took a bite. She moaned softly as she chewed.

"Is it that good?" Jan asked as she dusted cheese and pepper flakes on her slice.

"The moan wasn't for the taste. It was because I got to choose."

"When didn't you get to choose your pizza?" Jan chuckled. It was hard to believe Elise wouldn't demand what she wanted on a pizza.

"It's silly. It's nothing." She sprinkled a little cheese on the slice and took another bite.

"Tell me."

"Okay, but you're going to think this is childish. Ginger used to order the pizza and she didn't like white sauce or thin crust. So we always had thick doughy crust and red sauce on supreme pizza."

"Why didn't you just get two small ones? Each one of you could have had your own." Jan looked down at the two pizzas they'd ordered.

"The place she liked to get pizza didn't have small ones. Just large and extra large."

"Okay, why not get two large and have leftovers? Or maybe alternate. One time her choice. Next time yours."

"See? I told you it was childish. There are lots of logical and reasonable solutions. It was just easier to let her have her way."

"To settle?"

"Yes."

"May I make an observation here?" Jan asked gently.

"I'm listening."

"I think Elise Grayson is a virgin." She took a bite, leaving Elise to ponder her statement.

It didn't take long before Elise burst out laughing. Then she leaned in and whispered so only Jan could hear.

"I assure you I am not a virgin."

"I think you are." Jan took another bite, a devilish twinkle in her eye.

"That's ludicrous." Elise folded her pizza slice into a roll and took a bite.

Jan watched Elise obviously mulling over what she had said.

"Why in the world would you think I'm a virgin? And please don't say that idiotic notion that only penile penetration can take a woman's virginity. That is so chauvinistic."

"I'm talking about emotional virginity. I think instead of committing to a relationship that fulfilled you, you settled for a relationship with Ginger. And I'm guessing it's always been that way for you."

"Possibly."

"I also think you were more humiliated and embarrassed by Ginger's cheating than brokenhearted about it."

"How would you feel if your girlfriend openly admitted she had slept with another woman? And not just slept with her but had an ongoing relationship with her? She wasn't the least bit ashamed or repentant about it. Like it was my fault." Elise's chin quivered ever so slightly.

"I think she was an idiot." Jan reached across the table and placed her hand on Elise's. "I can't believe anyone would do that to you. That's not what love is."

"Thank you." Elise drew a deep, cleansing breath then shifted on her cushion. "You know what? Move over." She slid out of the booth and in on Jan's side. "There's a particularly invasive spring in that bench and I'm not interested in having a relationship with it."

Jan scooted over but Elise's thigh still pressed up against hers.

"Do you want me to find another table?"

"No, this is fine." She broke off a piece of her pizza and set it on Jan's plate. "Here. Try the good stuff." Jan took a bite.

"I'd offer you mine but you said you didn't like red pizza sauce."

"Can I try it? I'd hate to pass judgment without benefit of a sample." Elise leaned against Jan's shoulder and watched as she tore off a slice.

"Cheese?" Jan asked, poised to sprinkle.

"Yes. But no peppers."

Jan scattered the cheese then held the slice up for Elise to take, but Elise opened her mouth instead, ready to receive a bite. Jan obliged, feeding her the point of the slice.

"Hmmm, hey, that is good." She chewed and swallowed then opened her mouth for Jan to feed her another bite.

Jan offered another but Elise shook her head. "Nope, that's enough. I'm full."

Jan could feel Elise's thigh bumping against hers. Every time an electric shock raced up her body, bouncing from one sensory nerve to another like the silver ball in the pinball machine.

Elise heard laughing and glanced over at the skeeball machine. "Looks like somebody won," she said, watching a school-age girl jumping up and down with delight.

"You really can't lose at skeeball."

"It involves a ball and a certain degree of hand-eye coordination. Yes, I probably could."

"Slide out." Jan motioned for her to climb out of the booth. "I think the boss lady needs to spend her tokens."

"You're kidding. It's a game for kids."

"Not necessarily. Come on. I'll show you how to play."

"You play." Elise slid out. Jan took her hand and pulled her toward the now vacant machine.

Jan dropped a token in the slot. Nine softball size wooden balls were released and rolled down the shoot with a clatter.

"This is super simple. You roll a ball up the incline. It's sort of like bowling but instead of knocking down pins the ball will hop into one of the holes. The idea is to collect as many points as possible. The smaller the hole, the more it's worth." She handed Elise a ball then stepped back. "Don't worry. You can't look bad doing this. There's no skill involved at all. Just heave-ho."

"That from a woman who already knows how to do this. You obviously haven't experienced my athletic inability." Elise stood at the machine, rubbing her hands around the ball. She took aim and heaved it but it wasn't nearly hard enough. It rolled down the table, failed to hop over the incline and rolled back to her. "I thought you said I couldn't look bad doing this," she pouted, catching the ball before it fell on the floor. She placed the ball in Jan's hand. "Here. You do it."

"Try again. Give it a little more oomph." Jan gave it back and positioned Elise in front of the machine. "Full arm swing this time."

Elise tried again. This time the ball headed diagonally for the corner, hopped over the incline and fell into the scoreless slot. She turned to Jan with a disgruntled look.

"I'm glad you have a trade to fall back on." Jan chuckled and took another ball from the rack. She placed the ball in Elise's hand, positioned her at the machine and stood behind her. She put one hand on Elise's waist, the other guiding her arm. "Now swing nice and straight."

"Are you sure I have to do this?"

"Yes. Consider it a maturation process." Neither could hide her amusement and chuckled at the fun. "And remember, the more points you get, the more tickets will pop out of the machine. The more tickets you have, the bigger your prize will be."

"What kind of prize am I working toward?"

"There are lots of good choices. A stick of gum or maybe a plastic yo-yo."

"I always say you can never have too many plastic yo-yos." Elise allowed Jan to swing her arm back and forth. With Jan's help, Elise released the ball and sent it flying down the incline. It jumped the end of the barrier and disappeared inside the largest ring, scoring only ten points. "Hey, I got something."

"The object is to get the ball in that little hole in the middle. The one that says fifty."

"It's too small. No one can get the ball in there."

Jan rolled one of the balls down the table. It immediately jumped into the middle ring, adding fifty points to the total.

"Yes, you can. Swing your arm straight back and forth, right beside your body."

Jan stood behind her, guiding her arm. She could feel Elise's bottom snuggled up against her. Elise didn't seem to mind Jan's body so close or Jan's arm encircling her in a cradled embrace. But Jan was all too aware of what was within her grasp, enough that she felt her heart race. Elise finally released the ball. It rolled up the incline and hopped into the twenty point ring.

"How am I doing, coach?"

"Better. Much better. Are you ready to try it on your own?" Jan handed her a ball.

"Okay but I make no promises." Elise rolled a ball and seemed surprised it too hopped into the twenty point ring without any help.

"There you go." Jan discreetly wiped the nervous perspiration from her upper lip having caused it from the supple feel of Elise's body against her own.

Elise continued to roll the balls until she had used all nine. As soon as the last one disappeared several red tickets clicked out of a slot.

"Okay. Now it's your turn," Elise said brightly and pulled Jan in front of the machine. "Show me what you've got, kid."

Jan dropped in a token. It took her a moment to find a comfortable stance but once she began she rolled the balls with nearly robotic consistency. All but three of them hopped into the fifty point ring.

"Wow. Look at all the tickets," Elise said, watching the strip of red tickets flow out of the slot and onto the floor.

"Your turn." Jan moved aside with an awkward step. "I'm going to quit while I'm ahead."

"I think one game is enough for me too."

"Now you get to claim your prize." Jan tore off the strip of tickets and handed them to Elise. She pointed to the prize counter, where a teenager waited to redeem them. "What's it going to be? Plastic kazoo? Rub-off tattoo? Rubber ducky with sunglasses?" she teased. Her hand rested comfortably in the small of Elise's back as they stared into the case like kids at a candy store.

"The whistle looks interesting."

"Wait, I see the perfect prize and you have just enough tickets." Jan pointed at a key ring with a tiny seashell attached. "I think you should get that. Anyone who drives as much as you do should have a classy key ring."

Elise burst out laughing.

"You're right. Absolutely. That's exactly what I want." She grinned and handed over her tickets. "It's perfect. I'll always be able to remember my skeeball lessons at the Cape. Thank you."

"My pleasure."

"Shall we go?" Elise suggested as the noise in the café got louder.

"Yes. Good idea."

It had begun to spit rain, the wind whipping it sideways. Elise clung to Jan's arm as they crossed the parking lot.

"It's getting cold," Elise said with a shiver as she slid into the front seat.

"I'll have the car heated up in no time."

Jan started the engine and turned on the seat heaters. She followed the directions to the inn and pulled into the graveled lot in front of a two-story frame building. It had dormers and shutters and all the welcoming colonial charm found up and down Cape Cod. The back of the inn faced the ocean. From somewhere in the darkness came the sound of waves. Jan carried the suitcases into the lobby while Elise checked in at the desk.

"You have room eighteen. Corner room at the end of the hall on the right," Elise said, handing Jan a key. "Can you believe it? Actual room keys. Not cards you have to swipe. I'm in room twenty-one. Down the hall the other way."

Jan pocketed the key and set her suitcase next to the desk for safekeeping. She started down the hall to the left carrying Elise's bag.

"Twenty-one?" she asked.

"Yes, but I can do that." Elise followed.

"I've got it. You unlock the door."

Elise opened the door and snapped on the light. It was a large room with a four-poster bed and a bay window that looked out the back of the inn. Jan set the suitcase inside the door and stood in the doorway, her hand on the doorknob.

"Anything else?" she asked.

"No," Elise said as she scanned the room. "Thank you for carrying that for me. Let me know if your room is okay. If you don't like it we can change it."

"Elise, I'm sure it will be fine. Don't worry. So long as I have a bed to sleep in I'm good."

"I guess I'll see you in the morning then. Eight o'clock?"

"I'll meet you in the breakfast room at eight. Good night." Jan backed out and pulled the door closed.

"Good night," Elise called after her. "Call me if you need anything."

Jan started back up the hall but hesitated, leaning heavily against the wall. She and Elise had had a lovely evening together, enjoying each other's company. They were growing closer. She couldn't deny it. She'd love to take Elise to bed, to lay her down and feel her warmth and gentleness all through the night. She regretted not suggesting she stay. Before the accident she would have gladly accepted her Thanksgiving invitation. But not now. She had seen that look of disgust and horror in Allie's eyes. She didn't want to see it in Elise's eyes. Her gorgeous, radiant, sparkling eyes.

Jan's room was just as nice as Elise's, maybe bigger. It had corner windows and a sliding door that led onto the patio. The bathroom had support bars and a large shower with a bench. She might have called it handicapped accessible but she preferred to call it luxurious. And it was very generous of Elise to make such accommodations.

"Nice expense account, Ms. Grayson," she said as she touched the thick robe hanging on the back of the bathroom door. She undressed and removed her leg and liner. The stump was red and swollen, but it often was right after she removed the leg. She sat on the edge of the bed in her underwear and massaged it, stroking moisturizer up and down over the scars. Once she had worked it in she pulled out her phone and sent Elise a text.

The room is great. The bed is comfortable. The lotion even smells good. Plus I have a terrific view toward the ocean. Thanks again.

She had just plugged in her phone charger when she received a reply from Elise.

I'm glad you like it. Only the best for my chauffeur. I hope you sleep well. Seems like you're sure far away though. She added a dejected smiley face.

Jan wasn't sure how to reply. But she was right. Elise Grayson seemed miles away. Jan flopped back on the bed and stared up at the ceiling. Elise had planted seeds she was going to have trouble ignoring. She might only have one good leg but she had more than enough libido. What was between her legs hadn't been damaged in the accident. It was all in fine working order.

It was after ten and Jan still hadn't been able to close her eyes, much less sleep. She pulled on a pair of faded jeans, zipped her jacket over the thermal Henley she wore as pajamas, pulled herself up onto her crutches and stepped out onto the patio. The security yard lights from the inn illuminated the beach enough so she could make out the white breakers in the distance as they rolled ashore. A heavy, cold mist filled the air. Winter in New England, she thought. The smell of the ocean. The wind, crisp and cutting. An occasional feathery snow. She loved it. She leaned her armpits on her crutches and buried her hands in her jacket pockets, drinking in a deep breath of it.

"Glad your room is okay," Elise said.

Jan snapped a look down the patio to where Elise stood at the railing. She hadn't noticed her before or hadn't considered she'd be out on the patio this late. Elise was still dressed in her business attire but she was wearing slippers.

"Yes. It's wonderful. How long have you been out here?" Jan thought about stepping back inside but it was too late. Elise was already looking at the empty denim leg of her jeans.

"Not long. I thought maybe a little fresh air might help me sleep." Elise folded her arms over her sweater.

"I think I need to apologize for what I said earlier. I had no right to judge your relationship with Ginger. I didn't mean to offend you."

"You didn't. Everything you said was true. I don't think I ever truly committed to her. Or to anyone else I've dated." She smiled over at Jan. "Although I don't consider myself a virgin."

"I shouldn't have said anything."

"It's hard to admit a relationship was created out of desperation instead of love."

"Did you ever love Ginger?"

Elise gazed out toward the breaking surf. "No. I told myself I did. I told myself I was supposed to love her. But I don't think I ever felt that bond with her. How about Allie?"

"What about her?"

"Were you committed to her? Were you in one of those deep complete relationships?"

"I thought we were on our way to one. Maybe. We hadn't known each other that long when I had the accident. Less than a year. After the accident everything changed. I'm the one who broke it off. I didn't want or need a full-time babysitter. Haven't we stomped these grapes before?"

"I'm trying to understand." Elise came to stand by her.

"Understand what? That I don't need someone to take care of me?" Jan replied, teetering slightly on the crutches.

"How about someone who cares? Don't you need that?" Elise stared out at the ocean as a single tear trailed down her cheek.

Jan stood behind her and closed her jacket around Elise, folding her arms over her.

"Don't cry for me, Elise. I'm going to be okay. I can take care of myself."

"I'm not. I'm crying for myself because you won't let me in." She turned and looked up at Jan. "I want you to so badly." She looked down at Jan's pant leg then reached up and stroked Jan's cheek. "Please let me into your life," she whispered.

The chilly mist suddenly became a cold rain, blowing onshore and splattering against the windows.

"Elise, you make it sound like I don't have feelings for you. I do. More than I can express, I do. But I can't offer you what you deserve."

Before she could say any more Elise kissed her. She folded her arms around Jan's neck and pulled herself against her, rain be damned. It was a complete kiss, the kind of kiss Jan had dreamed of since that first moment she saw Elise Grayson step out of the elevator months ago. *This gorgeous woman, with her tongue in my mouth, is giving herself to me with no reservations.* It had been a long time since Jan had felt these kinds of emotions, but there they were, racing through her body and she didn't know how to fight them. Or even if she wanted to. When Elise pulled away Jan took her face in her hands and brought Elise's lips back to hers.

"Come inside," Elise whispered and backed them through the door, allowing Jan room to manipulate her crutches through the opening. The wind-driven rain whipped at the curtains as Elise slid the door closed. She turned to Jan and waited while she balanced on one leg and removed her jacket. She didn't interfere. She seemed to know Jan wanted to demonstrate her capability. Elise snapped off the light, bathing them in shadows. She stood before Jan, looking up into her eyes, swallowing back what seemed to be nervous apprehension.

"You don't understand," Jan said softly.

"Shh." Elise closed her eyes and looked away, then back, grasping for words. "I understand you want me as much as I want you. But I don't know how to do this. I'm forty-four years old and I don't know how to ask. I've always waited. My whole life I've waited. I don't want to wait anymore. How do I ask for what I want?" She asked her questions with an innocence that melted Jan's heart.

"You don't have to ask. You're a beautiful woman. Your lover should know." Jan brushed the rain-dampened hair from Elise's forehead. "She can read it in your eyes." Jan drew her closer as she sat down on the bed, setting the crutches aside. "She should always be able to read your needs, just like I can read yours now." Elise stood between Jan's thighs as they kissed. Jan slipped the sweater over Elise's head then unhooked her bra and let it drop.

There was no hesitation as Jan pulled her onto the bed, Elise melting into her arms. Jan cupped her hands over her eager breasts then stroked the long planes of her abdomen. With two fingers she released the button and zipper and worked Elise's pants down over her hips, their lips and tongues and mouths devouring each other.

Elise reached for the zipper on Jan's jeans but she pushed her hand away. Elise slid her hands up under Jan's shirt, seeking one of her erect nipples. Jan didn't stop her and eagerly waited for her to find the other one as well. Elise seemed to know where her boundaries were drawn and she didn't cross them.

Jan pressed Elise's arms to the pillow as she kissed first one breast then the other. Elise's moans and sighs guided Jan's sensuous journey down her body until she found that place where only the walls of the room could contain her. Elise released a guttural shriek as Jan inhaled her wetness.

"Oh my God, yes. You absolutely know. Yes." Elise lay on the pillow, writhing in ecstasy as Jan brought her toward orgasm; slowly, methodically, until rapture was inevitable. "I never felt anything like that before," she gasped breathlessly. "Never. Never."

Jan crawled up beside her, pulling the covers over them.

"You are one sweet woman," Jan whispered, drawing her finger up from Elise's crotch.

"I am your sweet woman." She snuggled against Jan's side. "Are you mine?"

"I know what you're asking but no, please don't. I don't want you to."

"Sweetie, I don't mind what it looks like. I really, truly don't. I know you have only part of that leg but it doesn't bother me."

"Well, it bothers me." Jan sat up and swung her legs out of bed. "I can't let you do that."

"Why? The lights are off. I will be gentle. I promise."

"I don't want you to see it or touch it." Jan glared back at her. "You don't want to see it or touch it, trust me. It's the only way I know how to do this."

"Sweetheart, I'm not Allie."

"I don't care. It's not happening." Jan struggled to retrieve her crutches and made her way into the bathroom.

"I'm not leaving," Elise called after her. "I won't ask again but I'm not leaving. Come back to bed. I promise not to touch or look. You can wear your jeans to bed if you want but please come back."

Jan opened the door and stood in the doorway, balancing on her crutches as she dried her hands on a towel.

"Promise?"

"I promise." Elise folded the covers open and patted the mattress. "Come back to bed."

Jan turned out the bathroom light and climbed into bed.

"Aren't you going to at least take off your shirt?" Elise asked, snuggling next to her and tugging at the hem of her top.

"Go to sleep, Ms. Grayson, or I'll go sleep in the car," Jan teased but there was half-truth in her tone. "Good night."

There was a long silence. Jan assumed Elise had drifted off to sleep.

"Is it okay if I say my chauffeur is one very talented woman?" Elise whispered then kissed Jan's cheek before rolling over and going to sleep.

CHAPTER SIXTEEN

Jan was already up, showered and dressed when Elise stretched and yawned herself awake.

"Good morning," she said, watching Jan tie her shoes. She was wearing her prosthetic and had black socks covering both ankles. "You're up early."

"Good morning. Did you sleep well?" Jan stood and pulled on her black suit jacket.

"Yes, I did. Did you?"

"Yep. Slept like a baby," Jan said as she stood at the mirror, combing her hair.

"Oh, then that restless person next to me wasn't you? I thought I was the one with the insomnia issues."

"I'm sorry if I kept you awake."

"You didn't. Your little moans and groans are cute. Gives me something to look forward to," Elise said with a lusty grin.

"The moans and groans are probably because sometimes I have dreams."

"You mean sometimes you have nightmares. The moans and groans didn't sound like happy sounds, sweetie."

"Yeah." Jan heaved a sigh.

"Bad ones?"

"Sometimes."

"About the accident?"

"That's just it. I never see the accident. I have no idea what happened. My dreams go blank before whatever happened happens."

"I imagine it's both scary and frustrating." Elise propped herself up on one elbow and tucked the covers over her bare chest. "Do the doctors think you'll ever break through that veil of darkness to see how you lost your leg?"

"They don't know. Some people regain their memory, at least parts of it. Some people never remember traumatic events that their brains have blocked out." Jan loaded her toiletries into the zipper pouch then folded the crutches on top of her suitcase. "Are you going to get up or stay in bed all day?"

Elise just smiled and winked.

"I thought you needed to be back at the construction site this morning."

"I do but I'm making the most of a very desirable situation. How am I doing?"

"Very nicely. I for one am enjoying the view." Jan leaned down and kissed Elise's exposed cleavage. "But it's almost eight o'clock. What time do you need to be there?"

"You're kidding." Elise sat straight up in bed. "It can't be eight o'clock. I'm always awake by six." She looked at the clock on the bedside table. "No, no, no. It can't be eight already."

She scrambled out of bed and pulled on her slacks and sweater. With her panties and bra wadded in her hand she rushed out the door and down the hall, promising to meet Jan in the dining room in fifteen minutes. It was closer to twenty minutes when Elise grabbed a bagel and a foam cup of coffee as she hurried out to the car.

The crew was already at work on the protective framing for the stained glass panel when she walked inside the building, her professional demeanor once again on display. She wished she could have leisurely visited with Jan over breakfast. Maybe she could have relieved some of her anxiety over their night together. But there wasn't time.

A few minor problems kept her on-site for several hours. By the time she and Jan started back for Boston a drizzly rain, interspersed with occasional snow began to fall. The weather delays meant they would hit rush hour traffic. Elise rode in the front seat but preferred to keep her eyes on her phone or laptop. She wasn't comfortable watching the bumper-to-bumper congestion through nasty conditions. Jan was a good driver but that didn't mean Elise wanted to watch.

"You don't mind if I do a little work in the car, do you?" she asked, hiding the real reason she wasn't interested in pleasant idle conversation.

"It's fine with me. You're the boss." Jan placed her hand on Elise's thigh reassuringly. "Don't worry. I won't make you drive in this weather."

They rode along to soft music on the radio. It was white noise. Neither of them seemed to be paying much attention to it. An incoming email chimed on Elise's phone and she opened it.

"Oh, sure. Now you reply," she grumbled and laughed at the materials estimate.

"What's so funny? Trouble at work?" Jan adjusted the wipers as the rain thickened.

"Not trouble. I requested a quote on some materials for a remodel and never heard back. Now I don't need them and I get the quote. Go figure." She shook her head disgustedly as she read down through the email. "I wouldn't be using this supplier anyway. He jacked up the shipping to double his profits."

"Was it for some big project you're already working on or one you're just planning?"

"It was a small project. Charlie Tuttle's little A-frame cabin at Lake Winnipesaukee."

"Sure. The one you said he decided not to remodel. You said he'd probably just sell it."

"That's right. I wanted a quote on an on-demand hot water system like you mentioned. And a whole-house emergency generator. I couldn't imagine Charlie wanted to be out in the woods with his grandkids without adequate backup systems."

"It sounded like he expected an awful lot of expansion for such a little cabin."

"Exactly." She deleted the email. "But I'm glad we got to spend some time there. It was very picturesque." She gave Jan a sideways glance. "Didn't you think so?"

"Let's see. No water, no central heat, no food and no functioning bathroom. Yes, it was interesting. Oh, let's not forget the bugs and cobwebs."

"Not to mention the long hike up and down the path and the fact your leg was bothering you." Elise bumped Jan's arm playfully. "It was being there with you that I enjoyed."

A slow grin curled the corners of Jan's mouth. "I did too."

"Okay, Jan. I have a very serious question for you and I expect a serious answer," Elise asked, with a challenging arch to her brow. "It'll be Christmas in two weeks and I need to know what you want Santa to put under the tree."

"A bag of jelly beans," Jan replied instantly.

"I said a serious answer."

"I want a bag of jelly beans."

"Well, too bad. You don't get one. How about a coffeemaker? One of those that grinds the beans then brews the coffee all in one machine."

"No. I don't make coffee at home."

"Okay, no coffeemaker. What size do you wear? I saw the most gorgeous leather jacket in the window of Neiman Marcus the other day. It would look great on you. Light tan with leather-covered buttons."

"No. Sounds like one I already have."

"I have another idea but I don't want it to sound stupid. Can you wear boots? Leather with an ankle strap? Very sexy."

"No, I want jelly beans. What do you want?"

"Jan, I want to get you something for Christmas. Something special. Tell me what you want."

"Thank you, but I really don't need anything. Promise me you won't buy something expensive."

"Why can't I buy my friends and employees Christmas gifts?"

"Promise me," Jan said sternly. "No big purchases. I swear, I'll send it back."

"Okay, but you're taking all the fun out of it."

The snow became thicker as they entered downtown Boston. The snowplows were out clearing the main arteries but Elise's street hadn't been touched yet.

"Do you want to come in? I'll fix us a sandwich or something, assuming my bread isn't green and fuzzy." Elise was following Jan as she carried her suitcase up the front steps.

"Not this evening. I need to get the car back before the roads are impassable."

"I have to agree. I don't want to worry about you driving on icy roads. We'll do it another time."

"Good night," Jan said from the doorway. She hesitated a moment then came back to Elise and kissed her before going out into the cold.

Elise watched from the window as Jan descended the steps, leaning heavily on the railing for support. Elise placed her hand on the windowpane, as if she could touch Jan's gentleness and vulnerability. With all her being Elise wished Jan had stayed.

* * *

"How was the trip to the Cape?" Lorraine asked as she followed Elise down the hall the next morning.

"Very productive. The stained glass panel has been installed and secured. I don't much care for the tile color in the restrooms but it's what they ordered and what they like." She peeled out of her coat and scarf as she opened her office door.

"That's not what I meant. How did the chauffeuring go? Any problems there?"

"Nope. No problems."

"You're not going to tell me the details, are you?"

"Correct. I'm not." Elise sat down at her desk and turned on her computer, ready for a busy day's work. "Can you find me the final corrections for the Hathaway project? I had an email from Mike. He's sure the closets in the corner offices aren't large enough."

Elise committed herself to work even though her thoughts occasionally strayed to Jan and their overnight together. Lorraine didn't need to know any of that. The smile that lit Elise's face was hers alone to enjoy. What she didn't enjoy was Jan's job sending her out of town for three days, chauffeuring a group of foreign dignitaries to Washington DC and back.

"Were you expecting a special delivery package?" Lorraine asked, carrying a box into Elise's office.

"I have no idea. What is it?" Elise said from the table where she was measuring a set of blueprints.

"I didn't open it because it says personal and private." Lorraine set the box on the table but stayed, her curiosity obviously getting the best of her.

"What's the return address?"

"It doesn't have one. It was delivered by messenger."

"If they're soil samples they should go to the lab. If they're color samples they need to go to Sherry." Elise opened the box and peeled away the tissue paper. It was neither soil nor color samples. The box contained a soft cuddly teddy bear wearing a hard hat and denim coveralls. The words Dirt Lady were handwritten on the front of the hard hat. The card attached read, *Tiny gifts from the heart, XOXO Jan.*

"Isn't that cute!" Lorraine said, trying to read the card in Elise's hand. "Who's it from?"

"It's from Jan." Elise clutched the teddy bear to her chest and read the card again.

"Really? From the chauffeur?"

"Yes. And I love it." Elise grinned wide enough to squeeze out a tear that trailed down her cheek.

"Are you surprised?"

"I'm surprised she sent a teddy bear, yes. It means she cares. I wasn't sure. But she does. She truly does." Elise danced the teddy bear over to her desk and placed him squarely in the middle, facing her chair. "Lorraine," she gasped. "What am I going to get her? I've got to give her something. What?"

"I'm sure you'll find something online you can order."

"That's just it. I can't. I promised not to buy her an expensive gift. If I do she said she'd return it. And I believe her. What can I get her?"

"Wow. You can't buy the gift? That takes it out of your wheelhouse, doesn't it? Sounds like you're going to have to make something. How about a wallet made out of duct tape? Macramé plant hangar? I know—macaroni necklace." Lorraine's laugh escalated with each suggestion.

"Will you be serious? I need to think of something I can give her that she'll like that doesn't cost a lot of money."

"You could always give her something of yours she's admired. But I'm guessing you've already done that." Lorraine snickered as she headed back to her desk.

Elise spent several minutes composing a text to Jan, thanking her for the gift and the sentiment but trying not to gush, to embarrass her at work.

* * *

Once Jan was back in Boston it took two days before their schedules allowed them a dinner together. Elise heard an incoming text chime on her phone but finished reading an email before she glanced at it. It was from Jan and all it said was *Hello*. She looked up from her work to see Jan standing in the doorway with her cell phone in her hand. She was wearing jeans and a leather jacket over a gray sweater.

"Hello," Elise said, leaning back in her chair to admire the tall woman.

"Hi. Am I interrupting something? You said to come up to your office, but you look busy. I can come back later." She turned as if to leave.

"No, wait." Elise hurried around her desk. "Come in here. I haven't seen you in a week. I missed you." She gave Jan a hug and a quick kiss.

"You look good, boss lady. I like the red sweater. Turn around." Jan watched as Elise turned.

"We had a Christmas party during lunch. I decided to be festive. Is it too much?"

"Absolutely not. Keep turning." Jan grinned fiendishly until she was interrupted by her cell phone. She unhooked it from her waistband and read the screen but didn't answer it.

"You can answer it. I don't mind."

Jan answered the call. She listened, then hung up and replaced the phone on her waistband.

"Wrong number or telemarketer?" Elise joked.

"Neither. It was an automated call reminding me of my doctor's appointment."

"Oh?"

"It's just a checkup."

"For your leg?"

"Yeah. I might need a new gel liner. You have to replace them every now and then. It's no big deal."

"I read about them online. The gel liner is the part that goes over your stump. It's custom-made to fit over your leg and fits down into the socket, right?"

"Yes."

"Did it take a long time to get used to wearing it?"

"Not really. It's learning balance that takes a little time."

"Do you need someone to go with you to the doctor?"

"Nope. It'll probably be a quick visit, then I'll have an appointment for a new casting. I usually spend more time in the waiting room than in with the doctor."

"I'll go with you if you want me to," Elise said reassuringly.

"Elise, it's no big deal. Honest. I'll be fine."

"But you'll let me know if you need something, won't you?"

"It's routine stuff, babe. Routine. Are you ready to go to dinner? You're sure I can't take us out someplace? The Pasta Barn reopened last week after the remodel."

"No, I told you. I'm cooking dinner. Well, I'm preparing dinner. For all you know I cooked everything from scratch. Let me get my coat." Elise shut down her laptop and loaded it into her briefcase. "It's a little early for dinner so if you don't mind I need to run by our equipment lot for a minute. Is that okay with you?"

"Sure."

They walked three blocks to where Jan had parked her car. Elise put her briefcase and purse in the backseat then buckled her seat belt. She noticed a backpack on the floor behind Jan's seat.

"I'm hoping that bag back there is what you'll need to spend the night. Is it?"

"Are you sure you want me to?"

"Yes, I want you to, and yes, I know your boundaries. But we can have dinner, then see what happens. No pressure. I have no expectations."

"Then yes, that's my jammies. And my crutches."

Jan took Elise's hand in hers and rested them on the console as they rode along. It took forty minutes to cross the river and wind their way to Grayson's lot where all the equipment was kept. It was surrounded by a ten foot tall chain link fence with coiled razor wire along the top. Jan pulled inside the fence with the sign that read Private Property, Grayson Construction, No Trespassing. She parked next to the brick building.

"Shall I just wait here?" Jan asked.

"No, come with me. There's Seth. He's our lot superintendent. He knows every piece of equipment we own. Everything from excavators to cement mixers."

A man in insulated coveralls was climbing out of the cab of a small white skid loader. He had parked it next to a pile of snow.

"Nice to see you, Ms. Grayson," he said with a jolly smile and moved a toothpick to the other side of his mouth. He had a scruffy beard and wore a stocking cap under his yellow hard hat. He turned his smile to Jan, looking her up and down.

"Seth, this is Jan Chase. She's the one I was talking with you about."

"Hello, Ms. Chase." He offered his left hand to Jan. The sleeve of his coveralls extended over his other hand, hiding all but the tip of a shiny mechanical hook.

"Hello." Jan noticed his prosthesis but didn't linger over it.

"How do you like the new toy, Ms. G?" he said, nodding toward the Bobcat. "It just arrived yesterday. Hardly had time to dirty the tires."

"What do you think, Jan?" Elise asked.

"It's like the ones at the construction site in Springfield. They look like fun. Is that the kind you know how to drive?"

"Yes." Seth laughed as soon as Elise said it. "Okay, I'm not an expert. But I can at least move it from one spot to another without running over people and small animals. Which brings me to why we're here. You said I couldn't *buy* you a gift, so I'm giving you something better."

"Which is?"

"Lessons. How would you like to learn how to operate a skid loader? Seth is going to teach you. What do you say?"

"Really? You mean it? You really think I could operate one of these?" She couldn't take her eyes off it.

"Sure. If I can do it you can do it. They aren't hard to learn, are they, Seth?"

"Nope. Easy as pie." He looked down at Jan's leg. "Nothing to it."

"Trust me, I wouldn't have offered if I thought you couldn't." Elise gave her an encouraging pat on the back. "I'd teach you but Seth is better at it than I am. He taught me."

"Don't they have foot pedals though?" Jan asked.

"Yep," Seth said, heading toward the machine. "They also have two hand controls. But I think you can handle it. If you know how to drive a car, I can teach you how to drive one of these babies."

Though hesitant, Jan finally climbed in the cab. Elise watched as Seth showed her how to lower the safety bar and start the engine. Elise couldn't hear everything Seth was telling her but she could see Jan listening intently with eager enthusiasm. She was a quick study. It took only a few minutes before she seemed confident enough to try it on her own. She looked over at Elise and gave a thumbs-up then raised the scoop, something Elise knew required the use of her left foot. Seth pointed to the small pile of snow then at a bare spot against the fence. It didn't take long for her to learn the delicate technique to scoop and move the snow. With each successful pass Elise cheered and clapped. Like a kid with a new toy, Jan continued until the little pile was moved and the job was done. It wasn't perfect but it was better than Elise had done her first time. Jan rolled to a stop and turned off the engine.

"How'd I do?" She raised the bar and hoisted herself out of the cab mostly by her arms.

"I'm impressed. Did you have fun?"

"Yes, I did. That was great. Wow, I can actually drive a Bobcat. Wait till I tell my dad I'm a heavy equipment operator." Jan grinned. "Thanks, Seth. And thank you too."

"I'll go put it away if you're done with it," Seth said and climbed in the machine. He turned the key to start the engine but it backfired, startling both Elise and Jan. "Oops," he laughed and tried again.

The loud bang seemed to grab Jan's attention and hold it fixedly. She continued to stare at the Bobcat as Seth drove it across the lot. Even after he parked it and turned off the engine she stared mindlessly at it.

"Are you ready, sweetheart? Shall we go have dinner?" Elise said, touching her arm to get her attention. "You can come back and drive it again anytime you want."

"What?" Jan's eyes were still on the loader. She seemed oblivious to her surroundings.

It wasn't until Elise took her arm and pulled her toward the car that Jan returned to reality. Jan started the car and headed out the gate, tossing one last look in the rearview mirror.

"What is it you see back there?"

"Nothing. I think."

They drove back across the river. Jan appeared preoccupied, her forehead furrowed in thought.

It was just after seven o'clock when Jan popped the cork on a wine bottle and Elise served their dinner, a meal she had pre-ordered. They sat at the counter on tall stools as they enjoyed their dinner together, laughing and chatting. It was after ten when they shared a piece of raspberry chocolate cheesecake, mashing their forks on the crumbs and moaning over its goodness. Twice during the meal Jan's focus drifted across the room with the same distracted and vague look she'd had after driving the Bobcat. When Elise asked about it Jan insisted it was nothing; She was just a little tired.

"I'm no expert but did something at the equipment yard bother you? Ever since you drove the Bobcat and heard it backfire you've been a little preoccupied about something."

"You noticed that, huh?"

"Was it Seth's arm? I thought you'd find a common bond with him while you learned how to play with the loader."

"How did he lose it? Was it an accident at work?"

"No, actually he was born with just one arm and what he calls a flipper. He said he was a thalidomide baby. But he's never let it slow him down. He's worked for us for twenty years. He can operate every piece of equipment we've got. I told him you were mesmerized by the little loaders working around the hospital site in Springfield. When I asked if he thought you could drive one he said, and I quote, hells bells yes. Actually, he said another word but I'd rather not repeat it. Did it make you uncomfortable to be around him?"

"No. I admire anyone who has similar challenges and conquers them," Jan said as she helped rinse and load the dishwasher, scraping the plates into the sink.

"The disposal switch is on the left."

Jan snapped it on. It was loud, louder than a normal garbage disposal and it startled Jan for a moment. She quickly turned it off.

"I'm sorry about that. I need to have that replaced but I'm never home long enough to have the repairman come do it."

Jan stood staring down into the sink, frozen by some unseen force.

"Jan, are you all right?"

"Did you see that?"

"See what?" Elise came to look at whatever had captured Jan's attention. "I don't see anything."

"I guess it was nothing. But I swear I saw…" She shook her head and turned away from the sink.

"You can leave that. I'll run the disposal later. Shall we go upstairs? It's getting late." Elise picked up Jan's backpack and trotted up the stairs.

There was a moment of hesitation on Jan's face but she seemed to resolve whatever it was and started up the steps.

"You'll be glad to know I'm having an elevator installed. The pantry is large enough to have it divided and a small elevator put in that will open onto the upstairs hall. I don't know why someone hasn't done it before. The stairs are so long." Elise smiled down at Jan from the top.

"Thank you for even suggesting it, but no. Absolutely not. Your home is perfect just like it is. It doesn't need an elevator. I can do stairs. Knowing you're upstairs waiting for me is all the assistance I'll need." It took a minute or two and a grimace Elise had seen before, but Jan finally made it upstairs and into the bedroom.

"What is that?" Jan asked when she stepped out of the bathroom a few minutes later, drying her hands on a towel. She was still dressed in her jeans and sweater. Elise had just pulled on her pajama top and was in her panties, searching through her dresser drawer for a suitable pair of pajama pants.

"Oh, the music? The previous owners had an elaborate intercom and security system installed." Elise went to the control panel on the wall just inside the bedroom door. "I can see who's at the front door or talk to any room in the house, including the garage. I can even turn up the furnace from my desk at work if I want. Very state-of-the-art, or so I was told. It also plays music. Ginger programmed it to play soothing stuff in the evening. Sort of white noise. She said it relaxed her." Elise smirked. "Not that I ever saw. Anyway, it comes on at nine and off at ten thirty. I'll turn it off."

"No, leave it. It's nice."

"Are you sure? I've gotten used to it. Sometimes I don't even hear it."

"I like the music and I like your outfit." Jan grinned at Elise's lacy black panties.

"I wasn't ready yet." She hurried back to the dresser to find the rest of her pajamas but Jan snagged her and pulled her into her arms. She started to sway to the music.

"You look fine just the way you are."

"If you say so." Elise slipped her arms around Jan's neck and looked up at her adoringly as they moved ever so gently. They weren't graceful dance steps but Jan did her best to keep them drifting around the room without losing her balance.

"Thank you for dinner by the way."

"You're welcome. Thank you for not commenting on the fact I didn't really cook it." Elise rested her head against Jan's shoulder as they danced.

"We had dinner together. Wasn't that the point?"

"Yes. Most definitely." Elise snuggled a kiss against Jan's cheek. "Do you think your family will share you with me on Christmas? I'd love to dance with you around the Christmas tree. I'll wear my red sweater and you can wear a Santa hat."

"They might if I was going to be here, but I'll be gone for four days."

"On Christmas?" Elise stood back from her, staring at her in shock.

"I know. I've heard it all from my mother and my sister. But Christmas is a busy time for us and I'm low on the seniority totem pole. I'm taking some foreign hotshots to New York City and back again."

"But Christmas?" Elise whined.

"If I told you how much I was getting paid you might not give me that look. Ninety-six hours of vacation overtime isn't hard to take."

"I understand, but I don't have to like it." Elise came back to her and held Jan a little tighter.

"No, you don't. Would you settle for New Year's instead?"

"Yes. And with great anticipation."

Jan winced and stumbled slightly.

"Maybe it's time I got changed. I get a little clumsy when I'm tired."

She disappeared into the bathroom with her bag and closed the door. Surprisingly it only took a few minutes for her to reappear in a Boston Strong T-shirt and flannel pajama pants. The left pant leg was cuffed and sewn shut so it wouldn't drag along the floor. She leaned on her crutches as she rubbed her hands together, working in a generous glob of lotion.

"Do you get winter dry skin too?" Elise didn't put on pajama pants, settling for the top and panties look Jan liked.

"I get alligator skin. They gave me this stuff in the hospital. Works pretty well on most of the scales."

"I like the smell," Elise said and redirected Jan's hands to her cheeks. She closed her eyes dreamily. "Almond and clove."

Jan rubbed her hands down Elise's cheeks and onto her neck. She slid her hands lower, up under Elise's top and massaged her abdomen then worked around to her back, stroking softly as if she still had lotion to offer. Elise's breasts were next, each one receiving Jan's tender touch.

"You're making me weak in the knees, you know," Elise groaned and leaned her forehead against Jan's shoulder.

"There was a time a few years ago if you had said that I would have swept you off your feet, carried you to the bed and had my way with you."

"I would have loved that." Elise gave a seductive grin and began tugging at the bottom of Jan's T-shirt. "But I think we can find a way for that to happen. What do you think?"

"I think I'm following a beautiful lady to the bed."

"I promise you'll be glad you did." Elise eased Jan down on top of her to the sound of crutches hitting the floor.

The soft music on the intercom provided a serenade to their foreplay. Jan's lips and caresses guided Elise to an orgasm that came so easily and profoundly. But Jan's leg was still off-limits. With gentle coaxing, Elise was allowed to slip her hand down inside Jan's pajama pants and reached for her wetness. But after only a moment, Jan stiffened as if she regretted allowing it. Elise withdrew her hand as Jan rolled away from her touch.

"It's okay, sweetheart. We'll wait. However long it takes, we'll wait." She pulled Jan into her arms. "There's no rush."

"I'm sorry. I just can't," Jan said, pulling the covers up around them.

"I'm here when you're ready."

They drifted off to sleep in each other's arms. For Jan it was a fitful sleep. Elise was a light sleeper and could feel Jan tossing and turning, her shirt damp with perspiration.

It was after three in the morning when Jan sat up in bed, her face drenched with sweat. She wore a look of sheer panic.

"What is it, sweetie? What's wrong? Are you in pain?"

"I saw it," she gasped. "I saw it all."

"Saw what?" Elise wasn't fully awake.

"I know what happened." She groaned. "I remember. God, I remember. I saw it."

"Tell me what you saw, sweetheart." Elise sat up instantly and took her hand. "Tell me what you recall."

Jan closed her eyes, remembering. "It was raining when I took off. I banked to the west. Once I got on top of the clouds I had unlimited visibility. Blue skies." Jan stiffened. Her eyes still closed, she frowned deeply. "I can see birds. Big birds. They're everywhere. Everywhere." She snapped her head back. "Oh God. I hit the birds. The windshield is broken. There's red bird guts everywhere." Jan grimaced as if reliving the moment. "The engine won't restart." She opened her mouth, panting as she gasped for breath. "I'm going down. I'm going to crash." She reached over the side of the bed, fumbling for her crutches. "I've got to get up. I can't stay here."

"Jan, tell me what happened." Elise pulled her into her arms, holding her from leaving. "Your plane crashed. Tell me what happened."

"The clearing was too short. I couldn't stop in time." Jan flinched then recoiled in pain.

"What is it? What happened?"

"The propeller. The blades of the propeller came through the cockpit. Oh God. It came through the cockpit." Tears began to stream down Jan's face. "It came through the cockpit and cut off my leg," she sobbed, shaking uncontrollably.

Elise cringed. She'd known whatever had happened to take Jan's leg would be something ghastly, but hearing Jan's painful memory of it made it all the more horrific. Elise felt her own tears welling up inside but she struggled to hold on to her emotions. She wanted to be the pillar of strength Jan seemed to need as she relived the terrifying truth.

"Let it go now, baby. Let it all go." Elise drew Jan to her and rocked her in her arms. "That's right. Let it go. Now we know what happened. Now we can deal with it."

CHAPTER SEVENTEEN

Elise leaned back in her desk chair and answered the call from Jan.

"Hello there," she said in a playfully husky voice. "Is this my chauffeur, the one with the dynamite kisses?"

"I certainly hope you mean me."

"It's you, believe me, it's you. How was Portland?"

"Cold. Thank you for the silk long underwear. They came in very handy."

"Aren't they great? Not as great as snuggling, but great." She spun her chair and smiled out at the bright blue skies. "Am I going to see you today? It's been over a week since we've had quality time together. One lunch and a quick dinner between meetings isn't nearly enough. And just so you know, Christmas was boring without you."

"We talk almost every day. Doesn't that count?"

"Talking on the phone is nice, but it's only second best. I was hoping you'd stop by during your lunch hour. I ordered a sandwich platter and fruit plate for the people in the office.

There's a great little deli on State Street that makes fabulous Monte Cristo sandwiches."

"I'm afraid not, sweetie. It sounds wonderful, but I can't. I'm not sure how late I'll be but may I call you this evening?"

"Yes, please," she said childishly. "With Dad out of town I'm snowed under or I'd have you drive me someplace."

"Where do you need to go?"

"No place in particular. Just have you drive around town so we can be together."

"Once we get past the holidays things will slow down. Babe, I've got to go. I'll talk with you later."

"Drive carefully."

"Always. And hey, I miss you." Elise thought she heard the faint sound of a kiss against the receiver.

Elise had just turned her attention back to work when her father called from overseas.

"Hi Dad. How's the cruise going?"

"Your mother says it's great. Dinner, dancing, socializing every night. She's in hog heaven."

"And you?"

"Sure is a lot of gray water. How are things at the office?"

"Humming along. They had some snow in Burlington that delayed the excavation but it's back on track now."

"Elise, I wanted to give you a heads-up. The inspector may want another look at those electrical panels in Springfield."

"I know. I took care of it. Barbara is meeting them this afternoon."

"And John Kruger says his crew will be ready to install the escalators by the first of the month. Will we be ready?"

"Don't worry. I talked with him yesterday. How are you hearing from these people? I didn't think you'd have cell service on a cruise."

"I'm paying an extra thirty-five bucks a day. We damn well better have cell *and* Wi-Fi service. By the way, Charlie Tuttle wanted me to thank you for getting him that estimate on his cabin renovation. He said it helped him sell it. He was able to convince the new owners it had possibilities. I think he passed our name on to them. I couldn't very well tell him not to, even though I'm not interested in doing that remodeling crap."

"I'll take care of it if they contact us. Enjoy your trip and don't worry. Kiss Mother for me. Talk to you soon."

* * *

Jan climbed into her car. Her left leg was sore from the doctor's examination and she had to use her hands to help lift it into the car, groaning as she tugged at her jeans. She leaned back against the headrest as she caught her breath and waited for the pain to subside. She hadn't gotten the news she'd expected from the doctor. She'd expected to need a new gel liner and maybe a new socket. Short downtime. Maybe no downtime at all if she could continue using what she had while the new pieces were made. She started the car, turned on the heater and pressed the button on the Bluetooth.

"Call Lynette," she said then waited while it rang.

"Hi Jan. Didn't you get my texts? You were supposed to let us know what the doctor said. We've been waiting for hours."

"I just finished." She pushed back against the seat and rubbed up and down on her thigh as another twinge of pain shot up her leg.

"I thought you went in this morning."

"I did but I had some tests done. Lynette, I have to have surgery."

"Why? For what?" Lynette demanded.

"I've got bone spurs in my stump. They call it heterotopic ossification. Abnormal bone growth. It's what's causing my pain. It's not phantom pain."

"I thought you said the socket was just too tight. Can't you get a new one?"

"The doctor said there are no conservation measures to address the problem. A new liner or socket won't help. I need a stump revision. That's what took so long today. They did x-rays and I talked to two different doctors. They agreed surgery is my only option if I want to continue to wear a prosthetic."

"When will they schedule it?"

"They had a cancelation this week. I go in on Wednesday." Jan could hear Lynette gasp. "The surgeon said the sooner the better. They've already done my pre-op lab work."

"The folks will want to be there."

"They don't have to."

"I'm not telling them that. Ma wouldn't listen to me anyway. Is Elise driving you to the hospital?"

"No. And she isn't to know about this. I'll tell her later."

"Why, for heaven's sake? You said you've had dinner with her. And more than once. She'll want to be there when you have your surgery."

"I don't want her there, Lynette. I'll be in a wheelchair or on crutches. The doctor said it could be a month or more before the swelling goes down enough for me to get my new leg. You can tell the family but that's all."

"So you'll be off your feet for a few weeks. So what? You said Elise has seen you on crutches."

"She hasn't seen my leg. And I don't want her to see it."

"Have you slept with her?" Lynette asked gently.

"Why am I having this conversation with my sister?"

"Jan, have you slept with her?"

"Yes."

"You've slept with her but she hasn't seen your leg?"

"No, and that's the way I want to keep it."

"Oh, honey. If you love her, what are you waiting for?" Lynette released an exasperated sigh. "You're making a mistake if you exclude her. I know your self-confidence has been damaged, but you need to give her the benefit of the doubt. Maybe she can accept you just the way you are. I'm telling you, Jan, she's going to be royally pissed if you don't tell her."

"Lynette!"

"You could lose her over this. Is that what you want? Believe me, there are easier ways to do it."

"I don't want to lose her. That's why I'm protecting her."

"Honey, you're not protecting her. You're excluding her from your life, a very important part of your life. If you love her, show her. Let her be part of who you are."

Jan could hear a scream in the background then crying. "Honey, I have to go. The boys are roughhousing and I need to see who broke what. Think about what I said, okay?"

* * *

"How was your weekend, Lorraine?" Elise called to the footsteps in the hall.

"I have a cheesecake hangover," she grumbled. "We had some friends over and we ate like it was our last meal. Then we played poker and I lost sixty-eight dollars." Lorraine appeared in the doorway. "How was yours? Did you and Jan go out?"

"No. She had to work."

"Bummer." Lorraine went back to her desk, humming the strains of "Auld Lang Syne."

Elise looked over at the poinsettia Jan had sent her for Christmas. It was still in full crimson bloom. She stroked one of the velvety red petals, imagining Jan's soft touch.

"Oh, I miss you, lady," she sighed.

She spent all morning buried in work. She had just sent an assistant out to a job site she didn't have time to visit herself when there was a faint knock at her door.

"Come in!"

The door opened and Jan was standing in the doorway.

"Am I interrupting?" she asked apprehensively. She had a smile on her face, but it seemed strained.

"No, come in." Elise beamed up at her. "I didn't expect you. Come in." She went to greet her with a kiss. "What a wonderful surprise."

"Elise, we need to talk."

"Sure," she said. A dozen topics raced through her mind, none of them good, if Jan's expression was anything to go by. She closed the office door to discourage interruption and motioned for Jan to take a seat, then brought a chair up next to her. "What is it, sweetheart? What's on your mind?"

Jan released a deep breath, as if preparing herself for whatever news she had. Elise gently covered Jan's hand. "Whatever it is, just tell me. We'll handle it together."

Jan snapped a look at her, as if there was something wrong in what Elise had said. "That's just it. We can't. This isn't something we can do together."

"Try me," Elise coaxed, squeezing her hand.

"I'm going into the hospital tomorrow. I'm having surgery on my leg."

"Oh my God. Why?" Elise gasped, tightening her grip on Jan's hand.

"The bones in my stump are developing abnormal tissue. It's called heterotopic ossification. It's like bone spurs. I thought I just needed new parts but they say that won't help."

"I knew your leg was bothering you. Why didn't you say something?"

"I occasionally deal with phantom pain. I was hoping if I got refitted that it would go away. The doctor said it will only get worse and could lead to infection if I don't have a stump revision."

"Then let's do it," Elise said, trying to sound encouraging in spite of her worry.

"It means I won't have a prosthesis to wear for at least a month. Maybe more. I'll be on crutches or in a wheelchair while I heal." Jan lowered her gaze. "I don't want you to see it."

"Sweetheart, it doesn't matter."

"Promise me you won't come to the hospital."

"No."

"Please." Jan slowly raised her eyes to meet Elise's.

"Don't even bother to ask. I will be there. I want to be there."

"I don't want you to see my leg." Jan's voice cracked and a tear rolled down her cheek.

"Jan, you don't need to hide it from me. I don't care what it looks like. Believe me, I don't. I love you. Whatever it is, however it looks, I love you. All of you."

"If you love me like you say you do, please respect this request." Desperation filled Jan's eyes.

Elise wiped the tear from Jan's cheek and forced a smile. "All right. May I at least be there during the surgery? Let me rephrase that—I *will* be there during the surgery. I'll just sit in the waiting room. You won't even know I'm there. I need to be there to know you came through the surgery all right."

"Okay. I can agree to that. Surgery is at seven a.m. Lynette and my mother will be there too." She handed Elise a piece of paper with Lynette's cell number on it. "Lynette said you'd insist on being there."

"She's a very smart woman. She's right. I love you and I'll definitely be there, sweetheart. I can't imagine being anyplace else."

Jan had errands to run before her hospital stay and finally had to kiss Elise goodbye, promising to call her later. As soon as she left, Elise went to her desk and sat staring at the computer screen but she couldn't focus on work. Jan's news was such a shock it was all she could do not to cry. As hard as it seemed to hold tight to positive thoughts and not worry, she'd stay strong. For Jan's sake, she'd stay strong.

* * *

It was six o'clock in the morning and breakfast customers were moving through the hospital cafeteria. Elise sat sipping her second cup of coffee as she watched the doctors and nurses blend in with the crowd, carrying their trays from the cash register line to a table then to the conveyor of dirty dishes. She had been watching the faceless mass for over an hour. She knew Jan was in the hospital somewhere being prepped for surgery. She probably had already been gowned and given an IV. She was also probably nervous, even worried about the outcome. How could she not be? Elise was. She hadn't slept more than twenty minutes all night. She wished she could be with Jan, holding her hand, reassuring her, right up to the moment they wheeled her through the doors into surgery.

"Elise," Lynette called, waving from across the dining room. She hurried over and gave her a warm hug. "I'm so glad you came. Jan said you'd be here."

"I wish she had let me be with her in pre-op."

"Don't feel bad. Jan really didn't want Ma in there either but she can be very insistent."

"Have they taken her back yet?"

"Not yet. She's been given something to relax her, so they sent us out. Ma's in the waiting room holding seats for us. I came down to get her some juice." Lynette held up a bottle of cranberry juice.

"How was Jan this morning? Was she nervous? I would be."

"If she was she didn't show it. She was joking and laughing about the surgery and how she expects Ma's home-cooking while she recuperates. But I think that was all for Ma's benefit so she wouldn't worry. I could see she was scared."

"I read some articles online about below-the-knee amputations. Revision surgery, especially with traumatic injury amputation, isn't unusual."

"You read about that stuff?"

"Sure. I wanted to know what she was going through. I wanted to be able to talk with her about it."

"I don't know what made Jan change her mind and decide to tell you, but I've never been so happy to see someone in my life. If she hadn't told you, I was going to. I thought you should know."

They headed upstairs to the surgery waiting area, already filled with families. Harriet was sitting near the window. She had her coat draped over her lap and was leaning back against the wall with her eyes closed. They exchanged pleasantries but Harriet didn't seem up for chatting. She closed her eyes again but her furrowed brow showed her concern. It was another hour before they were told Jan had been taken back to surgery.

The waiting room became noisy. People seemed to use conversation to hide their nervous impatience. Ladies in pink smocks manned the waiting room information desk. They checked in families and handed out pagers, answered questions, and received updates on patients. Harriet alternated between napping and walking the hall to the drinking fountain. Lynette played on an iPad. Elise fielded email on her cell phone, occasionally going in search of a quiet corner to make a call. She hadn't thought she wanted to be bothered, but work became a convenient distraction to her worry. Elise had just returned to her chair when the pager began to flash and buzz. All three of them hurried up to the desk, anxious for news.

"Ms. Chase has been taken to recovery," a white haired woman at the desk said. "The doctor will be out to speak with you in about fifteen minutes."

"Is she all right?" Harriet asked.

"Ma'am, they don't tell us that information. That all has to come from the doctor."

"Ma, she's fine or they wouldn't be taking her to recovery," Lynette said, walking her mother back to her chair. She tossed a worried look at Elise.

"Absolutely, Harriet. Privacy laws keep them from telling you everything went well, but I'm sure it did."

"Why did it take so long? She was back there four hours."

"Ma, don't worry. Stuff takes time."

The doctor finally summoned them into a small consultation room. He wore blue scrubs and had gray hair. He spoke quietly, explaining the procedure. Once Elise heard him say Jan was doing well and would make a full recovery, she heaved a sigh of relief. Little registered after that.

Jan remained in recovery for another hour before being taken to her room. Once she was settled in bed Harriet was allowed a short visit but warned Jan probably wouldn't be awake.

"You want to come in and see her?" Lynette asked, standing with Elise in the hall outside her room.

"I promised I wouldn't."

"I'm guessing you promised not to see her leg."

"Yes, she was very adamant about that."

"I'm taking Ma downstairs for lunch," Lynette said, wrapping an arm around Elise's shoulders. "In case you're wondering, Jan's asleep. She'll never know, if you want to go in for a minute." She smiled sympathetically. "I won't tell." Harriet stepped out of the room and they started for the elevators. Lynette looked back and nodded.

Elise stood in the hall, listening to the rhythmic beep of Jan's IV pump. A nurse went in and returned a few minutes later after taking her vitals.

"Is she still asleep?" Elise asked the nurse.

"Yes. She'll probably sleep all afternoon. You might as well go home, honey," she suggested in an understanding tone.

Elise stood listening another moment, then took a deep breath and went in. Jan's room was dim. The blinds had been closed and the curtain had been drawn partway around the bed. Jan's curly blond hair was mussed and matted against the pillow. She looked pale but peaceful as she slept, her heavily bandaged stump supported by a rolled blanket. Oxygen tubing ran from the outlet on the wall above the bed to her nose. Two bags of medicine hung from the IV pole, fed through the pump into the back of her hand. Elise had seen people after surgery before. She knew what to expect. But that didn't make it any easier. She wanted to take Jan's hand and whisper to her that she was there, and not to worry. But she'd promised. Jan stirred slightly. Elise stepped back behind the curtain and waited. After a moment she could hear the soft sound of snoring. Elise came to Jan's bedside.

She smiled down at her and whispered, "I'm here, sweetheart. I'll be here for you." She kissed her fingertip and touched it to Jan's lips before stepping out of the room.

* * *

Three days passed. Elise waited in the hospital lobby for the next elevator to take her upstairs. The bustling lunch hour crowd seemed too impatient to wait their rightful turn and pushed past her to fill the next one available. There was a time when Elise might have been part of the impatient herd, lurching for the open elevator even before those onboard could exit. But she was in no hurry. During those three days since the surgery, she had talked to Jan on the phone several times. She'd sent flowers and a balloon bouquet but out of respect for Jan's request, she hadn't been to her room since the day of the surgery. She'd promised. She could visit once Jan was discharged from the hospital, and able to dress and walk on crutches. That was the agreement. But there she was, waiting for an elevator, ready to disregard the agreement. She wasn't sure how she was going to handle it once she got upstairs. Hopefully she could peek around the corner and find her sleeping. But she had to at least see her.

Another elevator opened and a flood of passengers streamed out. Elise stepped out of the way, still wrestling with herself over going upstairs.

"Elise?" It was Keith filing out of the elevator. "Hello honey. I'm so glad you're here." He gave her a warm hug, blocking traffic and forcing others waiting for the elevator to walk around them.

"How is she?" Elise asked instantly and guided him away from traffic.

"She's okay. Still dealing with the pain but each day is a little better. She's anxious to be up on crutches. She wants to learn to use them on stairs. The therapist is with her now. They do stretching and range-of-motion exercises to keep her muscles limber."

"Is Lynette here today?"

"No, she's home. The twins are sick."

"Oh my. Is it bad?" She offered a concerned frown.

"Not really. They have colds and can't go to school." He laughed. "It's the only thing I've ever known them to share without a fight. I told her I was coming up to see Jan today. She can stay home and feed the boys Spaghettios. Are you going up?" He nodded toward the elevators.

"I was thinking about it but I'm not sure."

"Jan told me what she made you promise. She doesn't want you to see her leg."

"That's right. I've tried to reassure her I don't care what it looks like. I love her unconditionally."

"Awwww," he sighed. "That's so sweet."

"We all have flaws. But she absolutely won't allow it. I can't convince her."

"I know. It's stupid. I love my sister to death. She's better on one leg than many women are on two, but she's wrong about this. Wrong, wrong, wrong. She has to get past it."

"I thought once her memory of the accident returned she'd be able to deal with it. The trauma, the PTSD, would somehow diminish. But it hasn't made a difference. She can talk about what happened, but touching or seeing her leg is still off-limits."

"Her amnesia wasn't the problem." Keith rested his hand on Elise's arm. "Honey, everyone in the family has seen it. Even Baci. Once Jan came home from the hospital and stayed at the folks' house Baci helped Ma and Lynette change her dressings. She insisted they put two beds in her room so she could be nearby if Jan needed something in the middle of the night."

"If everyone else has seen it then why not me? I know I'm not family but I love her and I want to help."

"I know you do. And I'm sure she loves you too. And that's the problem. The last person who told her they loved her also told her the stump was gross."

"Allie?"

"Yes. At first she was helpful, kinda. She got Jan her meds and fluffed her pillows. That kind of stuff. She even ran errands once in a while. Sometimes I think she hung out at my folks' just to eat the food." Keith heaved a preparatory sigh and smirked. "I heard her on the phone. She was sitting in Ma's kitchen, talking with one of her friends. I don't think she thought anyone was around. Anyway, I heard her say Jan's scars were the most hideous thing she ever saw. She said her stump was so gross that even the thought of having sex with her made her want to puke. She told her friend that she doubted Jan would ever have a girlfriend again. Allie had Jan convinced she was damaged goods."

Elise gasped in horror.

"Not only did I hear it, but Jan heard it. Every word of it."

"Oh, Keith, she is SO not damaged goods."

He nodded. "She never told Allie she heard. She said there was no point. But I think she has lived in fear that it might happen again."

"No wonder she is so adamant."

"Are you going up to see her?" he asked softly.

"I don't know. I want to, but if I go up there against her wishes am I doing more harm than good?"

"I can't tell you what to do. Only you know what's best for you and for her. I know what I'd do, but I'm biased." He gave an understanding smile. "I have to go, honey. Call me if you want to talk." He kissed her cheek and walked away, leaving Elise with her decision.

She stood watching the elevators open and close and the lighted numbers change as they went up and came back down. She finally found herself stepping in and pressing the button for the fifth floor. When the door opened, she swallowed and stepped out.

The hall was lined with linen carts, lunch tray cabinets and empty gurneys. The faint aroma of antiseptic and fish filled the air. A nurse went into a room with the call light illuminated. A doctor stood at the nurses' station reading a chart. A woman with her arms folded leaned against the wall as if waiting for permission to re-enter a room with a closed door. The closer Elise got to Jan's room the tighter she clutched at her purse strap. She stood outside Jan's door, summoning her courage.

Before she could decide, a nurse hurried past her and entered the room. She was carrying a tray filled with rolls of tape and packages of sterile bandaging. From the muted conversation Elise could tell the nurse needed to change the dressing. Something to do with leakage around the staples.

This was the time. Elise knew what she wanted and she knew what she had to do. There would never be a better moment and she seized it. She stepped through the door. The curtain was drawn partway around the bed and Elise could see Jan's foot. She took a deep breath and stepped around the curtain.

"Hi," she said with as kind a smile as she could muster.

Jan had been watching the nurse cutting away the blood-stained dressing and snapped a look up at Elise. Her eyes instantly widened.

"What are you doing here?" she demanded, reaching for the sheet.

"No, no. Hold still," the nurse said. "Don't do that. I'll be right back. Don't let her cover that." She dropped her scissors on the tray and hurried out of the room as if she'd forgotten something.

"I asked you not to come. You promised," Jan said with a hateful scowl. "You need to leave. Now."

"Please let me stay."

Elise came around the bed and looked down at the exposed stump for the first time. A long suture line of metal staples extended from one side of her thigh to the other like a macabre jagged smile across the end of the stump. It was puckered and bloody. As Elise had guessed, Jan had lost her leg just below the knee. She had several other faded scars around her leg that Elise assumed were collateral damage from the accident. When she looked up tears were silently streaming down Jan's face as she sat frozen in the bed.

"Please leave," she said painfully, nearly choking on the words.

Elise placed her hand on Jan's thigh. She softly drew it down to within inches of the sutures. Jan stiffened, pressing herself back against the bed as if moving out of Elise's reach.

"Let me stay."

"NO!" Jan shouted. "I don't want you here. You promised not to come." She closed her eyes and leaned back against the pillow. "You broke your promise, Elise. Please leave."

Jan's words were like thorns. Hateful, angry thorns that cut Elise clear down to her soul. She could leave. She could turn and run out. But it wasn't the right thing to do. She knew it. Not until she said what Jan needed to hear.

"Jan, listen to me. I'm here for you. Me, Elise Grayson. I'm not Allie. And I'll never be Allie. You taught me what it's like to love someone. Not just settle for someone. I hope to God someday you love me half as much as I love you. But I can't settle for just part of you. I want the whole thing. I want your smile and your quirky sense of humor and your gentle touch and yes, your body. All of it, whatever it looks like." She stroked Jan's stump tenderly, smiling down at it. "That's what I'm offering. I know this is virgin territory for you, but when you're ready to accept me on my terms you let me know. I'm not settling again. I deserve more."

Elise turned and walked out. She was well down the hall when she leaned against the wall and succumbed to sobs.

* * *

Three days passed, three agonizing days without a word. Elise buried herself in work, or tried to. It was all she knew to do. Guilt over disregarding Jan's wishes and demanding Jan accept her on her terms had her pacing the office and had robbed her of sleep. She stood staring mindlessly out at Boston's skyline, when there was a knock on her open office door.

"Is it too late for an apology?" Jan stood in the doorway, balancing on crutches. She looked pale and tired. A visible bulge around the knee in the left leg of her jeans suggested she still had massive bandaging over her stump.

"Depends." Elise turned, breath catching in her throat. "What are you apologizing for?"

"Being a jerk. You were right. I was just too stubborn to see it. It's taken me three years, but I'm ready. I want to accept your offer. Can you forgive me?"

Unable to hold back her enthusiasm a moment longer, Elise rushed to Jan and hugged her.

"Yes, I forgive you. And I hope you forgive me for not respecting your wishes."

"I'm glad you were there. I was just too stubborn to admit it."

"Lorraine," Elise called, but kept her grin on Jan. "When my two o'clock meeting gets here will you have Barbara take it? I'm busy."

"I don't think you should do that," Jan said sheepishly. "It might be important. You always said work comes first."

"Barbara can handle it. I've got better things to do right now. It's just the new owners of that cabin on Lake Winnipesaukee coming to talk about a remodel."

"So you're going to renovate it anyway."

"I haven't met them yet but I understand they want to keep some of the charm of the cabin and just update it for convenience."

"Things like a generator and on-demand hot water?"

"Yes, as a matter of fact."

"And new appliances."

"Yes."

"And a railing and paved steps along the path. And repairs to the deck. Definitely repairs to the deck."

"How did you know all that?" Elise stared at her quizzically.

"And a new dock big enough for a pair of Adirondack chairs for watching the moonlight over the water." Jan grinned mischievously. "I really think you should take your two o'clock meeting."

Elise continued to stare in disbelief.

"Jan Chase, what did you do?"

"I bought Brighton Hollow."

"You bought Charlie Tuttle's cabin on the lake?"

"Yes. He's a very nice man." Jan pulled an envelope from her jacket pocket. "I made him an offer and he accepted. It's amazing what cash can do."

"You paid cash for it?"

"It's my insurance money from the accident. I thought it was time to invest some of it. I told Charlie I wanted a vacation getaway big enough for two and his cabin was just what I was looking for."

"You aren't kidding? You really bought it?"

"I had to," Jan declared flatly. "It's where we spent our first night together."

"We didn't actually spend the night together at the cabin, sweetie. We just spent a few hours there." Elise draped her arms over Jan's shoulders.

"It was long enough. Long enough for me to realize I love you."

"I love you too." Elise reached up to kiss her but was interrupted by her cell phone ringing on her waistband. She looked down at it then handed it to Jan. "Do you know how to turn this off?"

"I do." Jan pressed the mute button and tossed the phone on a nearby chair, then kissed her. "So you're willing to discuss my remodel?"

"Yes, I think we can handle it," she said, swimming in Jan's gaze. "Should we discuss it over dinner?"

"It might be a long, long discussion." Jan twirled a lock of Elise's hair around her finger. "I've got lots of ideas."

"I like long discussions."

"I should warn you about something first." Jan swallowed, as if preparing to deliver more big news.

"I'm listening."

"Before we have our discussion I may have to change my bandages. Is that going to be a problem?"

"I know the perfect girl for the job." She locked her arms around the back of Jan's neck.

"She's going to need a strong constitution."

"And a gentle touch?" Elise whispered.

"Sounds like my kind of woman."

"Oh, I hope so." Elise placed her head on Jan's shoulder. "I truly hope so."

"I can't believe you've put up with me this long."

"Oh, sweetheart, you don't realize how long we're going to have together. We're going to be putting up with one another for a long, long time. And I'm going to love every minute of it."

"Count me in, boss lady. Count me in."

Bella Books, Inc.

Women. Books. Even Better Together.

P.O. Box 10543
Tallahassee, FL 32302

Phone: 800-729-4992
www.bellabooks.com